A PENGUIN MYSTERY

Disaster at the Vendome Theater

M. L. Longworth has lived in Aix-en-Provence since 1997. She has written about the region for *The Washington Post*, *The Times* (London), *The Independent* (London), and *Bon Appétit*. She is the author of a bilingual collection of essays, *Une Américaine en Provence*. She is married and has one daughter.

M. L. Longworth's Provençal Mysteries

DISASTER
at the
VENDOME
THEATER

A Provençal Mystery

M. L. LONGWORTH

PENGUIN BOOKS

PENGUIN BOOKS
An imprint of Penguin Random House LLC
penguinrandomhouse.com

LIBRARY OF CONGRESS CATALOGING-IN-PUBLICATION DATA
Names: Longworth, M. L. (Mary Lou), 1963– author.
Title: Disaster at the Vendome Theater / M. L. Longworth.
Description: New York : Penguin Books, [2022] |
Series: Sun and Wine-soaked Provençal Mystery Series ; 10 |
Identifiers: LCCN 2022009018 (print) | LCCN 2022009019 (ebook) |
ISBN 9780143135302 (paperback) | ISBN 9780525506973 (ebook)
Classification: LCC PR9199.4.L596 D57 2022 (print) |
LCC PR9199.4.L596 (ebook) | DDC 813/.6—dc23
LC record available at https://lccn.loc.gov/2022009018
LC ebook record available at https://lccn.loc.gov/2022009019

Printed in the United States of America
2nd Printing

Set in Adobe Caslon Pro

Murder in Provence cover seal and artwork courtesy of BritBox

For Martin Crocker,
with thanks.

DISASTER
at the
VENDOME
THEATER

Chapter One

᷾᷾

Monday, August 7

Jean-Marc Sauvat hated being late. He walked quickly down the Cours Mirabeau, dodging the locals and tourists who were ambling slowly. Stopping to wipe his brow, he conceded that the tourists' sluggishness may not have been due to vacation mode but instead to the intense dry August heat.

Mercifully, the wide avenue's double row of tall plane trees with their fat leaves provided a tunnel of shade. He watched as a group of middle-aged friends, maps and guidebooks in hand, ran from shady spot to shady spot, dodging the sunny areas where the leaves couldn't quite cover the sidewalk. He was tempted to stop and rest; the café terraces were only half-full, as it was too hot even to sit down and order a drink. Most of the locals were home next to their pools, or hidden inside their darkened apartments, the shutters closed. Or vacationing in Scotland, as he had been last August.

Now he regretted, not for the first time, auditioning for a part in this stage play when instead he could be in Brittany, where, his friends bragged, it was sunny and barely 20°C. Every summer he took a trip with his former high school friends, all of them now married with children and over half of them now very Parisian. He was the only one who had managed to stay in Aix, although Corinne, who was also a lawyer, was nearby in Marseille. Every time he spoke with the Parisians they complained of Paris's gray skies and crowded streets and asked enviously about the weather in the south. But last night, on the phone, he was able to make them laugh with stories of Aix's heat. He was sorry not to see them, but not sorry to be the only single man in the group, trying to get their kids' names right and play board games, as if because he was single, he somehow liked that kind of activity. But he did love his old dear friends. He thought of the moment when he told them, at a dining table somewhere in the Loire Valley only a few years ago, that he was gay. Silence hung around the table for a few long seconds until Corinne walked around the table and kissed him on the cheek, then hugged him. One by one each of the others followed suit. The memory brought tears to his eyes now as he walked.

And because they were such good friends, they had been quite vocal about Jean-Marc's decision to skip the yearly vacation and take part in an amateur play. Why wasn't he with them, in Brittany? Was he making a career change? The questions were accompanied by loud snickers. He laughed along gamely and explained that the play, Marcel Pagnol's *Cigalon* (more snorts combined with his friends trying to mimic the heavy Midi accent), was supposed to have taken place in early July, but the lead actress fell ill with the flu. Jean-Marc happened to be at the theater, signing his contract, when the bad news arrived. He didn't know who the leading actress was, as the theater's owner, Anouk Singer, was cagey about it. Anouk hung up the telephone, swore a few times, then shrugged her shoulders, pulled a pencil from behind her ear, and changed the date on the free hardware store calendar to September. It had shocked him, her nonchalance, but he supposed that was the theater life.

So here he was in mid-August, stuck in one of the hottest cities in France, on vacation from his law office but having to show up on time for a play rehearsal. As he passed by the wedding-cake-like Rotonde fountain, he cursed the second-century BC Romans who'd thought it was a fantastic idea to build a city in a spot that was bitterly cold in winter and airless in summer; he cursed whatever writer, celebrity, or cultural influencer had spread the news that Aix was a beautiful place to visit and live, which made it now overcrowded; and he cursed himself and his pride in having won— and shamelessly accepted, as he was very much an amateur—a role in *Cigalon*. Looking at his watch, he realized he was now ten minutes late, but he didn't care. It was just too hot.

He walked on, across a vast square that was empty except for a kiosk selling flowers. The flowers sat, waiting to find a new home; the pavement below them was wet, as the florist obviously had to water his plants every twenty minutes or so. Waiting to cross the busy Cours Sextius, Jean-Marc frowned at the jaywalkers who ambled across on the red light even though traffic was still moving. Most of them were much too old to be behaving so dangerously.

To distract himself he tried to imagine his fellow actors. Today was the first time they'd meet each other; he hadn't seen anyone else around before or after his audition. On the audition day there hadn't been a busy waiting room full of nervous actors rehearsing their lines or doing warm-up exercises. There was only him, sitting on a stool, with Anouk facing him, dropping her book more than once and losing her place on the page also more than once. He had gone home dejected, drunk a glass of whisky and smoked a Cuban cigar that Antoine Verlaque had given him, and forgotten all about Anouk and her dingy Théâtre Vendôme.

But two weeks later he received an email from Anouk announcing, *with pleasure*, his successful audition for the role of the Count. The contract had been photocopied so many times it was barely legible. It surprised him that she hadn't specified which edition of the play they were to use, as it was more well known as a film, released in 1935. So he had ordered a copy at Goulard on the Cours Mirabeau and he expected that his fellow actors had done the same; they would all be on the same page, so to speak. The book was in a cloth bag hanging on his shoulder, along with a pad of paper, a pencil, a water bottle, and his cell phone. He really wasn't sure what else to bring, and he hoped he wasn't over- or underprepared. Was he having this so-called impostor syndrome that he'd read about in the papers and in magazines? Or was he just a worrywart as his friend Antoine often accused him of being? It had taken him over five minutes to choose the right cloth bag, and he had finally settled on one from the Centre Pompidou. He thought it showed that he was cultured and open to contemporary art and ideas, just in case Anouk wanted to put a modern spin on *Cigalon*.

The pedestrian crossing light turned green and Jean-Marc

walked across the street, his heart pounding as he got closer to the theater. Taking a deep breath, he told himself not to be so foolish. There was no reason to be afraid. He had passed the audition and had every right to be here. He may have been an amateur actor, but he was no slouch in life: He was a successful lawyer with his apartment paid off and a sports car sitting in a rented garage. His furniture had been bought mostly at the Paris auction house Drouot and he was considering buying a second home in Liguria. His best friend was Aix's well-known, if at times controversial, examining magistrate, who was now happily married to another of Jean-Marc's dearest friends, and they were expecting their first child. They had already asked Jean-Marc to be the godfather. He smiled. Yes, he had auditioned and earned his role fair and square.

His heart rate slowed down and he was just beginning to relax when he rounded the corner onto the tiny rue du 11 Novembre and saw the theater's front door. Above it hung an obviously home-made sign painted in garish colors, with an outdated, 1970s font. It was also slightly askew. It made him start to worry again: Was Anouk always as disorganized as she had been during the auditions? Would anyone even pay to see their performance?

Ahead of him walked an old woman who, despite her age, wore a short flowered skirt and a frilly cotton peasant blouse. She seemed to be singing. She was tiny but had a powerful clear voice, one that had been trained. He picked up his pace, trying to identify her song. For some reason he felt it was important. When he got closer he could pick out the song, one from the 1950s: Charles Trenet's "La Mer."

The woman stopped in front of the theater's front door and looked up at the crooked sign. She stopped singing, shook her head, put her hands on her hips, and slowly turned around to face Jean-Marc, who was now standing about ten feet behind her. He sensed that she knew he'd been listening. Her dyed blond hair was arranged in a large bun atop her small head and she wore a lot of makeup. Throwing up her arms in exaggerated frustration, she bellowed, "How the mighty have fallen!" Then she laughed, a very familiar high-pitched crackling laugh, opened the door, and walked in.

Jean-Marc stood still, unable to move. He realized that the woman had been referring not to the theater but to herself. She was Liliane Poncet, the once-great leading lady of the French stage and screen.

Chapter Two

✦

Monday, August 7

While Jean-Marc Sauvat was nervously meeting his fellow actors, Marine Bonnet was pacing back and forth in her country house kitchen, looking longingly at the sparkling swimming pool but knowing it was too hot and sunny to venture out. Why had they bought this beautiful house? Well, there was the pool, tempting her with its blue-green water and the wrought iron chaise longues lined up in a row, each with a tasteful white cushion edged in navy blue. But she missed their downtown apartment with its view of the city's rooftops. Putting her hands on her huge belly, she thought of their future child and which home would suit that child best. In the country the air was certainly cleaner, but in the city everyday life was so much easier.

Her cell phone began to ring and she picked it up off the kitchen counter. "Sylvie!" she exclaimed, seeing her best friend's name as the caller.

"Wine delivery!" Sylvie cried. "I'm outside your elegant abode."

"I'll be right there!" Marine said, making for the front door. "The automatic gate opener is broken."

Marine walked quickly down the laneway. She could see Sylvie's little green Twingo waiting in front of the elaborately carved iron gates. Although Marine was eight months pregnant, her baby was sitting high, like a little round ball, and she still found it relatively easy to move around. It was boredom that was setting in now; she so desperately wanted to meet this child. She got to the gate and waved, and began the slow process of undoing the combination lock and chains that Antoine had bought until the gate buzzer was repaired. Once the heavy iron gate was unlocked, Marine moved each side fully open so that her friend could drive in.

Sylvie rolled down her window. "Thank goodness you gave me your old car," she said. "And thank goodness it has air-conditioning."

Marine patted the roof of her old Twingo, quickly pulling back her hand because of the heat. "The salesman talked me into the air-conditioning, and boy am I glad I listened to him. Or was bullied by him." The women laughed, and Marine gestured for Sylvie to proceed up the long drive.

"Leave the Versailles gates open," Sylvie called. "I can't stay long, and it takes you ages to open and close them! Do you want to jump in?"

Marine gave her a wave of the hand. "I'd rather walk," she said. She smiled, happy to see her friend, and not surprised that she'd got a razzing about the pretentious gates, installed by the previous owner.

Sylvie drove on, parking the car next to Marine's new Range

Rover, a gift from Antoine. Opening her trunk, she pulled out a case of wine.

"What's this for?" Marine asked.

"For being such good friends. Plus the winery is doing a special deal right now, and I can't resist a bargain."

Marine saw the name of the winery—a posh one, about twenty minutes north of Aix and near their house, with an award-winning contemporary art installation on its grounds—and doubted that Sylvie got that good a deal. She was just generous. "Follow me into the house," Marine said. "It's cooler in there."

"I believe it."

Once inside the kitchen, both women kicked off their sandals, knowing that bare feet on the terra-cotta tile floor would cool them down. "Water?" Marine asked.

"Please," Sylvie replied. She looked around the vast country-style kitchen with its gleaming marble surfaces and six-burner old-fashioned oven and whistled. "I'm still having a hard time imagining you living here."

"Me, too." Marine handed Sylvie a glass of water and sat down opposite her. "The oven you're looking at cost the same as a small Japanese car."

Sylvie laughed. "Plus I can't just pop by now." She took a sip of water and said, "Sorry. That sounded egotistical."

"No, no. I completely agree. I honestly think that when the baby's born we'll spend more time in the apartment. But I haven't told Antoine that yet."

"You know what I think?" Sylvie asked. "I think that when Antoine sees that baby he's going to be so in love that he'll do anything you say."

Marine drained her water glass. "You could be right. Did I tell you that he's so obsessed by our child's education that the police officers and other employees at the Palais de Justice have a betting pool to guess where we'll send the child to kindergarten?"

Sylvie burst out laughing. "Does Antoine know you know?"

"No. I found out via my mother."

"What?!"

"Of course she overheard it during choir practice at Saint-Jean-de-Malte. Someone's son knows someone . . . That kind of thing."

Sylvie gave an exaggerated shiver. "Remind me to avoid that church. Nothing's a secret there."

"Would you like a coffee, or something to eat?" Marine asked.

Sylvie looked sheepish. "I wouldn't mind a dip in the pool."

"Of course! I hope it's okay that I stay here. It's too hot out there."

"No problem! I have my bathing suit in my purse."

"There are towels out there. Help yourself. You can change in the WC down the hall."

Sylvie walked down the hall, carrying a smallish purse with her that signaled just how small her bikini must be. Marine felt like a whale, but unlike whales she wasn't vegetarian: She'd been craving meat since almost the beginning of her pregnancy. Antoine, who seemed to want meat at every meal, was over the moon at this development.

Within minutes Marine could hear Sylvie splashing about and realized that when Sylvie called—albeit with a case of wine—there was often an ulterior Sylvie-styled motive. In this case, a swim. Marine shrugged, putting their empty glasses in the dishwasher. She knew that there was a part of Sylvie that was self-serving, but she had come to terms with it long ago.

Sylvie, meanwhile, was floating on her back, looking up at the blue sky framed by the tops of tall pine trees. She flipped over onto her stomach and did the crawl toward the house. She could see Marine's face in the kitchen window, watching her. Sylvie lifted a hand out of the water and waved, and Marine waved back, then disappeared. Sylvie did a few more laps, then lifted herself out of the pool, pleased she still had enough upper arm strength to not need the stairs or ladder. She shook the water out of her ears and short hair but resisted the temptation to lie down on one of the chaise longues; she didn't have much time, and she didn't want to get the fancy white cushions wet. Besides, it was so hot she'd dry off on the thirty-meter walk back to the house. She grabbed her purse and started back, admiring, however bourgeois, the manicured garden that had been so well designed that there was still quite a bit of color even in August. She dragged the palm of her hand along the top of the lavender, its flowers, purple in July, now turning gray. Lifting her hand to her nose, she took in a big, deep breath. "*Paradis*," she whispered, then opened the back door.

"That swim was heaven!" Sylvie called to Marine as she walked down the hallway at the back of the house that led to the kitchen. She walked on, now wanting a coffee, which she'd drink while drying off. "I'll make myself an espresso, okay?"

She turned on the coffee maker and set a demitasse under the spout, pounding a tune with her fingers on the kitchen counter. "I said I'm making a coffee! Do you want one?" She looked around the now empty kitchen. "Oh, I forgot! You hate coffee now! Right, Marine? Pregnancy did that to me, too!"

The coffee maker woke up and began to thump, pouring a deep black espresso into her cup. She took it and downed it in one gulp. "Where are you, Marine?" Setting the empty cup down, Sylvie walked through the kitchen and turned right, toward the living room. "Are you having a nap? I remember that. I used to sleep between giving classes at the fine art school. There was an old leather sofa in the faculty room, and I'd just head straight for it, and . . ."

In the living room she found Marine standing with her back to the stone fireplace. She looked at Sylvie, wide-eyed, then gestured with her head toward the sofa, now occupied.

"We have a guest," Marine whispered.

Sylvie turned her head, expecting to see Antoine, or perhaps Marine's parents. Instead, she saw a young woman sprawled across the sofa, her eyes closed. She whispered, "Who is it?"

Marine shrugged.

"Is she alive?"

"Yes, silly," Marine said, sitting down in an armchair. "I came in here and saw her walking up the drive, stumbling. Luckily we left the gate open. She fell asleep as soon as she sat down on the sofa."

"Heatstroke," Sylvie said. "I'll get a glass of water and a damp washcloth."

"Thanks, Sylvie."

Chapter Three

✑

Monday, August 7

Jean-Marc followed the bobbing blond head of Liliane Poncet into the theater. Mme Poncet was still humming as she zigzagged through the front of the house, which consisted of the front desk and a staircase that led down to the theater. They walked down a long hallway that was lined with posters and photographs of past shows. Here Jean-Marc normally would have lingered, given his nervousness, but since he was already late, he carried on, following Mme Poncet. She was a theater and film veteran, so no doubt she knew what to do and where to go.

Together they walked into the large back room that served as a salon and meeting area, where Jean-Marc had had his audition. Two sofas, both in faded velvet, faced each other; Jean-Marc tried not to turn up his nose at their shabbiness, complete with stains and cigarette burns. Behind them was a long wooden table with six mismatched wooden chairs, and near the west wall were two small round tables, each with four chairs. He imagined that theater patrons, after buying a drink at the intermission, might wander up here. On the walls were more framed posters of plays from both here and famous Parisian theaters.

"Hey!" Liliane suddenly yelled. "It would help if you told me, us, where we're supposed to go!" She turned around and winked at Jean-Marc, who smiled and managed to mumble *merci*.

"Down the back stairs!" yelled a voice from the basement. Jean-Marc thought it was Anouk but he couldn't be sure.

"I see you came prepared," Liliane said as she glanced at Jean-Marc's carrier bag. "A theater veteran?"

He coughed. "It's my first play."

She laughed and grabbed his arm. "You're in for an experience! Every play is magic."

They walked down the narrow stairs, and Jean-Marc followed Liliane's lead by holding on to the banister, as the wooden stairs were uneven and cracked in places. He hoped they wouldn't have to run up and down these stairs in between scenes; surely the changing rooms were downstairs behind the stage? He gathered up his courage and asked, "How many plays have you been in, Mme Poncet?"

She turned around and looked up at him. "I prefer mademoiselle. And I have no idea. Hundreds? No, let's say between one hundred and one hundred and twenty." She grinned, showing off the famed gap between her upper two front teeth, known to almost every Frenchman and -woman who ever took an interest in theater or film as Le Bonheur Poncet, a reference to that gap's nickname as good-luck teeth, *dents du bonheur*. Jean-Marc smiled back. Liliane Poncet, despite being an older woman, wanted to be greeted as mademoiselle, but in the same breath she had freely admitted to having appeared in over one hundred plays, exact proof of her advanced age. He put her at seventy-five, or possibly eighty.

Jean-Marc kept his distance as they walked into the theater and stage area, as he assumed that Liliane would make a grand entrance. To his surprise, she didn't; there was no sweeping in, or flourishes done with a hand, or a bit of song as he had heard outside in the street. She simply walked up to Anouk, shook her hand, and said, "Let's get started."

After half an hour the cast had been introduced to one another. Liliane Poncet, as Jean-Marc had suspected, was to play the principal female role of Mme Toffi, the rival chef to Cigalon in the quaint village of La Treille. Another professional actor, Gauthier Lesage, would be playing Cigalon, the former Parisian chef. Cigalon, after cooking for demanding clients for thirty-five years, runs a beautiful restaurant in La Treille, with a terrace sweeping over the green valley, but there's a catch: He refuses to serve guests. He cooks only for himself and his sister, Sidonie. Jean-Marc immediately disliked Gauthier, who sat back in his chair scowling during the introductions. Jean-Marc knew of him: He'd been known as a pretty boy in the French television world back in the nineties. He didn't have the physique for Cigalon, thought Jean-Marc. He'd always imagined Cigalon with a thick, round belly and double chin, an eccentric chef who reveled in cooking—and eating—the traditional and very fattening dishes of old France. Gauthier, on the other hand, was tall, slim, and wide-shouldered.

Jean-Marc had a soft spot for the youngest cast member,

ten-year-old Brigitte Vila, who would portray the village mes-
senger, a small boy known simply as Le Petit in the play and film.
"Brigitte will naturally be called La Petite," Anouk explained.
"Since this play has only four female roles, I've taken the liberty
to include another girl." A round of clapping followed, with the
cast smiling kindly at the girl, except Gauthier Lesage, who kept
his hands folded against his well-toned chest. But Brigitte beamed
with excitement. "It's my first play!" she said.

"Mine, too," Jean-Marc added.

"Same here," said Abdul Khattabi with his hand raised.

"Abdul," Anouk said, "you've been around theaters as long as
I can remember."

"Yes, but only as a lighting and sound technician," Abdul said,
smiling widely, his excitement matching young Brigitte's. "Never
as an actor!"

"Oh, good grief," moaned Gauthier Lesage.

"We'll pretend we didn't hear that," Liliane Poncet firmly said,
staring down Gauthier.

Jean-Marc's dislike of the man was confirmed. Was Gauthier
upset to be working with amateurs, or was he racist, or both? At
any rate, the fact that Abdul would be playing Le Brigadier, chief
of police, made Jean-Marc chuckle. He glanced over at Anouk,
who, instead of listening intently or even putting Gauthier in his
place as Liliane had done, was nervously playing with her long
reddish hair, twirling the ends around her long fingers. She suddenly awoke from her reverie and jumped up, clapping her hands
together. "Let's tour the wardrobe area upstairs!"

As if reading his thoughts, Liliane said, "The changing rooms
are upstairs?"

Jean-Marc thought of the rickety stairs. He was sure the other cast members had done the same, judging by their fallen faces, except for Brigitte, who kept beaming. Those stairs would be fun for a ten-year-old.

"You've got to be joking," Gauthier said, finally sitting up straight. "The costumes are two flights from the stage? We could break our necks!"

"No one's ever had an accident," Anouk said in a forced bright voice. "Follow me!"

The cast reluctantly rose from the mismatched chairs that made up the auditorium—seating for about sixty or seventy spectators, guessed Jean-Marc. They were effectively in the basement. The stage, semicircular in form, stood about a foot high in the northwest corner of the room. Because of the low ceiling, even lower onstage, the effect was claustrophobic, like the small basement jazz bar in Montmartre to which Antoine Verlaque once dragged Jean-Marc, who only listened to classical music.

At the far end of the theater space was an L-shaped bar lined with four barstools, and against a nearby wall were two small round tables with seating for four more people. Not quite enough room for the whole cast, Jean-Marc mused, but they could still have some fun there after practice. He imagined jokes and camaraderie, slapping each other on the back and so forth. His excitement for the play returned.

Before leading them upstairs to the changing rooms, Anouk took the cast backstage, in effect a narrow hallway behind the curtains that led to the back stairway. Abdul, as it turned out, not only would be acting in this production but was also designing the lights. He proudly showed the cast his small control box, which looked to Jean-Marc—who was not good with tools or technology—very old indeed. "Since much of the play takes place on the restaurant's terrace," Abdul began, saying aloud what they were all thinking, "I won't have to change the lighting that much. Two or three times should do it, in between acts or scenes."

"The stage will be split in two," Anouk added, "or rather, one-third will be inside Cigalon's kitchen, and the remaining two thirds on the terrace. We'll simply change the tablecloths and chairs when we want to change the set to Mme Toffi's rival café. The era will be mid-nineteen-thirties Provence, as Pagnol intended. I've even found a complete set of thirties dishes and glassware, which I'm thrilled about! Now, let's go up to the wardrobe, to Sandra's domain."

A woman in her late forties shyly raised her hand, waving it slightly. "That's me," she whispered.

"As you now know, Sandra will also be playing Adèle, one of the clients Cigalon refuses to serve," Anouk said.

"Amateur hour," groaned Gauthier Lesage.

"I once starred with Fabrice Dufort," bellowed Liliane Poncet, naming a famous actor. "It was also his first stage appearance. And no one, I mean no one, made anything of it! After that play he was signed up with the Comédie Française, and a few years later he won best actor at Cannes for his first film role!"

Gauthier mumbled his excuses as they followed one another single-file up the stairs, past the ground floor with the front of house and lounge, and up to the second floor. "Here it is!" Anouk said, with a wave of her hand. "As you can see, Sandra has a wide selection of clothes and accessories to choose from!"

It took some time for Jean-Marc's eyes to adjust to the large room's general shabbiness and chaos. The "wardrobe" that Anouk referred to comprised four clothing racks against the east wall, crammed with multicolored dresses, coats, jackets, pants, and shirts. Some purses hung at the ends of the racks, as did a bright pink feather boa. Anouk draped it around her bare shoulders and Jean-Marc cringed, embarrassed for her. How could this obviously chaotic woman ever put a play together? His excitement waned, and some of his earlier doubts came creeping back in.

At the far end of the room, there was a window overlooking the street, but it was covered with Post-it notes and small posters and photographs that cut off most of the natural light. Beneath the window, a desk, piled high with books, papers, coffee cups, and wineglasses. To the left of the desk was a small kitchenette, in the same state of chaos as the rest of the room. A half-eaten roast chicken sat on a platter; upon seeing it, one of the cast members let out a gasp of shock.

"There's another toilet up here, for the cast, with a shower," Anouk said, walking around the space. "Unisex, of course."

"Where are the changing rooms?" Gauthier asked.

Anouk motioned with her hand around the room, gesturing that the whole space could function as a changing room. When she saw the dejected look on the Gauthier's face, she added, "It's the twenty-first century, after all! And besides, this play doesn't require many changes of wardrobe."

"Thank goodness," muttered Gauthier.

"Oh, knock it off, Gauthier," Liliane Poncet said, pinching his arm. "You've always been such a crybaby."

The cast looked on, transfixed. It was finally Brigitte who spoke up. "Are you two friends?"

Liliane smiled while Gauthier shuffled his feet back and forth and coughed.

For twenty minutes Marine and Sylvie sat motionless, whispering to each other about the baby and Sylvie's upcoming photography exhibition and looking at the young woman. She was slight, as petite as Sylvie, and some of her light brown hair still stuck to her forehead from the heat. She slept with her mouth slightly open, and at times they could hear her breathing. The corners of her mouth rose at either side, as if she were smiling slightly.

"I'd love to take some photos of her," Sylvie said.

Marine murmured in agreement. "She does look quite angelic, doesn't she? Thank goodness I saw her. How old do you think she is? Thirty?"

"Nah. I'd say twenty-five, possibly less. Did she say anything?"

"Only thank you, and she mumbled something about the heat."

"In French?" Sylvie asked. "She could be a tourist."

"Oh yes, very French." Marine could tell from their slight exchange that their guest was educated, from a good school in Aix or possibly another city—Lyon, or Paris. Yes, probably Paris, Marine decided.

The girl stirred and Marine and Sylvie leaned forward, bracing themselves. She slowly opened her eyes. "I'm so sorry," she whispered.

"It's no bother," Marine quickly said. "You got too hot. It must be over forty degrees out there."

"Here, have some water," Sylvie added, wanting to be useful and perfect like Marine. "Can you sit up?"

"I'll try." The girl shifted and Marine reached under her elbow, helping her to sit up against the sofa's soft cushions.

Sylvie handed the girl the water. "Can you hold it yourself?"

She nodded, took the glass, and sipped. She smiled. "It's cold. Thank you."

"Take as long as you like," Marine said.

The girl closed her eyes and allowed herself to sink into the cushions. Sylvie looked at her watch.

"Try to drink a little more water," Marine suggested. The girl did as she was told, then handed the empty glass back to Sylvie.

"How do you feel?" Marine asked.

"Much better."

And in fact, Marine thought, she did look better. Some color had returned to her thin face, and she was no longer sweating. The girl felt herself being looked at and put a hand to her face. "I'm so embarrassed."

"Don't be," Marine and Sylvie said in unison.

"I should be used to this heat."

"Do you live nearby?" Marine asked. "We haven't lived in this house very long."

"Oh no, we live in Paris."

"But you said you're used to the heat," Sylvie reminded her. She was now getting a bit bored with the exchange, and she wanted to get home.

"It's our vacation house," the girl explained. "Up the road. I got too hot out walking, and a car drove by too close, too fast, and I fell. . . ."

Marine threw her arms up. "I can't believe it! That's the second time something like this has happened since we bought this place." She instinctively put a hand on her stomach.

The girl looked at Marine's belly and said, "A baby. Wow. Lucky. I have to go." She tried to get to her feet.

"Are you sure you're all right?" Marine asked.

"Yes, yes," she replied. She reached behind her back and felt the pockets of her shorts, and her face fell. "My phone!"

"I didn't see one when I helped you down onto the sofa," Marine said.

"You must have dropped it in the road," Sylvie said.

"I was reading something when I was walking. . . ."

Sylvie sighed and gave Marine a look. Marine closed her eyes and shook her head, giving Sylvie a signal that she didn't want her to give the girl a lecture about reading her cell phone while walking.

"I have to find it."

"I'll go out and look," Sylvie said, standing up.

"I'll come with you," said the girl.

"Then we'll all go," Marine said, helping the girl to stand. "I want to make sure you're all right."

As they walked out of the house and down the drive the girl seemed anxious. She kept her eyes fixed on the road ahead, and the closer they got to the open gates the faster she walked. "Whoa," Sylvie said, taking the girl's elbow. "If your phone is lying in the road, it won't have gone anywhere."

The girl didn't speak as they crossed the narrow country road. She immediately began scanning the dry grass at the road's edge. Sylvie did the same on the opposite side. Marine stood still, keeping an eye on the road, watching for cars arriving from either direction.

"Voilà!" Sylvie cried out. "The new iPhone! No wonder you were so worried!" She bent down and picked up the thin silver telephone, handing it to the girl.

"Car!" Marine yelled, putting her arms protectively around the women as the car, a new Mini, drove quickly past without slowing down or giving them space, then disappeared around a bend. "I won't even be able to take the baby for walks here."

"No," Sylvie said. "You won't." She turned to the girl, who'd quickly put her phone in her back pocket. "I'll give you a ride home."

The girl paused, as if wondering whether she should accept.

Marine cut in, "Yes, my friend will drive you home. No arguing."

"All right," the girl answered, and she followed Sylvie and Marine across the road and back up the cypress-lined drive. Sylvie unlocked her car and opened the passenger door. The girl obediently got in, adjusted her seat belt, and stared straight ahead. Sylvie closed the door and rolled her eyes at Marine. "No thank you. Spoiled millennial," she whispered.

Sylvie hugged Marine and walked around the car and got in the driver's side. Marine tapped on the passenger window and the girl rolled it down. "Thank you so much," the girl said, with sincerity, thought Marine. "You were so kind to me."

"I just realized we don't know your name," Marine said.

The girl smiled. "Aurore. Like the dawn."

Chapter Four

❧

Monday, August 7

Sandra Gastaldi left the theater with butterflies in her stomach. She'd worked on the wardrobe with Anouk for years; her apartment was just around the corner on rue de la Paix, so it had always been easy for her to come and go. During the day Sandra worked at a bank on the Cours Mirabeau. She enjoyed her job, but the theater was special; the energy and excitement stayed with her during each production even if it wasn't a sellout. But at times Anouk drove her crazy. It seemed no sooner had Sandra organized the clothes on their racks than Anouk arrived, disheveling everything. Sandra had learned to memorize where each piece of clothing was and to hide the better ones from Anouk's messy hands.

But Sandra had never acted before. Was that first meeting—it could hardly be called a rehearsal, as they hadn't read any lines— a typical one? Was it normal for the cast to look at one another bewildered? Perhaps they were just confused by Anouk's messiness. *It's easier for me,* she thought. *I grew up with Anouk.* They'd gone to school together, and Sandra had taken years of ballet classes when the dance school was still run by Pauline and Léo Singer, Anouk's parents. Sandra had always loved sewing and thrift-store shopping, so she just sort of fell into the costume job, at first helping Anouk find great clothes for the theater and then taking over the job once Anouk got tired of it, which was after the first play. Anouk was one of those people who got under your skin, and no matter how many times you tried to shake them off, they kept coming back into your life, perhaps because of their charm, or energy, or humor. In Anouk's case it was her ability to put together a play, get Aixois to pay to see it, have it run for a week or so, then break it down and start the process all over again a few months later. Sandra had no idea how she did it, but Anouk's enthusiasm was infectious.

Sandra opened the front door to her building and walked up two flights to her one-bedroom flat. Her front two windows, in the living room and kitchen, looked out onto the street, and from her sofa she could look right down the rue du 11 Novembre. She could even see the theater's front door. Sometimes she would watch people file out of the theater, laughing or animatedly talking, and it made her heart sing and her volunteer work at the theater feel all the more worth it. She'd been content enough working behind the scenes on the costumes. On the whole she was shy, and she considered most of the actors who passed through the theater's doors a little too narcissistic for her liking. Anouk had begged her once or twice to take on a small role so she could "discover the magic of theater," but Sandra knew it was only because an actor had pulled out at the last minute.

No, Sandra had never been tempted to join the cast, until now. Because of Marcel Pagnol.

A former bank manager had taken all the employees for a team-building day in the hills between Marseille and Aubagne. It was years ago, Sandra remembered, a Saturday, but they were paid—she was an intern then—so she was thrilled. The mid-eighties remakes of Marcel Pagnol's films *Jean de Florette* and *Manon des Sources* had just hit the cinemas and soon the whole world, it seemed, had fallen in love with the author. Unbeknownst to the employees, they were to spend the afternoon following a troupe of actors performing various scenes from Pagnol's plays and films in the very hills where he had spent his summers. That evening, happily worn out from walking and laughing and intently listening to the actors' thick Midi accents, the team had dinner in the restaurant Cigalon, named after one of the plays. The restaurant was in the village of La Treille, technically part of the 11th arrondissement of Marseille but only in postal code. Located in a nineteenth-century former grand house, the restaurant's terrace looked out over hills and valleys dotted with olive trees.

That day Sandra fell in love with Pagnol's work, especially *Cigalon*. It seemed that this restaurant was the exact same one that had been described in the play (it was, her boss later told her, and the chef in the play was based on a real chef in the village of La Treille who hated to serve clients). As much as Sandra enjoyed the other plays, *Cigalon* would always remain her favorite, no doubt because of that day, and because she loved cooking and eating. Anouk often chose what Sandra considered to be melancholy plays, but that spring over coffee she asked if Sandra could recommend a comedy. Perhaps one that takes place in Provence?

Anouk was so excited about *Cigalon* that Sandra had taken the plunge and offered to take on a small role. They agreed she would play Adèle, the mother of the party of four who try to have lunch, unsuccessfully, at the restaurant. The family appears only in the first act, so learning the lines was easy, and for the duration of the play Sandra could be backstage helping with the wardrobe changes.

It was finally getting dark, and Sandra opened her window so that hopefully some little bit of cooler air could flow through her apartment. She sighed; she wished they would have read through the play. Perhaps upon their next meeting? She went over some of her lines in her head, looking over toward the theater. A flash of something in the street caught her eye and she stopped rehearsing. There. She saw it again: A woman had turned onto the rue du 11 Novembre from a small side street, walked in front of the theater, stopped briefly, then turned left toward the busy Cours Sextius, disappearing from Sandra's view.

Sandra sat back, perplexed. Dozens of Aixois walked up and down the street every day; it was so narrow that only locals with special permits could drive on it. What had made her look twice at this woman? She felt herself getting anxious. It was too hot to eat, but she supposed she should nibble on something. She opened the refrigerator and pulled out a yogurt. While she ate she kept thinking of the woman. *Vas-y Sandra*, she thought to herself. *C'était quoi, exactement?*

As she threw the empty yogurt container into the garbage, part of her hair fell into her eyes. She gathered it and put it back in place with a barrette. Then she stopped and touched her head, still warm from the summer evening. It was a hat—the woman had worn a hat. And it hadn't been a summer hat (a straw one, for example); she was sure of it. It had been wool, or perhaps felt. A dark color. Much like the hat she had selected for Adèle to wear in the play. She sat down at the kitchen table. Greta Garbo, she realized. In the film *Ninotchka*. That was why she had been transfixed! It was a cloche, a bell-shaped close-fitting hat popular in the 1930s.

It was a warm evening and Verlaque and Marine sat side by side in chaise longues, their legs extended, their hands reaching across the gap between the two chairs. He squeezed her hand and turned to her.

"Should I cancel my trip to Paris?" he asked. "I leave tomorrow."

"No!" Marine said. "I'm three weeks away from my due date, and you'll be back in two days, right?"

"Yes," Verlaque said. "But the conference starts early in the morning, so my train ticket is for tomorrow late afternoon. So I'll sleep at my father's two nights."

"Sylvie already told me she can cover if there's an emergency," Marine said.

"Oh, I'm so relieved."

"Don't be so sarcastic."

"But you told me that during today's drama with the girl—"

"Aurore."

"Yes, Aurore, that Sylvie couldn't wait to be done with it."

"Maybe she had things to do downtown."

Verlaque snorted. "Well, Sylvie aside, I checked before we came outside and there's nothing to eat."

"There are olives," Marine suggested, laughing.

"I ate them," he said. "Why don't I go to the village and pick up a pizza?"

"You know, that sounds amazing. Plus, the baby will love that," she said. "Everyone likes pizza."

"Then we'll give the baby an Italian name," Verlaque said.

"Paolo," Marine said.

"Or Rosa," he countered. "Because I think it's a girl." He got up and walked toward the house.

Marine watched her husband. "Red peppers and sausage!" she yelled after him.

"I know, I know! And mushrooms!"

"Thank you!"

That night, no one slept well. Marine couldn't get comfortable, even with three pillows tucked behind her back. Verlaque, beside her, was conscious of her every move, worried that she'd go into labor after such a stressful day. But around 1:00 a.m. he felt her body relax and could hear her heavy, deep breathing. He turned over, thinking of that girl Aurore walking up the drive, and the open gates.

Sylvie, in her apartment in Aix, lay on her back with her arms folded behind her head. She thought of Marine's new house, with its cool white linen fabrics and polished terra-cotta floors. Back in Aix Sylvie's mattress was a decade or two old, and it was a miracle if she washed her sheets once a week. A car beeped its horn outside her window, and some kids walking down the street yelled at the driver to shut up, their cries louder than his horn. She imagined Marine's country house, quiet now, except perhaps for the hooting of an owl. She smiled, knowing that in a few short weeks their house would be busy at night, the baby crying for his or her night feeding, Verlaque pacing if the baby was unhappy. It made her miss her daughter, Charlotte, who'd been staying with a friend during their summer horse camp. The camp finished tomorrow. Sylvie would pick Charlotte up—she'd be on time for once—and they'd do something special that day, just the two of them. They had a week together before Charlotte would go to Berlin to visit her father, who, like Sylvie, was a professional art photographer. She rolled over, bending her right leg and slipping her hand under the pillow as she always did. In minutes she was asleep.

Chapter Five

﹏

Tuesday, August 8

The next morning Marine looked out the kitchen window at the manicured gardens, the rows of perfectly clipped lavender, the green-blue swimming pool. "We're prisoners," she said, setting her orange juice on the table.

"Sorry?" Verlaque asked, looking up from his newspaper.

"This house. The team of gardeners, the maid I now need because the house is so big. The gates." She laughed. "Or should I say the automatic gates that are always broken."

"I've never liked gates," Verlaque agreed. "It's something my mother would have wanted."

"Bourgeois?"

"Petty."

"Ah, yes. Nouveau riche."

"Bruno and Hélène don't have gates," he said.

"The Pauliks live on a farm, so no."

"Some farms have gates." He finished his coffee. "But we need them here. That girl, she walked up the drive and almost straight into the house. I kept thinking of that."

"No, I saw her, silly."

"Luckily. I can't think of what may have happened."

"Nothing did," Marine said. "She was too hot, we gave her water, Sylvie drove her home. End of story."

Verlaque nodded, not wanting to upset his wife. "So now that we've decided on baby names, I think you want to talk about where this baby will live. That's where this conversation is going, right?"

Marine reached across the table and squeezed his hand. "I've been thinking of it, even before yesterday."

"I thought so."

"It's just that school would be easier downtown."

"Yes," Verlaque said, getting up to make another espresso. "Although school is a long way off."

Marine smiled, knowing that her husband for months had been obsessing over which school their child would go to. She'd even overheard him at the fruit-and-vegetable shop asking the cashier, a young woman in her late twenties who'd grown up in Aix, where she had gone to school and if she'd liked it. Marine had turned away, embarrassed, when Verlaque asked the girl to rate it on a scale of 1 to 10. But the girl, bright but bored with her job (working because she loved fresh organic produce and wanted to save money to travel to Argentina with her boyfriend), giggled and gave École Sallier an 8.

"Even before our child goes to school," Marine said. "In town I'd be able to take him or her around on foot, and visit friends, and shops. The market. Out here I'd be lonely." She leaned back, looking at the swimming pool.

"What about the stairs?" Verlaque asked. "The apartment is on the fourth floor."

"So?"

"The stroller."

"Oh!" she said. "I'm not going to get one."

Verlaque swung around from his coffee preparation. "Pardon?"

"I bought a snuggly. One of those—"

"I know what they are. You're just like Sylvie, assuming I've never heard of Fendi, or Instagram."

Marine laughed. "Sorry."

"What about if *I* want to take the baby out?"

"Well, we can share the snuggly."

"Certainly not!" Verlaque cried. "I'd be a laughingstock!"

"Oh, come on!" Marine protested. "It's the twenty-first century!"

"You can use the snuggly, but I'm buying a stroller."

"Fine," she said, feeling the baby move. "I've waited a long time, so I want to feel the baby next to my skin." She put her hand up to her nose.

"Sorry about the coffee smell," he said, returning to the table. "Well, I suppose I could park the stroller downstairs in the front entrance. At least we've agreed on names."

"Yes, we have."

"So you can carry Paolo or Rosa in the snuggly, and they will throw up all over your lovely sundress. I'll use the stroller."

Marine laughed and gestured, tossing her napkin. Verlaque quickly put the cup to his mouth. "Hiding behind your espresso cup," she said.

"I can't wait until this little kid is born."

"Yeah, me, too."

Get comfortable with your character. That was the unanimous advice from three acting books Jean-Marc had read over the summer. Once he had plowed through those, he read the play over and over again, to the point that he knew not only his character's lines but most of the other ones as well.

It hadn't been difficult to learn the role of the Count, as he appears only halfway through the play. The Count—who is in fact a middle-aged petty crook—is first seen sitting with a fellow ruffian on a park bench. The two men complain of their woes: debts to pay off, arguments to resolve, hunger, and a continual lack of funds. They decide that it's only in prison that one is safe from the problems of the outside world. Six months in prison, clothed and fed and warm, while your adversaries forget all about those old grievances. The aging hoodlum thus decides to spend his last fifty francs on a fine suit and a taxi ride through Marseille, where he'll end up spending the afternoon eating a gourmet meal in a fine restaurant. The plan: He'll refuse to pay, and the chef, enraged, will call for the police. He will be arrested and sent to jail. Hopefully Aix's jail; he and his friend agree it is the best in the region. Unluckily for him, the taxi driver chooses Cigalon's restaurant. Of all the fine restaurants in Marseille! The hoodlum, with all his bravado and his well-thought-out plan, meets his match in the eccentric chef.

Jean-Marc decided he would ham it up in that first scene on the park bench. While walking to the theater, and only when no one could hear him, he tried to perfect a thick Marseillais accent. Cigalon takes the hoodlum for a count as he arrives in a taxi, wearing a fine suit and hat. The hoodlum, seeing he's been taken for a rich nobleman, exaggerates his wealth and prestige, behaving as an obnoxious snob. That would be fun, Jean-Marc thought. He'd met plenty of those throughout his life. For the restaurant scenes Jean-Marc would switch to a studied Parisian accent, keeping a bit of the southern accent, as the crook wouldn't be able to completely hide it. The accent would have to slip out now and again; how the actor who played Cigalon reacted to that would be their choice, for there was no note of it in Pagnol's play. It was Jean-Marc's idea, and he was quite pleased with it. He quickened his step and by the time he opened the front doors of the theater he was flushed with excitement.

He could hear their voices—and some laughter, he realized with relief—when he walked in the doors. His fellow actors were gathered around the sofas and armchairs at the back of the main hall on the ground floor. He saw Anouk first, flipping through papers and muttering, as if she were looking for something. Two of the actors were being led in stretching exercises by Liliane Poncet. The little girl—whose name, he remembered, was Brigitte—jumped in to join and easily bent down to touch her toes, laughing.

"My child, this is not a laughing matter!" Liliane cried. "Warm-up exercises are absolutely essential for actors!" She smiled and winked at Jean-Marc.

Jean-Marc had already done his exercises at home, so he looked around to see if there was anyone he could chat with. The costume woman was sitting alone, and he sat down beside her. "Good morning, Sandra," he said. Thankfully he remembered her name; he had a cousin about the same age—forties or early fifties—and with the same name.

"Good morning!" she answered brightly, turning to face him. "I'm sorry, I can't remember . . ."

"Jean-Marc."

"Oh, yes!"

"Who are you playing?" he asked.

"Adèle," she answered. "The mother of the family who first try to get served at Cigalon's restaurant. And you're the Count, right?"

"Yes." He leaned forward and whispered, "It's my first play."

"Mine, too. Well, I've worked on dozens of Anouk's plays, but only in wardrobe. This is my first role."

"It's too bad we don't have any scenes together."

"That's true, you come in at the second half, when I've already gone, unfed." They laughed. "Well, we can look out for each other, can't we?"

Jean-Marc smiled. "Exactly. Since we won't be onstage at the same time, we can give each other helpful hints."

Sandra smiled and then paused. For some reason she wanted to tell him about the woman she had seen last night. They could turn it into a shared joke. He was a teacher, she guessed, perhaps a classical musician at the conservatoire. Piano. But she held back; she didn't want to seem like she was overreacting. It was just a woman, dressed in vintage clothes. Sandra was disturbed by it, and she couldn't explain why, and since she couldn't explain it, it seemed silly to tell someone. "What do you do, when not acting?" she asked.

"I'm a courtroom lawyer."

"Oh!"

Jean-Marc laughed. "You hadn't guessed that, had you?"

"No, to be honest. I had you playing the piano. I work in home loans at the Crédit Lyonnais."

Jean-Marc was about to reply when Anouk called out, clapping her hands. "Okay, okay! Ready to begin!"

The actors sat down around Anouk, who remained standing. She rocked from side to side, her giant pink harem pants transfixing Jean-Marc, who, snapping himself out of his reverie, decided he hadn't had enough coffee. Anouk said, "Before we do a read-through, I'd like to give you my vision for the play. It's quite simple: The setting is nineteen thirty-five, on the terrace of a quaint Provençal restaurant. It is late spring or summer. As you've read the play by now, you know the story. Cigalon is a chef who, after thirty-five years of serving lunches and dinners to clients in Paris's best restaurants, now owns a restaurant in La Treille where he only cooks for himself and his sister, Sidonie. He refuses to serve clients, as we see in the first scene. Then, a neighbor, a former washerwoman named Mme Toffi, played by our own illustrious Liliane Poncet, opens a restaurant on the same street. Cigalon is enraged! The nerve of Mme Toffi! Things liven up in the second half when Cigalon finally agrees to cook for a client as he's impressed by the client's *apparent* wealth and prestige, *and* he wants to make Mme Toffi jealous. There's the story. I've made no changes to the cast, save for casting a girl in the role of Le Petit. I've made no changes to the text, but once we've done the read, there may be some minor changes, making certain words or phrasing easier for a contemporary audience to understand. We'll see how it goes."

Jean-Marc smiled and nodded, relieved that Anouk, despite the awful harem pants and the constant searching for lost items, seemed to know what she was doing as far as the play was concerned. "The first read we'll do will be what I call a pleasure read," she went on. "It's just to hear the script, to get a feel for the words spoken aloud. We don't even need to change our seats." She reached into her bag and got out the text. Jean-Marc, horrified, realized that it was a different edition than his own copy. Had she instructed the others on which version to buy? He was sure she hadn't told him.

"Anouk!" Sandra said, holding up her book, the same one that Jean-Marc had ordered at Goulard. "Mais alors!" The other actors murmured in agreement, each one holding up that same volume.

"I have the same book as the others!" Brigitte called out, holding up hers. "And Sempé drew the cover! I love his drawings!"

Everyone laughed except Anouk, who looked at her old book in bewilderment. "No matter!" she finally said. "I'll order the same one as the rest of you, and today if someone could share a book . . ."

"Really, *chérie*," said an old woman, leaning on a cane, shaking her head and clicking her tongue in disproval. "You found that on our bookshelf, didn't you? It's older than the hills. I think I bought it in the sixties."

"It's quite simple to instruct the actors on which book to buy," said a man the same age as the old woman.

"I'm sorry, Papa, but there's just so much to do!" Anouk said.

Jean-Marc looked at Sandra, his new friend, in confusion. "They're her parents," she whispered. "They each have a small role in the play. They couldn't be here yesterday."

Jean-Marc nodded, wondering why this information, like which text to buy, hadn't been communicated.

Anouk sat down next to her mother. "Let's begin even though Gauthier isn't here yet," she said. "I'll read the action prompts. Here we go." She coughed and lowered her voice. "It's a sunny Sunday. At the entrance to a village, a small group walks up the steep main street. There's a fat man, a boy of fifteen, a forty-year-old woman, and an old woman walking a dog. The group gets closer, leaning on a wall to admire the countryside."

The actors began reading their lines. The family exchanges remarks about the beauty of La Treille, the view, and how the fifteen-year-old boy, Chalumeau, is in a bad mood and, as usual, hungry. The actor reading the boy's lines did it with the nonchalance and boredom so common in teenagers that it made Jean-Marc and some of the other actors laugh out loud. The family sets off up the road in search of a restaurant, stopping when they see Cigalon's fine terrace and the green-painted sign *Café-Restaurant-Cigalon*. Anouk's mother, it was now clear, was playing the grandmother of the family, and she was just about to read one of her lines when Gauthier Lesage walked into the room. He bellowed, "Hello there, everyone!"

"Gauthier!" Liliane Poncet hollered back. "You know the fifteen-minute-early theater rule! Ten minutes early is on time. On time is late!" She looked at her watch, having to hold it very close to her face to read it. "And in this case, you're twenty minutes late!"

"I don't have to answer to you!" Gauthier replied angrily. "It's none of your business—"

"I didn't ask you where you were," Liliane said, glaring. "And anyway, I can only imagine . . ."

"Here's where we could use a courtroom lawyer," Sandra whispered to Jean-Marc, winking.

"You could apologize, Gauthier," Liliane said.

Gauthier sat down and sighed, stretching his arms out in front of him, as if that was all the exercise he needed to warm up. He cracked his knuckles.

"How about we continue reading?" Abdul suggested.

"Yes, let's go on. This play is fun!" Brigitte said. She looked at the boy playing the teenager. "And you're so funny, Mathieu!"

Mathieu looked flatly at her and shrugged, completely in character, his mouth wide open, his eyes fixed straight ahead at a spot on the wall. Everyone laughed.

"Okay, Maman, it's your line now," Anouk said. "Don't forget, you're a bit crazy."

Mme Singer looked at her daughter in exasperation and began to read.

Halfway through the play the actors took a break for tea and coffee. Miraculously, the refreshments were laid out on one of the large tables downstairs despite Anouk calling out at various points, "Where are the teabags?" and "There's no more sugar!" Teabags and sugar were found, and a lemon loaf—baked by Emile Leclerc's wife—appeared. Jean-Marc thanked him for the cake. "Your reading was excellent," he added to the giant Leclerc. "I already have a clear picture of Ludovic's character, even his physical appearance, just from listening to you."

"Thanks," Emile said, swallowing a piece of cake and brushing crumbs off his belly. "That's very kind. Do you play the gendarme?"

"No," Jean-Marc replied. "The Count."

"Fun role."

"Is this your first play?"

"No, I've done lots around Aix and Marseille. Usually small theaters like this one, but last year I was lucky enough to do two plays at La Criée."

"Really?" Jean-Marc asked. "That's impressive! La Criée is a Marseille institution. You're a professional actor, then?"

Emile laughed. "Hardly. I'm a butcher who's caught the acting bug."

Jean-Marc, about to take a sip of tea, froze. He thought he'd recognized Emile! "Here in Aix?"

"The butcher shop at the bottom of rue Espariat," Emile said, unperturbed. "I own it with my two brothers."

Jean-Marc nodded, grateful that Emile hadn't taken offense. "I go there sometimes!" he said, honestly. "To tell you the truth, I don't eat a lot of meat, but when I do, I shop at your place. I thought you looked familiar, but it's hard to tell . . ."

"Out of context," they both said in unison, Emile finishing Jean-Marc's sentence. The two men laughed.

"And you?" Emile asked. "When you're not acting?"

"I'm a lawyer," Jean-Marc replied.

"A lawyer!" Gauthier Lesage bellowed. Jean-Marc swung around to see the actor standing behind him, grinning. He cringed as Gauthier turned around to face the others. "Liliane! Did you hear that? This Jean-Marc's a lawyer! You can hire him for your next divorce!" Liliane Poncet, who had been speaking to Brigitte and Mathieu, turned red in the face. Unperturbed, Gauthier went on, "Or your next business venture!" He doubled over, laughing at his own joke.

"Listen, Gauthier," Liliane began, her voice wavering. "You're embarrassing yourself."

"Poor Guy Minoux. Bit it in a car accident. Then Stéphane was happy with you, but you got itchy feet once more," Gauthier said, now walking around the room, enthralled by the attention.

"That's enough," Liliane said. She sounded like she was about to cry.

Jean-Marc looked at the floor, unable to watch the famous Liliane Poncet reduced to tears. After a few seconds of staring at the concrete floor, he looked up to see Emile Leclerc towering over Gauthier. Emile said, "How about you sit down and finish your tea and cake?"

"I don't have to," Gauthier said sullenly, but with a note of fear in his voice. Jean-Marc watched, his teacup trembling in his hands.

Emile stepped even closer, so that his stomach touched Gauthier. "You'd better eat your cake," he repeated. "My wife made it especially for today." Gauthier sat down. "There will be no more nonsense during our rehearsals," Emile said. "Understood?"

Gauthier nodded, his eyes downcast. The room was silent. Someone shifted their position, their shoe making a squeaking noise across the floor.

Anouk said, "Let's get started on the second half of the play."

"Wow," mumbled Mathieu, the teenager. "That was cool." Jean-Marc, puzzled, looked at the boy, who remained straight-faced.

Did Mathieu think that he had just seen some improvisation? Or a scene already rehearsed by Emile and Gauthier? Or was he simply, like Jean-Marc, impressed by the butcher/actor's authority? At any rate, Jean-Marc was grateful to get back to the play. Real life was too messy.

Chapter Six

꿍

Tuesday, August 8

Emile Leclerc hated being the enforcer. But because of his height—six feet two inches, enormous for a Frenchman from the south—and his great girth, he had since adolescence been regularly called upon to settle skirmishes. At the butcher shop he appeared to be even bigger, as he and his brothers, behind their gleaming counters, stood on a platform raised about four inches. But clients weren't intimidated. They lined up to ask his advice: What makes your stuffed cabbage so good? *Chopped chestnuts, but I shouldn't be telling you, Mme Doudel!* What dishes can I prepare with those tender pig's cheeks you're selling? *Ah, in winter my grandmother's bourguignon, very simply done with onions and carrots; or, in the summer, cook them with fennel, white wine, and olives.* Emile's brothers didn't begrudge his notoriety. Far from it, as his older brother, Gustav, loved the business end of the shop, keeping the accounts in order and the staff happy; and Louis, the youngest, made the orders, visiting the farms and getting the best prices for the most organic meats he could find. Louis's good looks meant that a number of the clients came to see him, too, including Jean-Marc.

Emile smiled as he walked down the rue Victor Leydet toward his apartment, conveniently located between the theater and the butcher shop. He considered himself blessed. He loved his job, although at times his back ached from the physicality of it: the cold of the meat locker, the constant cutting and chopping, bending over to chat with customers, getting up before dawn almost every day. But it was his passion, too, and one that he constantly sought to inform himself about, going over ancient recipes, watching cooking programs, talking to fellow butchers while traveling around France during his precious time off. His acting passion had happened by mistake, during a weekend when his wife, Claire, who taught French literature at a local high school, needed his help as she prepared the play *Tartuffe* for her students. That play, combined with the advice of his doctor to work less and find a hobby that had nothing to do with meat, preferably one that didn't send him into a refrigerated room every few minutes, hooked him on theater. As he read the role of Tartuffe along with his wife, she had tears in her eyes. "You could have been an actor," she said, hugging him. "Your timing is perfect."

Both his brothers lived on the outskirts of Aix, and with the growing success of the business, they installed swimming pools and manicured gardens. But Emile and Claire preferred being able to reach everything, especially their jobs, on foot. From their little rooftop terrace they could see the delicate wrought iron spire of the neighboring chapel of Les Augustins; in the other direction, if they placed themselves perfectly between a neighbor's two chimney pots, they could see the Gothic stone steeple of Saint-Jean-de-Malte. They grew herbs to use in the kitchen, and every five years or so they replaced the olive tree, which got too big for its terra-cotta pot.

But as he walked, Emile found his smile turning into a frown. He was thinking of Gauthier Lesage. He opened and clenched his fists, trying to stay calm. How dare Gauthier show up late, especially when he had the principal role! And the way he had spoken to Liliane was unforgivable. It didn't matter that Liliane was famous.

The actors had carried on with their reading, but the jolly ambiance was lost, all thanks to Gauthier. And Emile wasn't even impressed with his reading; he stumbled over a few of the passages, as if he was reading them for the first time. Emile supposed that Gauthier had got the role because of his appearance in a number of silly made-for-television films and a few horrendously bad game shows.

When Emile walked in the front door of their apartment he felt an enormous relief. Claire met him in the hallway and wrapped her arms around him, her two hands not quite meeting. "How was it?" she asked. "You look exhausted. Sit down in the living room and I'll bring you a pastis. It's too hot on the terrace."

Emile took off his shoes and collapsed into his favorite armchair, rescued from his grandparents' farm. Claire came back carrying a tray with two glasses of pastis, a bowl of black olives, and some cashews, and sat down across from him. "Cheers," she said, holding her cold glass up to his. Emile mumbled in reply and after a few sips told Claire all about the rehearsal. They laughed as he described Mathieu's taking on, full-heartedly, the role of the bored teenager, and little Brigitte's enthusiasm for just about everything; Anouk's absentmindedness and yet her well-organized reading and thoughtful advice; Liliane Poncet's warmth, despite her bossiness. He thought that Jean-Marc and Sandra did particularly good readings, and they had obviously prepared. He sighed, and Claire said, "You're leaving out the principal player. Cigalon."

Emile sighed. "Gauthier read that role as if he were bored!"

"But Cigalon *is* bored of cooking, isn't he?"

"No, not at all. He's bored by serving fussy clients. He's bored with running a restaurant. But he still loves cooking."

Claire laughed. "Just for himself. Now I remember the story."

Emile drained his pastis and went on, "And why not just cook for himself? I can't imagine serving lunch six days a week, then having to cook dinner two hours later! Name me a harder job!"

"I can think of some—yours and mine, for example—"

Emile cut in, "Cigalon should be played with bravado! Passion! Even rage!"

Claire nodded and resisted saying aloud, *Cigalon should be played by you.* She knew it was what they were both thinking.

At this same moment Abdul Khattabi, at fifty exactly the same age as Emile Leclerc, was also in his living room. In his hand was a glass of freshly made lemonade. He hesitated before taking his first sip, looking at the pale yellow liquid, in which several plump pieces of pulp floated, ice cubes hitting the glass when he moved it in his hand. Two children ran around him, but for the moment all he saw was the lemonade. He closed his eyes and took his first sip. The frustration of the play reading washed away with the tart-tasting juice. Reaching out, he patted one of the heads that ran past him.

"Let your father relax," his wife, Rachida, called after the children, who in turn squealed and chased each other into another room of their crowded flat. He and Rachida had three older children, one of them still at home with them but nowhere to be seen, and two smaller ones born many years later. It was Rachida's idea. There was no saying no to her, once she had an idea. He was dying for a cigarette, but had to wait for the children to go to bed.

"What's wrong?" Rachida asked as she walked by carrying a hamper of folded laundry. "Normally you're chatting a mile a minute after one of your play rehearsals, and this time you're acting!"

"One of the actors is causing problems, that's all," Abdul said.

"It was just your first read-through. It will get better, I'm sure."

"No, it will get worse."

Rachida set down the hamper and sat next to Abdul. "Are you being a pessimist? My Abdul? The same man who convinced me to buy this apartment, even though we were refused by every bank in Aix for a loan?"

Abdul managed a smile. "Until the branch office of Crédit Agricole in Les Milles said yes. No, today I'm being a realist. This actor will cause problems."

The children ran back into the living room and Rachida told them to say good night to their father, and ushered them into their bedrooms. As she left, she turned around to Abdul and mimed smoking a cigarette. She winked and laughed as she walked out of the room.

Abdul got up and walked to the long narrow balcony—one of

the reasons why he had wanted this apartment so much—and stepped out, taking a pack of cigarettes out of his pocket and ritualistically tapping the bottom to release one. He smiled, with love for Rachida and the children, and for this moment of pleasure. He didn't feel guilty about smoking, as he never drank alcohol and Rachida cooked the healthiest and tastiest food in all of Aix. He looked out at the other apartments in his view, all of them hastily built in the 1990s and all of them full of people like them: immigrants. Not even the students lived out here.

As he smoked, leaning his arms on the metal railing and watching the sun go down, he thought of his family in Tunisia. He knew exactly why he was out of sorts this evening: Gauthier Lesage reminded him of his older brother, Brahim.

On paper, Brahim and Gauthier had nothing in common. Abdul had looked up Gauthier's biography on the way home on the bus, on one of those film database websites that his two eldest children used. Gauthier Lesage was the son of a rich industrial family from Lyon. Brahim, on the other hand, was the eldest son of six children, born into a poor farming family in southern Tunisia. But Rachida always said that Brahim was a "man child," and Gauthier showed all the signs of belonging to that rank, too. They were both spoiled and lived in a childish world, partly encouraged by the way their parents treated them. Both men were egotistical. They couldn't help others, as they only thought of themselves. Brahim could never do wrong, even when it was obvious to everyone, even neighbors, that he made no effort to improve himself or help out the family. The rest of the five children just got on with their lives and moved away, as Brahim inherited the family farm. "Your parents didn't help him, spoiling him like that," Rachida would remind Abdul. "You are much better off here, in France." And Abdul would answer in the same way he always did when he and Rachida had a heart-to-heart, reminding them both of the random chances in life that allow one to meet the love of their life coming home from work: "Thank goodness for the thirty-one bus."

Chapter Seven

❧

Wednesday, August 9

Verlaque pulled closed the red doors of his father's house on the rue des Petits Pères, glad to have had late-afternoon coffee and cakes with his father and his father's girlfriend, Rebecca, but equally glad that it—and the never-ending talk of the new baby—was over. The conference that day had been even duller than he had feared, and now he wanted to walk. Luckily he had slept well the night before; he always did in his father's big gloomy house. His father and Rebecca were dining with friends that evening—it had been booked ages ago—and so he was on his own. Tomorrow he'd get up early so as not to bother them, head straight for the conference, put in an appearance, and then get on a train back to Provence. He could even try to change his train ticket, if he cut out of the conference a bit early. He suddenly felt better. He had a plan.

Outside, on a tiny paved square, the red doors, while large, gave no clue as to what lay behind: an immense four-bedroom house with a small courtyard, in the middle of Paris. Technically this was the 2nd arrondissement, but the family had always considered it the 1st. It was on the border between the two, just behind the imposing Banque de France and Jardin du Palais Royal. Miraculously, the street hadn't changed much from when Verlaque had lived at the house. It was so central, and so pricey, that new shops didn't have the money to open here, and certainly not restaurants. Those were farther north and to the west, in the trendier part of the 2nd arrondissement.

He looked up and saw that the religious bookstore was still there. Its wood facade had been given a new coat of rather pleasing glossy burgundy-colored paint, and at first glance it looked more like an antique shop—for there were plenty of those around—and not a place to buy books of the saints' lives, rosaries, and votive candles. His mother had been the only family member to shop there; she was of a noble but impoverished family, and although she had never seemed to care about anyone around her, she somehow remembered to buy Communion and confirmation presents for nephews, nieces, and children of her posh friends.

Dammann Frères, the tea shop, was next door, and he went in to buy a tin of Lapsang Souchong tea. He was sure he could buy it in Aix, but he felt restless, as if he needed to do errands instead of just walking aimlessly around the city, which is what he knew he would do after buying the tea. Outside the shop he looked up and saw an oratory of the Virgin Mary, protected by a painted wooden niche, and now he remembered how the religious bookstore could afford to have stayed open all these years: It was part of a large convent. He had no idea if the nuns were still here;

he doubted it, as the upper-story apartments had bright flowers in their window boxes and what looked like modern windows. One or two had terraces with cheerful striped awnings.

He bought his tea and then walked south, toward the Louvre, the bag swinging awkwardly beside him. Could he do more shopping in order to fill the bag? Maybe he could buy a small bottle of water, as the tourists always seemed to have. He could use some water; the lunch had been heavy—Maria, his father's cook and housekeeper, was Spanish and believed in hearty lunches—and they had finished two bottles of wine between the three of them. His father had never been a great drinker, but Rebecca loved wine and took it upon herself to refill the cellar with those she researched using various wine magazines. Verlaque supposed he should refer to Rebecca as his father's partner; they weren't married, and *girlfriend* was too infantile for a Cézanne scholar from Yale and someone in her midforties, thirty years younger than his father. But *partner* was too lacking in affection, too businesslike, and Rebecca had brought so much happiness and ease to the elder Verlaque.

Before he knew it he was at the busy rue de Rivoli, waiting to cross the street with hordes of tourists and locals. He turned briefly around and saw that a large purse store still had items on sale. He considered going in and buying something for Marine, but she was choosy about handbags, and she always chose comfort over luxury or fashion. Her friends teased her that she was a martyr and should buy more luxurious things for herself, and she shook it off with her usual good grace. And soon she wouldn't need a handbag at all; it would be too cumbersome with the snuggly and the baby.

He crossed the street and walked through the stone archway

of the Louvre, and was duly impressed, as always, by what was beyond: the gigantic open square and its glass-and-steel pyramid. People were lining up to get into the museum or taking pictures of the pyramid. A young man stretched out on the pavement, his whole body flat out on the hot concrete, to get a dramatic shot of the building. Verlaque was proud when he saw this kind of enthusiasm for his hometown. He realized he didn't feel the same way in Aix, probably because he hadn't grown up there.

There was no place to light up a cigar around here, so he moved on. His father had offered up the courtyard for Verlaque to smoke in, but he had wanted to get out and walk. Besides, he would be sleeping there tonight, in his old room now transformed in tasteful beiges by a well-known interior designer. Tomorrow the rest of the meetings at the Ministry of Justice would be painful, full of back-and-forth arguments that went around in circles until they decided that they would resume the discussion in their next meeting in three months. Those who didn't work in it criticized France's penal system—but, Verlaque always argued, didn't that happen in every country? His colleagues in Italy, England, and even Germany faced the same criticism that he did. In France the questions revolved around the magistrate's role—his role. Could a magistrate lead an investigation and also participate in it? Would they remain neutral, or become the accuser? Still, he was happy to have an excuse to be in Paris, even if he felt guilty being away from Marine. He hoped that didn't mean he was an egoist, like his mother and certainly like his real estate mogul younger brother, Sébastien, who had been absent that afternoon even though he'd been invited. Something about "the deal of the century in Montreuil," or perhaps it was Montrouge; Verlaque had only half listened when they spoke on the phone.

Walking over the Pont du Carrousel and into the 6th, he decided that he'd smoke his cigar in a new bar he had heard about, hidden behind a barbershop. A few of the guys in his cigar club, most of whom had to come regularly to Paris for business, had been there and raved about it. He picked up his pace, having finally decided upon a destination.

By the time he arrived at the twirling red-and-white barber sign he was lightly sweating. It wasn't as hot in Paris as it was in Aix, at least not today, but he was no longer used to Paris's humidity. They had joked about it at lunch, relieved to be inside. Rebecca told them it was even more humid in Connecticut.

Most cigar bars, even in luxury hotels, were hidden. Usually he found himself asking employees for directions. Smoking was now an evil pastime and cigars were something enjoyed by Mafioso and crooked right-wing politicians. He smiled and thought of Virginie in his cigar club, a pharmacist and outspoken socialist. This bar was an extreme case: All he could see through the window was a thirtysomething man getting a beard trim. He quickly walked in and a barber smiled and nodded toward the back of the shop. "The bar?" Verlaque asked.

"Through that black door, then a second one," the barber answered.

Verlaque nodded his thanks and opened the door, which led to a short narrow hallway and another door, which he opened to reveal a sunlit bar styled with furnishings inspired by the 1920s. A man in a dark blue three-piece suit stood behind the bar, polishing glasses. He gave Verlaque a big smile and welcomed him in. "Can we smoke cigars here?" Verlaque asked as he approached the bar. The bartender pointed to a set of large glass doors and Verlaque laughed, amazed he hadn't seen them. "How stupid of me," he said.

"It's amazing how many people don't see that," the bartender said, "despite that the entire wall is glass. I think it's because the glass is partly frosted. Just tell me what you'd like and I'll bring it in. You can buy a cigar here if you want."

"How civilized." Verlaque now saw a glass-fronted humidor and went over to it and had a look. "I'll have a Quai d'Orsay 54," he said, pointing to the big Robusto. "And a double espresso."

"Coming up."

Verlaque turned toward the large sunny windows. "It's surprising to walk back here and see so much light. It wasn't what I was expecting."

"When I saw this place I knew it was perfect," the bartender said. "Those windows look out onto a courtyard."

"Are you the owner?"

"Max," he said, extending his hand.

Verlaque shook it. "Antoine. Congratulations on this place. I live in Provence, but I think I've found my home away from home in Paris."

"Go on in," Max said, smiling. "There's an available armchair on the left as you walk in. I'll follow you in with the coffee and cigar."

Verlaque opened the surprisingly heavy door and went in, saying hello to the three others, all men, all smoking cigars. He sank down into the soft leather armchair and crossed his legs, at once comfortable. Max came in carrying a small tray with his coffee and cigar and, to Verlaque's relief and delight, a large glass of water. "There are lighters and cutters on the coffee table," Max said.

Verlaque thanked him. He cut the tip of the cigar, lit it, and took the first few drags, relishing the peppery flavors that hit his mouth. He leaned back, in that half-delirious state cigars always put him in, thankful that the three other men present seemed to be colleagues or friends, and were quietly speaking among themselves. Bits of their conversation floated to his ears, along with the soft jazz that Max had piped into the smoking room. Verlaque guessed that his father would be having a nap now, possibly Rebecca as well, although she had mentioned something about editing an article. Marine would be in Aix, trying to stay cool, with Sylvie at her side keeping her amused. He checked his phone in case there was news, but there were no messages. Bruno had also promised to check in with Marine this evening before he went home to his farm east of Aix. Verlaque knew he shouldn't feel guilty—he could do nothing about tomorrow's meeting, and he would be in Aix in time for dinner. It had been Marine who suggested he come to Paris a day early to see his father. She was forever thinking of others, how to make them happy. The martyr. She made him feel even more guilty.

He heard Max speaking to someone and looked through the frosted glass to see a tall brunette standing at the bar. Max poured her a glass of champagne and set it on a tray. To the happy surprise of Verlaque, she chose a cigar. She didn't appear to be a Mafioso or a crooked politician. He smiled, glad to see someone else battling cigar stereotypes, and turned back to his phone, checking to see if it would be just as hot tomorrow. He dreaded the possibility of no air-conditioning in their meeting room. He vaguely heard the door open and saw a set of long manicured feet in elegant brown leather sandals standing before him.

"Well, Antoine Verlaque," the woman said in French with a British accent.

He looked up, startled. He noticed that the three other cigar smokers had stopped talking. "Emily," he said, half choking as he said her name. He composed himself, changing into his Verlaque of years ago. He switched to English. "Or Lady Emily, should I say?"

Chapter Eight

❧

Wednesday, August 9

She sat down in the vacant armchair next to him. "This is a surprise," she said, "but I'm very glad about it. You know, I find that my title comes in ridiculously handy in Paris. You French executed the nobles but are still in awe of them."

Verlaque shrugged. "Murky territory. It isn't black-and-white, you know."

"It certainly isn't."

Max came in carrying the same elegant black tray and set down Emily's champagne and her cigar. He smiled and discreetly walked out.

"Also a Quai d'Orsay," Verlaque said.

"I've always liked this one," Emily said, expertly snipping the end off her cigar. "Had you forgotten?"

"Yes."

"Liar."

"How is your father?" he asked, quickly changing the subject but also curious.

Emily smiled. "He's very well, thank you. He's taken up watercolors, which thrills my mother. He was spending too much time hunting with the neighbor's wife."

Verlaque took a drag of his cigar and thought, but didn't say, just how bizarre the English upper class was.

"Since you're being quiet, I'll just sit here happily chatting to myself," she said, taking a drag of her now lit cigar. "Green peppercorns. Mixed with oaky spices. Do you remember when Daddy had us fill out tasting charts while smoking our cigars?"

He laughed. "I do. He wisely had us drink sparkling water or tea with our cigars. I'm sure we would have been ill had we drunk alcohol." He didn't add that he often thought of Lord Watford when he drank smoky Lapsang teas. With his foot he nudged his Dammann Frères bag, making sure it was still there.

"We would have been in trouble had we figured out that cigars go well with champagne," she said, taking a sip. "It was already my favorite beverage, even though we were still teens."

"Do you often drink champagne and smoke in the middle of the day?"

"Pardon me?"

"I'm sorry," Verlaque said. "I'm not judging. I'm curious, that's all. And I love this spot. I've never been here before."

Emily nodded. "I come here often, I must admit. Our magazine offices are down the street and when I'm stuck on a problem I come here to smooth things out in my head."

"So you're still in the fashion business?"

"Yes, and this morning I was promoted to editor in chief,

hence the champagne. I needed to get out and away from all the backslapping. Plus the Art Director was fuming—he was sure the job was his."

"Congratulations," Verlaque said, smiling. "I'll join you in a glass." He got up and walked out into the bar, where Max was slicing limes, no doubt for the evening's cocktail hour. Verlaque saw the champagne bottle sitting in an ice bucket and asked for a glass. Max lifted the bottle, still almost full. "Did you just open that?" Verlaque asked.

"Yes, I opened it for Mlle Watford."

"We may as well take the whole bottle."

"I'll bring the bucket in for you," Max said.

"Thanks." Verlaque walked back into the smoking room, convincing himself that they would probably have more than one glass, so the wiser financial option was to buy the whole bottle. By the glass was always a rip-off. He tried not to stare at Emily as he sat down, but he quickly noticed her long thick dark brown hair, athletic wide shoulders, and toned legs. He wished it was winter and her body wasn't so exposed.

She looked up and saw Max enter with the bucket and bottle. "Oh goodie!" she said. She looked at her watch. "It's almost five. I'll text the office that I'll see them tomorrow. They never ask where I am, probably because I work so much." She bent her head and sent a quick text message, then put the phone into a woven straw bag that looked like it could have been bought in Capri in the sixties but he knew was probably made this year and cost a fortune.

Max poured Verlaque a glass and refilled Emily's, then went over to the three other clients and began chatting with them. For a split second Verlaque imagined himself doing the same job, in another city, and how pleasant that might be. "And how are things at Durrington Hall?" he asked Emily. "Do you get back often?"

"Not as much as I'd like to," she replied, with what Verlaque saw as real regret. "Devon isn't so easy to get to from here."

The image of Emily's family home came into his head, as always accompanied by the sound of crashing waves, as the vast manor house looked onto the sea.

"I assume you're still in Aix," she said, sitting back. "And, judging by your left hand, you're married."

"Yes," Verlaque answered.

"Any children?"

"No." He drank some champagne. "We are . . ." At that moment Max walked over and emptied their ashtray, replacing it with a clean one. "Everything okay here?" he asked.

"Just fine, Max," Emily said. "Thank you."

Once Max was gone Verlaque asked, "And you? Married?"

She laughed. "I did actually try that, about five years ago. We lasted eighteen months. No children, thankfully. Not that I don't like children, but it wouldn't have been fair to them. Plus Octavia has three. You remember her?"

"Of course," Verlaque answered. "Your sister was always changing the wallpaper in her room. It drove your father crazy, but every time she'd manage to get him to help her." He laughed wholeheartedly now, thinking of Emily's father, his hands covered in wallpaper paste, and Octavia, the bespectacled plump teenager ordering him to keep the strips straight.

Emily laughed. "She's still doing that! She and her husband, Rupert, and kids live in one of the estate's cottages. Well, the rectory, to be exact. She's quite a famous interior designer now. You can follow her on Instagram."

"I'm not on social media."

"No, I didn't think you would be. In fact, I would have been disappointed if you were." She gently kicked his shin. "My glass is empty."

"Righto," he said, refilling their glasses.

Emily got out her phone and scrolled through her photographs, stopping at one. She leaned over to share the images with Verlaque. "The garden in winter," she said. "Isn't it beautiful?" She muttered something about Octavia's newly renovated house, and as she searched for the photos Durrington Hall came back to him, precisely the sloping garden and the fabulous view of the sea through a hole in one of the tall hedges, called the Gothic Window. Emily's mother, a noted horticulturalist, had found the pointed arched window frame in the attic and told the gardener to cut a hole in the hedge in the same shape. During the summer that his grandmother Emmeline—who knew the family and the house— had arranged for him to spend at Durrington Hall, he and Emily would stand before it for what seemed like hours, nudging each other to knock the other person off balance and ruin their view. They'd quiz each other on wine and cigar facts to prepare themselves for the evening's lecture by Lord Watford. "For heaven's sake, Monty," Emily's mother would cry at the dinner table. "Leave the children alone! They're only eighteen!" It had been the happiest summer of Verlaque's young life.

It was at Durrington that he saw how a family could behave, a family where love poured out daily. "I love you, Daddy," Octavia would say, wrapping her arms around her father's large waist. Or,

"My beautiful girls," Lady Watford would mutter as she fluffed the thick hair of her two daughters. And of course what went on between him and Emily—in the stable's hayloft, as cliché would have it—had forever marked him. It took him years to forget her, after she dumped him for a Scottish lord's son and didn't return his letters, only to turn up at his apartment in Aix one evening, unannounced, after he had started dating Marine.

He shook himself back into the present. "The Gothic Window?" he asked. "Is it still there?"

"Oh yes," Emily answered. "We used it for a photo shoot last year for the magazine."

Verlaque cringed, saddened by the fact that hundreds of thousands of fashionistas now knew the view and that special place. He remembered the gardener's flat cap, in battered green tweed, but couldn't remember his name. He knew he was being rude not speaking to Emily, but for some reason the name seemed important.

"You've gone to your quiet spot again, so I'll keep talking." She went on to give him news of their mutual friends from that long-lost summer, most of them doing extremely well and living in Kensington or Chelsea or Hong Kong. The cook was retired, living in a granny flat in a suburb in Birmingham behind her daughter's house. Emily's mother had ripped out the all-white garden and replanted it with dahlias of every color imaginable. Everyone thought Rupert, Octavia's husband, "a bit of a twerp." Except Octavia, thankfully. And the gardener—"You remember him, don't you? Tom?"—was dead, but had worked up until his ninety-first birthday. Through all this Verlaque listened, leaning back in the soft leather chair, imagining the cool wet air of Devon.

Emily didn't speak of her work, or her ex-husband. Verlaque enjoyed being taken away for a ride, as Emily had always excelled at storytelling. After a while he noticed that the three other clients were gone. The evening crowd would arrive soon, but he had no idea what time it was.

"Another cigar?" he asked.

Chapter Nine

Wednesday, August 9

Pauline Singer sat in her favorite chair and watched her daughter move furniture around on the small stage with Gérard Richet, their usual handyman. Gérard was a fine actor, too, and would be playing the policeman in the play. Above the scene was a hand-painted sign that read *Café-Restaurant-Cigalon*. Anouk had managed to borrow patio tables and chairs from friends and neighbors so that the stage was really beginning to look like a restaurant terrace. On one of the tables sat a yellow Ricard pastis jug and two glasses. The perfect touch, she thought. She hoped that the actors were better behaved for this rehearsal. At least Gauthier, that spoiled brat. She wondered if it was a coincidence that Liliane and Gauthier were acting in this play together, because she remembered their connection but hadn't told anyone else. Liliane and Gauthier had been lovers, about twenty-five years ago, Pauline thought. It had been all over the glossy papers back then, but she doubted any of the cast would remember. She thought that her daughter would have been performing on the cruise ships back then, or was she already in Paris? Gauthier would have been in his midtwenties, and Liliane in her late forties. Pauline giggled, thinking that the contemporary term back then for Gauthier would have been "boy-toy." Or was it "toy-boy"? Well, what of it? Pauline didn't have very many rules as far as love was concerned. She just wanted everyone to get along so that they could put on this play.

"Anouk!" she yelled from her first-row seat. "Did you hire Gauthier along with Liliane? Was that the deal?"

"Maman! I'm busy!"

Gérard set down the chair he'd been carrying and laughed. Anouk turned red in the face.

Pauline tried again. "Well?"

"What on earth are you talking about?" Anouk asked.

Pauline looked at the dark walls of the theater. Oh dear, she thought. She had forgotten her train of thought. "The set looks great!"

"Thanks, Maman!"

Pauline remembered. "You haven't answered my question about Gauthier and Liliane!"

"Whatever happened long ago is not our concern," Anouk said. "Now if you don't mind, we'll get back to it."

"That's the answer to your question," Léo Singer said, sitting down next to his wife.

"She didn't say if they were hired together," Pauline huffed. "Besides, what do you know about it? You don't even know what I'm talking about."

"Liliane and Gauthier were lovers long ago," he replied, grinning. "Even I remember! It was all over the papers!"

Pauline shrugged. "Not the real papers." She heard a noise at the back of the room. Her memory may have been playing tricks on her, but her hearing was pin sharp. With Léo, who, like her, was eighty years old, it was the other way around. She turned and saw some of the actors arriving for the rehearsal, and her heart leapt for joy. This was the exciting bit for her, even after all these years. For decades the Singers had made their money by holding dance classes in this space, but theater was Pauline's first love. She jumped up and ran to greet them.

"This isn't the Senior Olympics!" Léo called after her.

Anouk motioned for the actors to come up onstage. "Ten minutes early is on time!" Brigitte announced. The other actors laughed.

"Except Gauthier," Emile said. "He isn't here yet."

The cast looked at each other, some rolling their eyes in exasperation.

"I thought it best that we rehearse the first few scenes together, even though you're not all in them," Anouk told the cast. "It will give us a sense of the play, and my vision for it. Then we can split up into groups and rehearse in pairs. So, I'd like the Sunday walking party to arrange yourselves stage left, facing the terrace, and we'll begin there. You'll all see that Gérard, Abdul, and I have made a mini-kitchen stage right, beside the terrace, separated by a folding screen so that the audience can see the kitchen scenes."

"Ingenious," Pauline said.

Liliane Poncet stood back, her arms folded, looking at the scene. "Yes, this works."

"Thanks," Anouk said. "And we'll need Cigalon and Sidonie

standing in the kitchen as the walking party arrive up the hill. Jean-Marc, could you step in as Cigalon?"

Jean-Marc nodded and walked over to the kitchen space. Anouk went with him, as she had cast herself as Sidonie, Cigalon's admiring sister. "We'll do a proper technical rehearsal later, but if you find that some of the furniture isn't in the right place, please let me know. Or just kick it out of the way. Okay, let's begin!"

Emile, Mathieu, Sandra, and Pauline took their places off-stage and slowly began walking toward the stage. Anouk said, "Just to remind everyone, Emile plays Ludovic, father of the family; Mathieu is his bored teenage son, Chalumeau; Sandra plays the mother, Adèle; and Pauline, my *maman*, is their great aunt, Coralie. Go!"

The group began to walk and Emile stopped and said, "This is charming and picturesque!" He swung his arm around, as if they were in the middle of a great vista. "I'm not unhappy to have been thrown off course; this is the prettiest village around these parts!" He slapped Mathieu's shoulder. "And what do you think, Chalumeau?"

Mathieu shrugged. "I'm hungry." They walked on.

Anouk raised her hand. "Now all of you stop walking at that spot, the second row of chairs."

Emile stopped and said, "Chalumeau, you're just not artistic. Here you are on a gorgeous Sunday facing a sunlit valley and all you can say is 'I'm hungry!'"

Sandra, playing Emile's wife, Adèle, said, "I'm hungry, too. Are you, Aunt Coralie?"

Pauline let her shoulders fall, looking old and tired. "I'm hungry, too. Ludovic must be hungry, too."

"Well of course I'm hungry!" Emile yelled, cutting Pauline off, the timing perfect.

"Plus it's noon," Sandra said. "We could very well enjoy the countryside from the terrace of a restaurant."

Pauline said, "If the restaurant has a terrace."

Mathieu mumbled, "If there's even a restaurant."

Emile looked helplessly around. Spotting something in the distance, he gloated. "Well, Chalumeau, turn your head thirty degrees. What do you see over there, written on that wooden sign?"

Mathieu squinted and answered, "Café-Restaurant-Cigalon." His diction was so perfect—a combination of bored and sarcastic— that the cast broke into laugher and applause.

"That's perfect!" Anouk called out. "While we're waiting for Gauthier, let's try our lines in pairs, or groups of three, no matter if you're in the same scene or not. You're listening to your partner's reading, and giving advice. Pay attention to their body language as well. I'll make the rounds and check on all of you. You can spread out over the three floors."

The cast put themselves into small groups, most of the selection done by simply choosing the person who happened to be standing next to them. Anouk saw that Jean-Marc was teamed up with her mother, so she added, "Jean-Marc and Maman, could you two please rehearse the next scene, of Cigalon in the kitchen with Sidonie? You can use the text as a guide." They nodded

Anouk was happy to see that there was no favoritism, or popularity contests, as had so often occurred at school. The comedy musicals in Paris had been the worst, the cast either bickering or playing favorites. This reminded her of Gauthier. It was clear that after all these years he didn't even remember her. True, she was much heavier now, no longer the slim dancer she had been over twenty years ago. Liliane didn't remember her, either. She knew what her mother had been trying to ask at the beginning of the rehearsal: Did she know that Liliane and Gauthier had been an item? Oh yes, she knew.

Anouk looked at her watch and saw that Gauthier was now forty minutes late. She walked up the stairs to the kitchen and wardrobe area, figuring she would start at the top, then make her way down the next two floors. Besides, she had seen Jean-Marc and her mother go upstairs, and she was curious to see how they would get on. Jean-Marc, she knew, was clever enough to be able to temporarily act out the role of Cigalon along with his own role of the Count, who appears only in the last act.

To her surprise they were standing beside a row of costumes, acting out the scene without their books. It *was* a short scene, in the kitchen, where Sidonie tells her brother that they have clients on the terrace, but still she was impressed with Jean-Marc and her mother. She watched as Cigalon tasted his tripe stew, saying it needed ten, no, fourteen, no, exactly twelve more minutes to cook. Cigalon isn't bothered about the clients at all; he is entirely focused on the stew, made for him and Sidonie. Jean-Marc was completely believable. Anouk thought she could even smell the food.

It wasn't going to help breaking up the rehearsal this way, she now realized. Gauthier's no-show had thrown her for a loop, but when she saw how well Jean-Marc knew the script she immediately realized they should just carry on with the rehearsal as planned. So when Jean-Marc and her mother were finished, she told them to go back to the basement, to the stage, and they would carry on rehearsing. She saw her mother roll her eyes, but Anouk stood straight and quickly walked down the stairs, instructing the actors who were rehearsing in the lobby to go down to the stage. "Already?" Brigitte asked.

"Yes," Anouk said in her best loud, clear voice. "We will carry on with Jean-Marc playing Cigalon."

"Forever?" Brigitte asked.

Anouk coughed; she hadn't been prepared for the little girl's frankness. "No, no, just until Gauthier gets here." She paused and then added, "It's more important that we carry on with the scenes in order, as a group." She made her way down the back stairs to the stage area, where Abdul and Gérard were acting out the scene where they appear together. "We're going to continue with the play," Anouk announced.

"Already?" Gérard asked, as if mimicking Brigitte.

"Yep."

Footsteps pounded down the back stairs and the rest of the cast gathered around the stage. "Okay, Jean-Marc and I will go back into the kitchen, and the famished family, you all walk toward the terrace, then gather around that first table, the wooden one." Anouk walked onto the stage, aware that she was sweating. She hoped it wasn't showing, but these days she broke out sweating about every thirty minutes. It was menopause, she knew that much, and she noticed that the hot flashes were often brought on by stress.

The rest of the rehearsal went on seamlessly, and Anouk was thrilled at how well she had played Sidonie next to Jean-Marc's Cigalon. They acted out a very long scene in which Cigalon, knowing the family is famished but that he will never cook for them, teases them by eating his stew right in front of them with Sidonie. Furious and desperate, the family finally leaves. Anouk felt energetic acting with Jean-Marc, and she could tell that he was having a great time. Jean-Marc was even better than Gauthier, and now she was in another dilemma, as it was obvious that the cast could also see Jean-Marc's talent.

Chapter Ten

∼❧∼

Wednesday, August 9

I was a femme fatale," Liliane said to Sandra, taking a long drag of her cigarette. "Women in their forties are at the height of their sexual powers."

"Well, not me," Sandra said, and added a chuckle so that she didn't sound too desperate. Liliane didn't respond to Sandra's comment, nor did she encourage her with a false, "Oh no, don't think that way." Sandra was thankful for this.

Liliane went on, "We were in a few plays together, back in the day, in Paris, of course. Gauthier was just starting out. I used to think he got into acting to irritate his uptight Lyonnais family. At any rate, it was love at first sight. He was beautiful back then, and I was in between husbands."

Sandra nodded, remembering Gauthier's claim that Liliane had started dating number two while still married to number one.

Sandra had also heard that Liliane then dated Gauthier while still married to number two.

Sandra looked out at the Cours Mirabeau and saw that some people stopped and whispered when they saw Liliane. *Really*, she thought, exasperated. The Aixois were *so* obvious sometimes, so shallow. Why couldn't they just let Liliane sit here and enjoy her drink? On the other hand, it was true that she and Liliane could have had a quiet drink at the café around the corner from the theater. It would have been closer to Sandra's apartment, too. But Liliane had insisted they come to the cours, because it was on the way home for her. So maybe she liked the attention? That certainly went along with all the stories Sandra had read over the years about elderly actresses.

Sandra took a small sip of her beer. She had been so nervous that when Liliane ordered a beer, she ordered one, too, but she really didn't like the bitter taste. "You don't like beer, do you?" Liliane asked.

Sandra laughed, relieved. "No, not really."

Liliane snapped her fingers—Sandra couldn't believe she did that!—and the waiter, Frédéric, appeared. "Oui, Mlle Poncet?" he asked, adding a slight bow for effect. Sandra had been coming to this café for years, but Frédéric still had no idea what her name was. "My colleague would like to order a different drink," Liliane said. "I'll finish your beer," she added, winking at Sandra.

Frédéric asked, looking at Sandra, "A Martini Rosso, as usual?"

Flustered, she nodded and smiled. So Frédéric had noticed her. Liliane turned around and watched him walk back into the café. "He's sweet on you."

"No, I really don't think so," Sandra said, turning her head to also watch the tall elegant waiter walk to the back of the turn-of-the-century café to place his order with the bartender. She turned back to face Liliane and, wanting to change the subject, said, "I wonder what happened to Gauthier. Surely he'll show up to tomorrow's rehearsal."

"I highly doubt it."

"Really? Why do you say that?"

Liliane dropped her cigarette on the marble table and quickly picked it up. "I only meant that, knowing Gauthier, he'll think nothing of it, and tomorrow he won't even apologize." She took a large sip of beer and said, "You know he's a lousy actor, don't you? You've been around the theater for a long time, I can tell. You're observant."

Sandra was relieved when Frédéric set down her drink. She quickly took a sip. Yes, it was so much better than beer. "I haven't really seen much of Gauthier's acting—"

Liliane cut in, "You've heard of the casting couch?"

Sandra nodded, shocked. "But are there many women in casting and producing? I thought it was mostly men."

Liliane laughed. "Gauthier isn't particular who he sleeps with, as long as he gets work." She leaned back and took a drag on her cigarette, watching the crowd ambling along the cours, as if daring them to stare at her. Liliane's direct stare—a kind of challenge, the one she was doing now—had been captured years ago by a newspaper photographer. Sandra even remembered her mother showing it to her. She couldn't remember what the article was about, but thought she could pinpoint that date, as she had been studying for her bac exams and was annoyed that her mother, lovable but frivolous, was shoving a newspaper clipping under her nose when she was trying to concentrate on calculus. Her mother loved scandal, while Sandra knew she didn't have time for that. In order to survive she'd have to study hard. She was good at math and got a job straight out of high school when banks in Aix were growing and hiring. *What was that article about? Did it have to do with a man?* Sandra mused as she looked at Liliane. *Or money? Or both?* Liliane was right; Sandra was observant and had always been. But why had Liliane felt the need to say that? Sandra worried that Liliane was watching, flattering her (unnecessarily) yet also sizing her up, as if she would need Sandra's help, or endorsement, someday.

Sandra helped herself to another olive and saw a young woman two tables away staring at Liliane. Sandra grinned, thinking it funny that Liliane, as famous as she was, was sitting here in a café where all of Aix could see her.

"You didn't hear my question," Liliane said as she motioned for the waiter.

"Pardon me?" Sandra asked, embarrassed to have been daydreaming.

"Are you sure we haven't met before?"

"Oh no," Sandra said. "I doubt it."

Anouk walked down the bank side of the Cours Mirabeau, casually scanning the cafés and bars across the street as most Aixois do, when she saw Liliane and Sandra, laughing over beers. She set down her shopping and leaned against a plane tree, watching them. *Sandra, drinking beer?* she thought to herself. *Sandra hates beer!* But then Frédéric came and set down a glass of what she assumed was Martini Rosso. Either there had been a mix-up and he got the order wrong—not likely!—or Sandra was so tickled to be with Liliane Poncet that she'd ordered the same drink as the famous star. Poor Sandra. She was always so anxious to please others.

Anouk moved on, not wishing to be spotted by Liliane or Sandra. She tried to remember where everyone had been at the end of their rehearsal earlier, and why she hadn't been invited out for an aperitif. She stopped walking, realizing she'd been called away by the ringing telephone just when the cast were saying goodbye to each other. That explained it well enough, although, as she was Sandra's oldest friend, she was hurt by the omission. And she didn't trust Liliane. Sure, Anouk had been thrilled when she found out that the famed actress was living in Aix, and that she was openly looking for roles to "pass the time." Anouk laughed out loud. Everyone knew of Liliane's desperation to act again—after several disastrous small films in Hollywood, she had returned to France much more humble than the day she left. Liliane made a big show of it when she came back to live in Aix, "city of her youth," and the mayor made sure the press came out in droves.

Liliane obviously didn't remember Anouk from the play they were both in all those years ago—a remake of *West Side Story* set in Paris during WWII, where Liliane played Maria (she was already too old for the role). Anouk was hidden in the background, one of the singers and dancers connected with Maria's family. And they'd both been in love with Gauthier, who played one of the Jets. The big difference was that Gauthier ended up sleeping with Liliane, not Anouk.

By the time Anouk got back to her apartment overlooking the

Cours Sextius she was red with rage. She set her shopping down on the kitchen floor, opened the fridge, and poured herself a large glass of rosé. She could have won Gauthier over. He *had* been interested in her! More than once during their rehearsals he had looked over at Anouk and smiled. Once, when she had finished a particularly taxing dance routine with a not-very-talented male dancer, Gauthier had winked at her. She still remembered the tingles she'd felt. The problem: Liliane Poncet saw the wink, too, and moved in for the kill. Thank goodness Anouk hadn't told her parents about her crush on Gauthier, for back then she'd shared everything with them. They didn't even remember that she and Anouk and Gauthier had been in that musical together. She finished her wine and began to put the groceries away, feeling a little better.

Chapter Eleven

❧

Thursday, August 10

Verlaque pulled the heavy glass door closed behind him and looked around. He had never been on the rue Marbeuf, but at the top of the street he could see the Champs-Élysées, already full of speeding cars, mopeds, and motorcycles despite the fact that it was only eight o'clock in the morning. He stepped onto the sidewalk and looked up at the building where he had just spent the night: 1980s, glass and concrete with large windows that led out onto small square balconies, one per apartment. It was in impeccable condition, given its prestigious location and no doubt a full-time concierge, but he would hate to live there. It had nothing to do with the building itself—he liked contemporary architecture. It was just too close to the Champs-Élysées. But despite his aversion to the Champs he began walking toward it, as his meetings at the ministry were beginning in thirty minutes and he needed to get there via a route he was sure of. As he got closer to the grand boulevard, he felt his body stiffen and his nose twitch, something Marine swore she could see happening in real time in his body. Antoine the Snob, he could hear her whispering. He winced and felt his face redden.

Once on the Champs he walked quickly, staring straight ahead, purposely ignoring the luxury clothing boutiques and fast-food restaurants on either side of him. He had never been able to understand how or why one could shop at Louis Vuitton and then cross the street and eat at Burger King. Bad taste, he supposed, didn't care about your budget. He felt his snob alarm nose twitch again and he picked up his pace, veering around a bunch of tourists taking pictures of themselves with the Arc de Triomphe as a backdrop. "Original," he muttered in English as he focused his gaze on the roundabout at the bottom of the street.

Once at the roundabout, whose fountains had been broken for as long as he could remember, he continued straight ahead, the crowds thinning out, and he cut a zigzag across the Place de la Concorde. He turned right onto the rue Saint-Honoré, where hopefully he could pick up a coffee to go and a croissant. He looked at his watch—8:17 a.m. Had it taken that long to walk down the world's ugliest and most famous street? He stopped, waiting for a light to change to green, and took off his jacket, as his shirt was beginning to stick to his back. He preferred Aix's choking summer heat—at least it was dry. He was relieved to be going home, and that last night his old friend Axel had arrived at the cigar bar when he did.

By a miracle Verlaque was sitting at a large mahogany oval-shaped table one minute after 8:30. He hadn't found a place selling coffee or pastries, but there was coffee on hand for the meeting's participants. He quickly drank one, and then took a second into the meeting room with a large glass of water.

A colleague from Bordeaux, sitting across the table, smiled. "Antoine," he said, lifting his coffee cup in a salute. "Good morning."

Verlaque smiled and raised his glass; he was sure his colleague was mocking him, his eyes lowering—the half smile still present—to Verlaque's now wrinkled white shirt.

A female colleague quickly sat down next to him, papers flying, almost spilling his coffee in the process. "I'm so sorry!" she exclaimed, reaching out to stop Verlaque's cup from tipping. "The Metro stopped at Châtelet and didn't budge for ten minutes." She organized her papers and sat down, turning to face him. "Antoine!" she said.

Verlaque looked at her and vaguely recognized her glasses—the sort without frames—and her wiry blond hair now turning gray. She saved him by saying, "Karine. Karine Boin. I went to law school with Marine." They gave each other the *bises*.

"Exactly!" Verlaque said, feeling slightly queasy. His stomach gurgled. He regretted the late-night whiskies.

"And congratulations, by the way!" Karine continued. "You're having a baby!"

He felt his face go red. "Yes, in a few weeks."

"Please pass my greetings on to Marine."

"I will."

The event's organizers walked into the room, said hello, and began introducing themselves. They seemed to be former psychologists, now consultants, who worked with government agencies and ministries on employee well-being and enrichment. Verlaque hoped they wouldn't be forced to play any games.

Karine leaned over and whispered, "We have three. It's the best thing we've ever done."

He realized he must have looked puzzled because she added, "Children."

Verlaque felt his stomach tighten and he began to sweat. He reached for his cell phone, still thankfully in his jacket pocket. He tried turning it on, but the battery was dead. And his charger was at his father's house. He sat still, breathing deeply. The lights dimmed. Apparently they were going to look at slides. Or was it a short film? He closed his eyes and waited for the agony to stop.

The cast arrived at the Théâtre Vendôme at more or less the same time and gathered downstairs near the stage. Abdul and Gérard were already there, in a corner, discussing the lights and how to use them, considering the play takes place during the day.

During the first rehearsal the cast agreed not to do the *bises* every time they met—it would take too much time, and it was an awkward tradition when people worked together but didn't really know each other. So the actors stood around making small talk and waiting for Anouk to come down the stairs. Jean-Marc drifted over to Sandra, who he thought was looking very assured, poised. While they spoke, she looked anxiously toward the stairs, and he saw that neither Liliane nor Gauthier was there yet. Was Sandra in awe of one of them? He then realized that Anouk wasn't there yet, either. Perhaps Sandra was just waiting for Anouk, her long-time friend and associate.

Suddenly Anouk's voice rang out from the top of the stairs: "Never fear! I'm here!" She came running down the stairs, waving flyers in her hand. "Fresh off the press!" she called out.

The cast gathered around Anouk as she passed out the flyers. "It's in a month!" Sandra exclaimed.

"We'll be ready," Anouk replied, smiling from ear to ear.

Jean-Marc looked at his fellow actors, most of them, like him, in shock. They all knew the opening date, but now, seeing it in print, it was a shock.

Léo Singer took the stack of flyers and set them aside. "We'd better rehearse, then!"

"We can't," Gérard said. "Liliane isn't here yet."

"And neither is Gauthier," Abdul added.

"Maybe he has quit?" Mathieu suggested.

Anouk looked up the stairs, as if willing them to appear. "Oh dear," she mumbled. She swung around, facing the cast. "Well then, we can rehearse the next scene, when Cigalon comes storming out of the kitchen to speak to the family sitting on the terrace."

"Without Gauthier?" Sandra asked.

Anouk nodded. "Jean-Marc, would you mind taking his place once more?"

Jean-Marc shrugged and looked around. He was honored, but he felt like he was stealing someone else's role. He also thought they were wasting time, practicing without the two major actors. Whenever Liliane and Gauthier showed up they'd just have to do the same scenes all over again.

"You know the lines, don't you?" Anouk asked.

"Um, yes," Jean-Marc said. He walked toward the stage, followed by a few of the other actors.

"Such a waste of time," Emile said under his breath but loud enough for Jean-Marc and Sandra to hear.

"Liliane might be a little sick this morning," Sandra said,

wanting to explain and lighten the air a bit. It was also a good moment to mention that she had been invited out with a famous star.

"Oh really?" Emile asked. "How do you know?"

"We went out last evening" Sandra said. "And she drank quite a bit of beer."

Emile laughed. "I think Liliane can hold her liquor."

"Did you also see Gauthier last night?" Jean-Marc asked.

"No," Sandra said. She didn't add that they had both seen Anouk, leaning against a tree, watching them. And she especially didn't reveal Liliane's secret: that she remembered Anouk from a musical in Paris years ago. "Anouk thinks I don't remember her," Liliane had said. "It's true I can't remember names." She sighed and then tapped the edge of her right eye. "But I have an outstanding visual memory. Of course, Anouk was much thinner back then. It was so obvious she had a sad little crush on Gauthier." She drained her beer. "But his attentions were elsewhere." She winked at Sandra, who choked a little on her drink, pretending to cough.

Sandra was jolted out of her reverie by none other than Liliane's famous booming voice. "*Salut*! Sorry for the delay!"

Emile turned to Jean-Marc. "Sorry for the delay?" he whispered. "Of course she'd say that, and not 'I'm sorry for being late.' As if the delay wasn't her fault."

Jean-Marc nodded, wanting to stay out of any clash.

Liliane stumbled coming down the stairs. Luckily Abdul was quick to help her manage the last two steps. "Careful," he said, giving her his arm for support.

"Maybe she *is* a little hungover," Emile whispered.

"Anouk!" Liliane hollered. "Those stairs are going to be the death of me yet!"

"Nonsense," Pauline Singer said. "I've been taking them two at a time for decades." Everyone stared at Pauline, who looked between seventy and eighty years old. Her husband, Léo, snorted. "Well," Pauline went on, "at least I *used* to."

The rehearsal, despite its bad start, went off without any more mishaps. People seemed to be able to remember their lines, and more or less their positions onstage. The café tables had to be rearranged after Pauline twice bumped into one and bruised her shin.

Gérard had spent days painting a backdrop of the valley spread out beyond the café's terrace, dotted with olive and cypress trees. The effect was enchanting: The landscape was at once dreamy and yet realistically Provence. Abdul stood on a stepladder and adjusted the lights, some focused on the tables and others lighting up the valley. Jean-Marc felt that the set helped the actors, inspired them. At least that was the case for him as he acted next to the great Liliane Poncet. Liliane played Cigalon's former cleaning lady turned rival, who opens a restaurant in the same village. He knew they played well against each other, Liliane with her bravado and energy and rage when Cigalon steals her client from under her nose. "Thief!" she yells. "This man is only dressed as a chef! He'll never cook for you!" And in return Jean-Marc puffed out his chest, imagining that he had a large stomach. He crossed his arms and glared at Liliane, trying to put her in her place as a cleaning lady and not a rival chef. He was Cigalon! Celebrated chef from Paris! In fact, Jean-Marc imagined that he was Antoine Verlaque, and that bit of method acting did the trick. He and

Liliane, at the end of their scene, had the rest of the cast in tears of laughter. He couldn't wait to perform the scene in front of a proper audience.

"That was fabulous!" Anouk said, applauding. She looked at her watch. "It's already five o'clock! Who'd like a drink?" She turned around and gestured toward the bar.

Jean-Marc looked at his watch, too. He couldn't believe that the day had gone by so quickly. They'd rehearsed almost nonstop, save for an hour-long break for sandwiches at lunch. Perhaps they really would be ready in a month's time. Once again, Anouk had proved that despite her flightiness, she did know what she was doing.

"Come on, everyone!" she called out. "I'll pour out the wine. We have cold rosé on tap!"

"I'm so thirsty!" Brigitte announced.

"I'll bet you are!" Léo Singer said. He lifted her up and placed her on one of the barstools. "I'm sure we have a juice for you. Anouk, do we have juice?"

"Of course!" Anouk answered. "I bought apple and grape." She busied herself with pouring the wine, and Sandra jumped in to help.

"I'll get the juice out," Sandra said. She opened the bar fridge and bent down, looking through the shelves. "Is it cold?"

"Oh, I may have put it in the cupboard," Anouk said. "Behind me."

Sandra closed the fridge and went to the cupboard, moving aside boxes of napkins and glasses. "Nope."

"I bought some, I know it," Anouk said, taking a sip of rosé and making no move to search for the juice herself. She opened a bag of chips and poured them into a bowl, and the actors descended upon it.

Léo said, "Brigitte, Mathieu, and Abdul have nothing to drink while we're all having wine in front of them. Maybe it's in the storage room?"

Anouk shrugged and grabbed another bag of chips, as the bowl was already empty. "How about sparkling water?"

"That's fine with me," Abdul said.

"I'll go look," Léo said, rolling his eyes in exasperation.

"Stay sitting, Léo," Gérard said, putting his hand on the old man's shoulder. "I'll check." He walked over to a black metal door just to the right of the bar and tried to push it open. "It's stuck," he said, looking over his shoulder at Anouk. "It will only open a few inches."

"It sticks!" Léo and Pauline yelled in unison.

"You really have to give it a good push," Sandra added.

Gérard pushed harder. "It's blocked by something."

"By the boxes of juice!" Brigitte said, laughing.

Gérard slipped his hand in the door and switched on the light. Then he backed away and quickly closed the door again. He leaned his back against the door, looking wide-eyed at his fellow actors.

"What on earth?" Sandra asked, walking out from the behind the bar. "You don't look well." She looked at Gérard and suddenly realized that he was quite good-looking despite his unstylish eyeglasses and bad haircut.

Gérard said, "Call . . ."

"What?"

"Call an ambulance," he said. "But I think it's too late."

The cast quickly gathered around him. Jean-Marc took Pauline's hand, as he saw that she was trembling. He asked, "What is it? Is there someone in there?" He looked over and saw that Mathieu had the presence of mind to wrap his arms around Brigitte, who was still sitting on a barstool.

"Gauthier," Gérard said, looking pale. "It's Gauthier. He's lying on the floor, blocking the door."

Anouk picked up her cell phone and punched some numbers in, her hand shaking.

"Is he . . . ?" Léo asked.

"Yes," Gérard said, putting a hand to his stomach.

Jean-Marc was amazed that no one cried out. The room was silent. He could hear Anouk on the telephone with the police, who in turn called an ambulance. Emile set his full glass of rosé on the bar and the other actors followed suit. Someone coughed.

"Why is he in there?" Brigitte asked, looking around.

"We don't know, *chérie*," Pauline said, having recovered. She helped the girl descend from the stool and led her up the stairs by the hand.

Jean-Marc looked over at Liliane, realizing she had stayed silent throughout the event. She was sitting on a chair at one of the small round tables, her head in her hands as she began to weep. She looked up, her face streaked with mascara. "I feel sick," she said.

"I'll help you," Sandra said, immediately at her side. "Let's go to the toilets."

Anouk ran across the room and headed for the stairs. "I hear cars outside," she said.

"Let's all stay here," Jean-Marc suggested. "We shouldn't move until the police come downstairs."

Sets of feet pounded down the stairs and two uniformed male officers came in, Anouk following.

Jean-Marc nodded hello to the officers. "We haven't moved from here," he said, "but Mme Singer has taken a little girl upstairs." The older of the two officers said that they had seen them, and thanked him. They said that an ambulance was on its way.

Gérard stepped aside so they could get to the body. He gestured to the closed door, mumbled something about apple juice, swayed, and then promptly fainted.

"Tell me everything in detail," Sylvie said as she slurped her tea.

Marine breathed in, exhaling through her mouth as she had been practicing in her birthing class.

"According to his WhatsApp he's been off-line since seven last night," Marine said.

Sylvie bit her lip. "Did he take his phone charger with him?"

"I can only assume so. At any rate it isn't on the kitchen counter where it's usually plugged in."

"He could have forgotten it on the train on the way up to Paris. I did that once. The cord is black, as is the wall on the train, with that black faux carpeting, impossible to see."

"Too much detail, Sylvie. But thanks. So then why didn't he tell me straightaway?" Marine asked. "As soon as he realized, before the battery ran out?"

"And you called his dad's house?"

Marine sighed again and said, "Yes, I spoke with Rebecca, Antoine's father's girlfriend."

"I remember her," Sylvie said. "She's an art historian and looks like a supermodel."

Marine nodded. "They're quite worried. Antoine's bed wasn't slept in last night, and early this morning his suitcase was still there."

"The charger is probably in his suitcase."

"Yes," Marine replied glumly.

Sylvie looked at her watch. "It's just after two. Is his stuff still at their house?"

"I don't know," Marine said. "Rebecca and Antoine's father, Gabriel, had to leave early. I spoke to her as their taxi was pulling up. They're flying to Venice for a few days."

It was Sylvie's turn to sigh. "Ah, to be rich."

Marine looked out the window, toward the spire of Saint-Sauveur, her forehead wrinkled with worry. She leaned back and rubbed her fully distended stomach, watching the starlings dart in and out of the steeple's open pointed arches.

"I'm thirsty," Sylvie said. "Mind if I have some white wine?"

"Help yourself."

Marine stayed sitting as Sylvie went into the kitchen, mumbling to herself. Marine knew it was only a matter of time before Sylvie would want a cigarette. Wine always did that to her. She'd have to go up onto the terrace.

Sylvie walked back into the dining room carrying her glass of wine. She took a sip. "Recap," she said. "Antoine was going up for a meeting?"

"At the Ministry of Justice."

"Did you see the information for this supposed meeting?"

"Supposed?"

"A pamphlet? An invitation?"

"Sylvie!" Marine said. "I don't have to check up on Antoine."

Sylvie stood up, taking her glass with her. She began to pace as Marine sighed. "Unfortunately, we do with men."

Marine bit her lip to stop herself from speaking. Sylvie's track record was dismal, and her relationship with the father of her daughter, Wolfgang, who lived in Germany, was once again on the rocks.

"What was he doing last night?" Sylvie asked.

"I assumed he would eat dinner with Rebecca and Gabriel."

"Did you ask Rebecca if that was the arrangement?"

"No," Marine said. "I didn't think of it." She rubbed her forehead.

Sylvie began pacing again. She drained her wine. "So typical!"

"What do you mean?"

"They're covering up for Antoine!" She walked into the kitchen and Marine heard the refrigerator open and more wine being poured. "Do you have snacks?"

"The cupboard above the fridge." She could hear the cupboard door open.

"Pistachios. Excellent."

"That doesn't make sense," Marine said.

"What doesn't?" Sylvie asked as she came back into the room.

"That Rebecca would hide the truth from me."

"She's a Verlaque now."

"They're not married."

"Yeah, but she'd stick up for Antoine, for Gabriel's sake. He's how old now? Seventy-five? She doesn't want him to keel over from a heart attack over the stress."

"Really, Sylvie," Marine said, sighing once more. She laughed, not being able to contain herself. "You should have been an actress."

"I considered it," Sylvie said, taking a handful of pistachios. "Or a psychologist."

Verlaque could see the TGV sitting on the farthest track in hall two, of course the farthest hall at the Gare de Lyon, a good seven-minute sprint from hall one. The train always left from hall two when he was late. He began to run, silently begging the train to stay at the quay. As he got within a few meters of the train he waved his ticket at the conductor. "First class," he hollered. "I'll get on here and walk through the cars."

"You just made it," the conductor said, putting the whistle to his mouth.

"No kidding." Verlaque heaved himself onto the train as the whistle blew, lifting his small suitcase behind him. He looked at his ticket—car three—and began the long walk toward his seat, desperate to sit down, plug in his phone, and get something to eat to settle his stomach. Something—anything—greasy.

When he finally got to car three he was relieved to see that he had booked a solo seat. He'd be able to plug in his phone without having to share the outlet with someone else. He took off his jacket and laid it on the upper luggage rack, then set his suitcase down on the seat and took out his phone charger. He plugged it into the wall socket, closed his suitcase and set it on the luggage rack behind his seat, and took off for the bar car.

The bar car had just opened but there was already a line. Verlaque shifted from foot to foot, wishing he had come straight here instead of taking the time to plug his phone in. He peered ahead, trying to see what people were buying. Lots of coffee and cookies, it seemed. Perhaps they had eaten dinner before getting on the train. He looked at the colorful menu printed on the wall behind the barman. A combo meal of salad, risotto, and a brownie? Verlaque wrinkled his nose; he didn't need the salad. A croque monsieur! He hadn't eaten one in years, and that would feed his appetite for something fatty and greasy. His stomach was still making unhappy noises from the amount of whiskey he'd drunk the previous evening.

"Un croque monsieur," he said as he got to the front of the line. "S'il vous plaît."

"Nothing hot today," the barman replied.

"Pardon me?"

"The oven isn't working."

"That is really bad news," Verlaque said, frantically scanning the menu board for something else to eat. A salad? No, that wouldn't do. He looked at the several small packages lined up on the counter and grabbed two packs of mini salami and a bag of chips. He heard the woman behind him snicker. He pushed the packages toward the barman. "And two Cokes, please." He looked over his shoulder at the woman, giving her his best self-congratulatory smirk.

When he got back to his seat he was careful to keep the food hidden in the paper bag, embarrassed by his dinner—especially the Cokes, which he hadn't drunk in years. He opened the chips and salami and began to eat. His phone, now partly charged, began lighting up and he was surprised by the number of messages: several from Marine, two from Rebecca, two from Jean-Marc, and one from Emily.

He decided to listen to the non-Marine messages first, beginning with Rebecca. In the first one, from last night, wanting to know if he'd be there for dinner; in the second, from this morning, asking where he was. He sent a text reply, apologizing for not getting her messages, and wished them a good Venetian holiday. They didn't need to know more than that. Next, a text from Emily. She joked about their evening and said how nice it was having bumped into him. He replied with the same sentiments, wishing her family in England all the best. Then over to Jean-Marc. In his first voice mail he was speaking so quickly that Verlaque couldn't understand him. Verlaque's heart raced, worried that something was wrong with Marine. He listened to the second message; it was calmer, but the train went through a tunnel and the message was garbled. Something about an accident at his theater?

Now for Marine's messages. The first, a text, wished him a good train ride and trip to Paris. The second, another text, was a photo of her dinner, a delicate Italian soup she liked to make with chickpeas, fennel, and leeks. It looked especially pretty in the Tuscan soup bowl, hand-painted in Deruta, that he had given her one year for her birthday. He smiled, missing her, and angry at himself for not taking his cell phone charger with him last night. In the third, a voice mail, she wished him a good night, and told him that the baby was moving more than ever. The next, this morning, another voice mail, in which she sounded a bit worried that she hadn't heard from him. In the fifth message, Marine sounded tired and upset, but not accusatory, saying that she, Rebecca, and Gabriel were worried. The final was also a voice mail but contained no actual message—just a click of the receiver.

He drank one of the Cokes, amazed at how awful the sensation of a thick layer of sugar coating his teeth was. No wonder he hated it. He ate a few chips and set the bag down on the tray in front of him, closed his eyes, and fell into a deep sleep.

He woke up as people around him started to make noise, lifting their suitcases and leaving the car. "Aix?" he asked a woman who was walking past his seat, pulling her suitcase behind her.

"Yes," she said. "We just pulled in."

He quickly got up, relieved he hadn't slept through his stop.

Chapter Twelve

✷

Thursday, August 10

In less than three hours the theater had been cordoned off and the medical examiner, who had rushed to the site in the middle of shopping for dinner at Monoprix, had examined the body. "He's been dead for over twenty-four hours," she whispered to Bruno Paulik. "And he was strangled from behind. That always surprises me."

Paulik looked at Dr. Cohen. He was always impressed that she arrived at a crime scene with her cropped gray hair impeccable. He liked her bright blue glasses, too. "Pardon?"

She held her hands up in front of his face, palms facing him. She pushed her thumbs toward him. "The thumbs, on the victim's neck. Easier than from behind."

"Did he fight back?" Paulik asked.

"Yes, there are bits of colored something under his fingernails. Fabric, I would guess."

"Thank you. My guys have finished with their photographs, so the morgue attendants can take the body away. The forensics team will come tomorrow morning."

"I'll let them know," she said. She looked down at the body. "Was he a famous actor? Like Liliane Poncet?"

"I couldn't tell you," Paulik answered. "I'm an opera man."

"Right, I forgot. I saw you at this summer's opera festival, but with the crowds I couldn't say hello. Please say hello to Hélène for me."

Paulik almost asked Dr. Cohen how she knew his wife, but then he remembered that she and her husband bought Hélène's wines and often came to their winery parties. "I will. Thanks for coming." He accompanied her out of the building, then said a few words to Brigitte, who had been crying, her head resting against the chest of an old woman. A junior officer told him that the old woman and her husband were the parents of the theater owner and he spoke to them, jotted down some notes, and then told them they could leave as soon as Brigitte's parents, who were on their way, arrived. They seemed relieved.

He walked upstairs, where Anouk had cleared some space in her office for interviews. "No one left the theater?" Paulik asked Jean-Marc, who now had a coffee in his shaking hands.

"No, not even Brigitte, our youngest actor."

"I spoke with her downstairs," Paulik said. "Her parents are on their way to take her home."

"Thank goodness," Jean-Marc said, forcing himself to take a sip of the lukewarm coffee.

"Tell me what happened here," Paulik said.

"We rehearsed all day and finished at exactly five p.m., when Anouk said it was time for a well-deserved drink."

"So you went to the bar area, which I saw is next to the theater."

"Yes. And there was a kerfuffle over the juice, as Brigitte and Mathieu are too young for wine, and Abdul doesn't drink it either." Jean-Marc saw Bruno writing this information down in a small notebook. He wondered why he didn't use his cell phone recorder. Maybe he was low-tech; Antoine certainly was.

Paulik looked up, seeing Jean-Marc's eyes following his pencil strokes. "I've found over the years that note-taking is still the most efficient way to record an interview. If I do it on my phone, I still have to transcribe it all when I get home. And that's family time."

Jean-Marc smiled. "I was wondering why, I must admit."

"Nice to have such an honest witness, although I had no doubts." Paulik turned a page in his notebook. "So why the kerfuffle?"

"Sorry?"

"The juice . . ."

"Oh, right," Jean-Marc said. "Sandra couldn't find it behind the bar, and Anouk was too busy pouring our wine to go look for it. Multitasking isn't her thing, and I think she really likes wine, if you get my drift. So Gérard volunteered to get it, out of the storeroom next to the bar."

"The fellow who fainted."

"Yes, he's our handyman," Jean-Marc said. He quickly corrected himself. "Set decorator."

"Did you know the deceased well?"

"Gauthier? No, not really."

"Did you like him?"

"No, not really."

Paulik asked, "Would it be your general impression that he was not liked?"

"Yes."

"Why?"

Jean-Marc finally set his coffee cup down, realizing that it was now cold. He had been holding the cup too tightly, so he flexed his hand, as it was now cramped. "Gauthier was rude, for one. Always late for rehearsals, but not apologizing for keeping us waiting. He was especially cruel to Liliane. You'll have to ask her, but they knew each other long ago, in Paris theater circles." Jean-Marc sat back, reflecting. "But the weird thing is, no matter how rude he was, I got the feeling that some of the women rather liked him. Even Liliane."

"A handsome guy?"

Jean-Marc was surprised by the question. But he then realized that Bruno Paulik had only seen the dead version of Gauthier, and they weren't sure how long he had been in the storage room. He shuddered.

"Are you okay?" Paulik asked.

"Yes. And yes, Gauthier was handsome in a nineteen-eighties Hollywood kind of way. Big hair, big teeth. I forgot you don't watch too many films." At least, thought Jean-Marc, not the sort of television variety and game shows that Gauthier often appeared in.

As Paulik waited for the next appointment he thought of the innocents—in his opinion, so far—in the case: Brigitte, the teenager Mathieu, and Jean-Marc. Probably the old couple, too, given their age. Gauthier Lesage would have been stronger than even the two of them together.

He tapped the edge of the old wooden desk with his pencil, waiting. He checked his phone to see if Verlaque had called, but there was no message. At 8:00 p.m. it was now, no doubt, too late in Paris to call. Or perhaps Verlaque was on the train. Paulik saw that his wife, Hélène, had left a text message that his dinner was in the oven, keeping warm. One thing about interviews, he mused, was that you were so busy and focused that you didn't notice your empty stomach.

Someone ran up the stairs two at a time and Paulik guessed that the feet belonged to the troupe's teenager. He looked at the list of names that Anouk had printed out for him. Mathieu Marsal was the boy's name, age sixteen. Student, Lycée Zola. Paulik saw the top of Mathieu's thick black hair emerge from the top of the stairs. "Hello," he said.

"Hi," Mathieu replied, flopping down in a chair with a thud—unintentionally, realized Paulik, as the boy then tightly gripped the sides of the chair.

"This won't take long."

"Thank goodness. My parents are waiting outside for me."

"Okay," Paulik said, pulling his chair up closer to the desk. "How long have you been involved with this theater?"

"Well, I auditioned in July and we began just a few days ago. I'm not sure of the date. I wrote it down on the calendar hanging in our kitchen."

"That's fine," Paulik said. "Did you know anyone in the troupe before then?"

Mathieu shook his head. "Nope."

"Including the deceased—"

"Gauthier, you mean? I didn't know him, either."

"Did you get along with him?" Paulik asked.

Mathieu shrugged. "I suppose so, but he hardly did any rehearsals with us. He was either late, or . . . didn't show up." He looked down at his hands.

"When he did show up, what was his behavior like?"

"Not very nice, to any of us." He paused and Paulik let him have time to think. He went on, "But I thought it might be normal, for actors, you know. The snooty thing."

"Thank you, Mathieu," Paulik said, putting down his pencil. "You can go now. Thank your parents for the wait."

"Sure thing." He got up like a bolt and did a half jog to the stairs. He turned around and asked, "Should I send someone else up?"

"They have a list down there." He looked at his own list, which he'd quickly made up with Anouk's help. They had agreed that Anouk would go last. "Mme Poncet," he said. He thought a few seconds and realized that although Mathieu was clearly innocent— no connections to Gauthier and no motive—he might have something more to add than his shrugs. "Mathieu," Paulik quickly said, just as Mathieu had put his right foot on the top step. "One last thing." Paulik got up and walked over to the boy so that he wouldn't have to yell. "Did you notice anything unusual today, or yesterday, here at the theater?"

Mathieu came back up to the top of the stairs, realizing that he had just been asked an important question. He looked at Paulik in a way that assured the commissioner of his intelligence.

"After the rehearsal tonight," he said, then stopped. Taking in a deep breath, he continued, "I'm not sure, but Anouk was being weird."

"How so?"

"She didn't seem to want to help with finding the juice." Paulik stared at the boy and waited, not wanting to put words in his mouth. Mathieu went on, "What I mean is, it was as if she didn't want to go into the storage room."

Paulik thought about Mathieu's comment. Jean-Marc had said almost the same thing, blaming it on Anouk's love of wine. Perhaps that was simply it? She was a bit of a wino and wanted to get her own glass of wine as quickly as possible. Or maybe the room was a mess and she was embarrassed by it. He and Hélène used to have a storage room like that at their former house in Pertuis, a charming village house that was really too small for three people. He'd go and have a look once his men had finished with their inspection.

"Dear and glorious commissioner," Liliane Poncet said as she walked into the office and wardrobe room.

Paulik couldn't help but smile. Mme Poncet was over-the-top, as most of the internet sites that he had quickly browsed said she was. He'd never seen her famous *Mimi in Montmartre* films, but his sisters had, multiple times. He did know that those films had made her rich and famous. "Please, have a seat," he said, gesturing to the chair across from him.

As she sat down, she said, "Gauthier was murdered, wasn't he?"

"Yes," Paulik answered. "Our medical examiner thinks strangling, but we'll know more tomorrow. Please don't speak to the press for now."

"I hate the press." Liliane closed her eyes. "I've already cried, in case you think I'm heartless."

"Why would I think that?"

"Oh? Anouk didn't tell you, I see. I knew Gauthier, over twenty-five years ago. We were in a play together, *West Side Story* set during World War Two."

Paulik tried not to show his horror at the idea of such a play. "I understand that you and M Lesage also had a relationship off-stage."

"Oh, people *have* been talking, I see." She straightened her back with pride.

"How long did your relationship last?" Paulik asked.

Liliane looked at the ceiling. "A few weeks, six perhaps, including the two-week run of the play."

Paulik mused that the play didn't last long. No big surprise there. "Did you see him after that?"

"No. Well, once or twice we'd show up at the same party, but I'd leave as soon as I saw him."

He didn't ask why. He'd find out sooner or later. "Did you know he was going to be in this play?"

"No," Liliane said. "I didn't even know he was living in Aix. So it was a surprise."

"A good surprise?"

She paused, again looking at the ceiling. "At first, yes. He was just as handsome as ever, and all those memories came flooding back, when we were both young, and I was . . ."

Paulik leaned forward, hoping she'd finish her sentence, but she took a sip of coffee and made it clear that she would not.

Famous? He wondered. *At the top of my game? Beautiful?* "Was he happy to see you?" he asked. "Here, in Aix?"

He saw sadness in her eyes. "No, I don't think so. He treated me like any other cast member."

"Was he doing well?"

"I'm not sure what you mean."

"Well, since you were at one time close to him, you might notice if he was in some kind of trouble, had worries and such," Paulik suggested.

"Ah, I see your point, Commissioner," Liliane replied, her eyes at once livelier. She was a well-practiced flirt. "I did think it odd that Gauthier was routinely late for rehearsals."

"That was unusual, back in your Paris days?"

"Oh yes," she replied. "He was always quite professional." She paused and then added, with the trace of a smile, "Professional in the sense that he was on time and knew his lines from day one."

Once again, Paulik decided not to follow up. He didn't want to get off topic, and he could easily find out what she was referring to by looking at some back issues of *Gala* and *Paris Match*. "Were you worried when he didn't show up for today's rehearsal?"

"Yes, we all were. It was embarrassing for me, as we are both professional actors. It doesn't look good if the pros are slacking off."

Paulik nodded, taking her comment not as pretentious but as more matter-of-fact. "Did Gauthier have family?" he asked.

"Oh, right," Liliane answered. "I didn't think of that. They need to be notified. He has a sister, not in the business. She used to live in Brittany. They never got along. His parents are dead."

"What is her name?"

Liliane looked up at the ceiling. "Starts with a *C* . . . Claire. No! Clara. Don't ask me what her last name is. It may still be Lesage, or she may have taken her husband's name. She did get married at one point."

"Do you have any idea what happened?" he asked. "Last night, I mean. You knew him best from what I can tell."

"No idea," she answered. "And I didn't really know him, not then, and not now. But I can tell you that Gauthier Lesage would do anything for money."

Sandra stared at Bruno Paulik wide-eyed, twisting her fingers together. "Please sit down, Mlle Gastaldi," Paulik said. Sandra sat down and kept staring. Paulik was amazed that she didn't seem to be blinking. He decided that on her next blink he would begin speaking.

"Are you all right?" he finally asked. She nodded, still twisting her hands. "Had you met M Lesage before this play began?"

"No," she said, clearing her throat. "Never."

"Did you speak with him very much? General chitchat while waiting for rehearsals to begin, that sort of thing?"

Sandra permitted the commissioner the vaguest of grins. "No. I don't think we exchanged any words, just the two of us, that is."

"So you can't say you knew him?"

"No." She paused, picking at her skirt. "Although I've met men like him, I think I can say. Even here in Aix." She paused again. "Especially here in Aix."

Paulik leaned forward, as Sandra was almost whispering. And

yet, aware of his bulk, he didn't want to intimidate, so he brought his voice down a notch. "Could you explain?"

"Well, he seemed pretentious. No, he *was* pretentious. He thought only of himself. It seems terrible to say that, now."

Paulik said, "You paint him as a very disagreeable man. A man who would easily have enemies. Can you think of any?"

Sandra went back to her wide-eyed stare. "Here? At the theater?"

"Yes."

She wrung her hands and coughed. "I wouldn't know," she said uncertainly. "I couldn't say."

"Can't or won't?"

She looked down, picking at her skirt once more. She wasn't a very good actor, Paulik thought. But then again, Anouk had written beside Sandra's name "wardrobe designer," so maybe she normally didn't act.

"We've only just begun. . . ."

"Okay. That'll be all for now," he said, feeling sorry for her. He'd ask more questions in the coming days.

As Sandra got up to leave, Anouk ran up the stairs and peered over the banister, out of breath. "I'm sorry to interrupt, Commissioner, but Gérard still isn't feeling well and would like to go home, and Abdul needs to catch the last bus."

Paulik looked at his watch. "It is late. I'll come down and speak to everyone. We can meet back here tomorrow morning at ten a.m., but the bar area will be roped off. Anyone who needs a ride home this evening will be provided with one." He looked at Sandra.

"I live up the street," she said, pointing in the direction of rue de la Paix. He nodded, interested that Sandra lived so close to the theater. She may have seen people coming and going. He jotted it down in his notebook.

"And Mlle Singer," Paulik continued, "once I've spoken to people downstairs, I'd like to ask you a few questions that can't wait until tomorrow."

"Fine," Anouk said.

"Mlle Gastaldi," he said, looking at Sandra. "I'd like to continue our discussion tomorrow."

Sandra swung her head in Anouk's direction as if she needed permission. She looked terrified. "Oh, okay."

Paulik told them that the theater was now a crime scene and they would have to hand in their keys. Anouk did so grudgingly, which didn't surprise him. What did surprise him was how many of them had keys: Sandra, Gérard, and Abdul. Plus Anouk, of course, and each of her parents. He explained that meeting times would be sent to them via text message or phone call, and they would meet in the front foyer of the theater before being told by an officer where to go. It took ten minutes to put Abdul and Gérard in two separate taxis and arrange an officer to walk Sandra up the street to her front door. Emile shrugged off offers of assistance and said he lived near his butcher shop, less than ten minutes' walk on foot. But Paulik insisted, and a young male officer accompanied Emile on his walk home.

Once everyone had gone, Paulik decided he and Anouk could have a conversation in the lounge on the ground floor. For the time being, no one would be permitted in the theater and bar in the basement. The forensics team were coming tomorrow to continue their dusting and general inspection.

Anouk had anticipated this arrangement, and a minibar miraculously appeared in the lounge. She poured herself a glass of rosé and gave Paulik a small bottle of sparkling water. They sat back on the sofas, facing each other. Various magazines were strewn about on the coffee table that separated them: one about current French theater that Paulik had never heard of, a *Paris Match*, and a few of those free color real estate magazines that he knew Antoine Verlaque liked to browse. "Cheers," Anouk said, lifting her glass in the air.

Paulik nodded and watched as she took a big swig. Perhaps being comfortable on sofas wasn't a good idea.

"What about the play?" she asked.

"I'm sorry," he said. "But you'll have to cancel it. At least for the time being."

"Merde."

"The sooner we clear this up, the sooner you can get back to the play." He hoped he wasn't lying; he just wanted to throw her some hope. "Any idea what happened?" he asked.

"We stopped rehearsal at five p.m.," she began.

"That's not what I mean," he said. "I have that information. Do you know what happened to M Lesage?"

Anouk drank more of her wine. "No, I don't."

"Have you seen anyone suspect hanging around the theater?"

"No. And I do pay attention, as a few years ago some local kids broke in here."

"Tomorrow if you could give my officers that information," Paulik said. "That date and such. What did they take?"

She looked around and forced a smile. "Nothing. They drank some of the booze in the bar, that's all. And made a mess."

"What was Gauthier doing here last night, and how did he get in?"

Anouk paused longer than he thought the question deserved. "I gave him a key, but I don't know why he was here."

"Why give one of the actors a key to the theater?" Paulik asked, genuinely surprised. "Is that normal?"

Again, a long hesitation. "No, not really. He told me he wanted to rehearse without the other actors."

Paulik nodded, feeling that this attitude of Gauthier's fit with what everyone had told him that evening. That he was a snob and considered himself above the others. He flipped to the next page in his notebook. "When did you first meet Gauthier Lesage?" he asked. "Early this summer for the auditions?"

"No." She gripped her wineglass and stared into it. "I knew him years ago in Paris. Twenty-five years ago."

Paulik looked up, surprised. "For a play?"

"*West Side Story* set during the war."

He nodded, taking in the information. Liliane Poncet hadn't mentioned Anouk being in the play. Had she not known Anouk back then? The coincidence was alarming, the three of them in the same play years ago. He said, "Go on."

"Well, I was just starting out, and I was in the chorus."

"Do you remember the exact dates?"

Anouk reached into her back pocket and unfolded a pale green piece of paper. She handed it to him.

Paulik looked at it, surprised. It was the flyer from the musical. He jotted down the name of the theater and the dates in his book, handing the flyer back to her. "Thank you," he said, finding it curious, sweet even, that she had kept it all these years. And a bit odd.

"I fetched it out of my office this evening," she explained. "I knew you'd want the exact dates."

"So you knew Gauthier Lesage back then."

"No, not really. We were in the play together, but he had a bigger role than me." She gulped and breathed in. "We exchanged glances once or twice, but never spoke. I was too shy."

"And he was . . . ?"

"One of the stars!"

Paulik continued, "Did he act like one, too?"

"I don't want to speak ill of him now. . . ."

"It's just that some of the other actors have been telling me of his negative behavior here. Showing up late . . ."

"They don't understand," she said. "He couldn't take a little theater like mine seriously."

"Why not? It seems to me that Liliane Poncet does, and she's even better known." He didn't add *at least to me*, as he didn't follow the careers of cinema or theater stars.

"Liliane!" Anouk said, huffing. "She's had it in for Gauthier since we began rehearsals."

"Because they dated all those years ago?" Paulik suggested.

"Oh, so you know."

"Mme Poncet told me," he said. "Do you know why M Lesage moved to Aix?"

"No," she answered, almost too quickly. "I never saw him, even on the cours, where you tend to see everyone."

How true, he thought. "And so you don't know anything about his life here in Aix?"

"No, nothing. I have his address in my files, which I gave to one of your officers. That's all."

"Did M Lesage remember you?"

Anouk looked directly at the commissioner. He now saw that she was exhausted. He should have left the questioning until tomorrow. "No," she answered, rubbing her eyes.

"Did Mme Poncet remember you?" he asked, already knowing the answer.

"Not in the slightest."

Chapter Thirteen

✧

Friday, August 11

Bruno Paulik and Antoine Verlaque, who had arranged to walk together to the theater, met at the Palais de Justice just after 9:00 a.m. Verlaque gave a wave as he saw the commissioner standing on the front steps of the building, his giant arms crossed, watching the people come and go on the square opposite. They shook hands.

"How's the coffee at this theater?" Verlaque asked.

Paulik thought of Anouk and the general chaos. "I would guess not that good."

"Let's stop on the way, then," Verlaque said. "I need more than usual this morning."

"Paris was that bad?"

"It gets more difficult every time I go," Verlaque said.

As they began to walk Paulik glanced sideways at the judge,

trying not to make his curiosity too obvious. Verlaque was impeccably dressed, as usual, with his thick salt-and-pepper hair freshly washed. But his eyes looked tired, and sad.

Verlaque went on, "Thank you for your message this morning. How is Jean-Marc?"

"He was doing all right last night," Paulik said. "But I often find that it's the next day that the seriousness of the situation hits home."

Verlaque swung his head around and Paulik realized he might have just said something wrong. *Did Antoine and Marine have a fight?* he wondered. "When a dead body is found," he quickly continued, "that night, when the ambulance and police come, you're full of nervous energy."

"And then the next day," Verlaque cut in, "exhausted."

"Ah, yeah," Paulik said. He pointed to a café they both knew, where the coffee was good and the service fast. They could stand at the bar and not have to mingle with the other clients; if they were sitting at a table, half of Aix could come by and chat. Standing at the bar meant off-limits—a sign that you were busy, doing business.

Over their coffees and croissants Paulik filled in the judge on the previous day's events and his night's questioning. They had a good spot at the bar's far end, where no one could hear them.

Verlaque listened, his head bowed. He nodded from time to time. "It seems like you got some good information," he said when Paulik had finished. "Even the teenager was able to tell you something."

Paulik nodded. "I found that interesting, too," he said. "Anouk didn't want to open the storage room."

"She has a good motive," Verlaque said. "Lots of free publicity. Was she still in love with Gauthier?"

"After twenty-five years?" Paulik asked, leaving some coins on the counter and waving goodbye to the barman. They walked out into the sunshine and heat.

"It can last a long time," Verlaque said. "That kind of unrequited love."

Paulik looked at Verlaque, who had his head cocked up to the sky, looking at the top floors of a building they were walking by. "I don't think you'd still be vengeful."

"Look at that apartment," Verlaque said, still looking up. "They have a great south-facing terrace."

"It's odd, too," Paulik went on, ignoring Verlaque's architecture commentary, "that Liliane freely offered the information that Gauthier would do anything for money. It was an add-on to the end of her sentence, one of those disconnected comments left hanging in the air. I also doubt Anouk was telling the whole truth. What if she'd not only seen Gauthier Lesage since Paris, but they had kind of gotten together?"

Verlaque grunted. "Do you think that's possible?"

Paulik thought of Lesage's movie-star good looks and Anouk's messy presence. "Not really, I suppose."

"Rue du 11 Novembre?" Verlaque asked.

"Yes, just around the corner," Paulik said. "Le Théâtre Vendôme. It was a dance studio in the late seventies, eighties, and early nineties run by Anouk's parents."

"Ah, so they likely own the building outright." Verlaque turned to Paulik as they approached the theater.

"That's important?"

"Everything in Aix revolves around real estate."

"I'm afraid you're right."

They nodded to the young officer guarding the front door and went inside. Verlaque followed Paulik through a lobby lined with framed play posters to a large back room kitted out with sofas and armchairs. Gathered around were the actors—at least, that's who Verlaque assumed they were—and two uniformed officers. From Paulik's description over coffee, it was fairly easy to pick out who was who.

Paulik introduced the judge and reminded the cast not to go downstairs, as it was a crime scene and was being scrutinized. He explained that he would interview Abdul, Gérard, and then Emile upstairs in the wardrobe area, and that Antoine Verlaque would speak to the others as he felt necessary. "M Khattabi?" Paulik said, looking at his list. "Could you follow me up the stairs?"

"Yes," Abdul said, setting down his coffee.

Once they were comfortably facing each other, Paulik began. "How long have you been working here?" he asked.

"It's not really work," Abdul said. "I volunteer. But for about ten years now."

"Where do you work?"

"I do maintenance work at the university."

"Ah, that's a good position, isn't it?"

Abdul nodded. "Yes, very good benefits." He didn't bother to add that it paid minimum wage. The commissioner would probably be aware of that.

"And so you come here some evenings . . ."

"Exactly. I passed the theater one day, by chance, and came in and asked for work. It was before I got the university job. Mlle Singer—Anouk, that is—was very kind. She told me they didn't have paid work, but if I could volunteer it would look good on my résumé."

"Did it help?"

"I think so, yes," Abdul said. "And I really liked the work here, so I stayed. It's a break for me."

"From work?"

"No," Abdul said, smiling. "From my five children."

"Ah," Paulik said, returning the smile. "What kind of a person was M Lesage?"

Abdul's smile quickly left his face. "Not a kind one."

"Go on."

"He ridiculed some of the actors in front of us all. It takes a small man to do that."

"Whom did he ridicule?"

Abdul hesitated, not wanting to create a false suspect. Paulik picked up on this right away. "Gauthier Lesage and Mlle Poncet knew each other long ago, I hear," Paulik added. "Was it her?"

Abdul nodded. "Yes, and he made it clear he didn't like working with first-time actors. That would be most of us, including me, and Sandra, who usually works on costumes."

"You're also acting in the play?"

"Yes, I'm playing a brigadier."

Paulik smiled.

"The play will now be canceled, will it not?" Abdul asked.

"For the time being," Paulik answered.

He thanked Abdul for his help and Abdul left, sending up Gérard after him.

Paulik looked carefully at Gérard, who looked a good deal better than he had the previous evening. Paulik said so.

"Thanks," Gérard answered. "I'm sorry about fainting."

"No need to apologize. It happens frequently."

"Does it?"

"Yes, to both sexes, and all ages," Paulik replied truthfully. "How long have you been working here?"

"About ten years."

"Really? So you must have started around the same time as M Khattabi."

Gérard thought for a few seconds. "Just before him, I think. I've always dabbled in the theater, and my sisters went to the Singers' dance school when we were kids."

"Where's your full-time job?"

"I work at a small hardware store downtown."

"The one near the Palais de Justice?" Paulik asked. It was one of the only remaining independent hardware stores downtown; the rest were mega chain stores out in the suburbs.

"That very one, behind the Gap."

"Can you tell me what happened last night?"

"Well," Gérard said, taking a breath. "We stopped rehearsing and were all ready for a congratulatory drink. It had been a hard day, but good, too. So we all went over to the bar area and Anouk began pouring out the wine."

Paulik stopped him and turned to a fresh piece of paper. He sketched out the bar area as he remembered it, with the storage room to the far side. "Does this look about right?" he asked, showing Gérard the drawing.

"Yes. There are tables, too, and some chairs."

"Can you draw them in?"

Gérard took the pen and drew in the rest of the furniture. With a few lines he was able to render the furniture in three dimensions. "Impressive," Paulik said.

"I went to art school," Gérard explained. "Which is why I now work in a hardware store but still volunteer in a theater."

Paulik smiled and nodded. "Can you fill in for me where everyone was? Where they were sitting?" He watched as Gérard drew. The man was clearly observant and detail-oriented. He bit his upper lip as the pen flew across the page. After a few minutes he handed it to the commissioner. "That's about it."

Paulik looked at it. Gérard had labeled each person. "Anouk and Sandra were behind the bar," Paulik said, looking at the drawing. "And you were on the far side, closest to the storage room."

"Yes, that's why I offered to get the juice."

"Who's that sitting alone at a small round table?" Paulik asked.

"That's Liliane," Gérard replied. He paused. "No, wait, she went to the toilets. But I can't remember when. Wait, I do now. Sandra took her to the toilets after I found Gauthier. Gauthier's body . . ."

"Liliane was upset?" Paulik asked.

"Very."

"And you've never seen any odd goings-on here?"

"No," Gérard quickly replied. "Well, Anouk is odd, but a good person." He paused and added, "And so is Sandra, come to think of it. But I understand what you're asking and no, I've never seen any odd, or wicked, behavior here."

Verlaque stood in the middle of the bar area, his arms folded, watching the forensics team pack up their equipment. "Quite clean," the head of the team said as he shook Verlaque's hand. "Except for the cobwebs. More importantly, we do know that the victim was dragged in there."

"Ah. Can you tell where from?"

"From the bar area is my guess right now. There are some black scuff marks on the floor that may match the bottom of the victim's shoes. We've gone over the foyer and front door and there's nothing. Unfortunately the actors were all gathered around the bar last night, so the site is fairly contaminated."

"Okay, thanks. Will we be able to use the rest of the theater for questioning?"

"I don't see why not. And another thing, there's a small window that was open. It sticks, so it appeared shut, but the latch wasn't fixed."

"Can you show me?" Verlaque asked.

"Sure, follow me."

They stopped at the open door of the storage room, still taped off. The technician shone his small flashlight at a far wall, revealing a window at shoulder height. Labeled packing boxes were stacked against the wall. "The window is bigger than it looks from here," he said.

"Big enough for an adult?"

"Yes, a slim one. And coordinated."

"What's on the other side?"

"A narrow alley between the buildings."

Verlaque said, "So it's nicely hidden."

"Yes, and dark. One of the guys went out there and there's no light, and it's far from the closest streetlight."

"That's unusual in Aix," Verlaque suggested, "to have an alley between two buildings. They usually didn't waste space."

The officer nodded. "You're right. But over here," he said, motioning with his hands, "the Cours Sextius would have been the outer limits of the seventeenth-century town. Back then Sextius was lined with inns and shops, and behind, like where we are here, tanneries and *cardeurs*."

"*Cardeurs*?"

"Wool-combers," the officer explained.

"Ah, La Place des Cardeurs," Verlaque mumbled.

"And the Place des Tanneurs."

"Right," Verlaque said, almost thanking him for the mini history lesson. The forensics director had a reputation as a history buff.

"I'll write up a report as soon as I get back to the office," he said. "Anything else?" He looked at his watch and coughed, shuffling from one foot to the other.

"Any other places of historical interest in this neighborhood?" Verlaque asked, trying to break his uneasiness.

"Ah, yes. La Chapelle des Pénitents. Or, more correctly, La Chapelle des Pénitents-Gris-d'Aix. It's around the corner; just cross Sextius and walk toward the Place des Tanneurs. It's finally open."

"It's usually closed?"

"Yes, permanently closed. But it's open for a week's visit for the general public, as the city just spent a few hundred thousand euros on renovations. The chapel was built in the early sixteenth century for an order of local monks. Their name comes from the homespun sackcloth robes they wore. . . ." He paused, self-conscious. "Anyway, there's some wonderful wooden sculptures of the crucifix and death of Christ in there. Just the kind of art for repenting brothers."

Verlaque smiled, appreciating the director's reference to the word *pénitence*.

"We're ready," one of the forensics guys said as he walked by.

The director nodded. "Try to get a peek at the chapel," he said to Verlaque. "It's worth it, and this may be your only chance for a while." He tapped Verlaque on the shoulder in a playful way. "You can also unload some sins at the same time, eh?" He laughed and waved goodbye as he walked away.

Verlaque felt the need to sit down and drink a large glass of water. He thus thought it strange when a voice behind him said, "Would you like something to drink? I'm just getting myself a glass of water."

He turned around and saw a middle-aged woman looking at him, wide-eyed. "Thank you, I would," he said, surprised. He composed himself and added, "Antoine Verlaque, magistrate." He held out his hand.

The woman coughed. "Sandra. Sandra Gastaldi." They shook hands. "I do wardrobe here, and I'm a home loan officer at the Crédit Lyonnais on the cours."

"Could we chat?" Verlaque asked. "While we drink our water?"

"Of course. There's bottled water in the lounge."

He followed her to the lounge and watched as she poured out two large glasses of bottled water. Her hands shook slightly, but he thought it normal, given the circumstances.

"Thank you," he said as she handed him his glass. She pulled over a stool and sat next to him.

"You were also acting in this play, I understand," he began.

"Yes, for the first time. Normally I just do the costumes."

Verlaque smiled. "My wife is always distracted at the theater by the costumes," he said. "She loves them."

"It's a complicated task," Sandra said without bragging. "How the costume relates to the play and its era; how the actor will be able to move around in it, hopefully comfortably; and how the audience will see the outfit, many of them from a distance." She laughed. "Although at our theater everyone is sitting up close."

Verlaque smiled. "It's a small theater." He was impressed with her professionalism in costuming. "Did you get to know M Lesage during rehearsals?"

"Not really," she said without hesitation. "He was usually late, or not here. And no, I didn't like Gauthier, but I've already told the commissioner that."

"Was M Lesage not very likable?"

"No. He was a snob and condescending." She paused. "I'm not sure why he was even in our play, as apparently he couldn't act, either."

Verlaque looked up. "Oh really?"

Sandra took a huge gulp of water, evidently embarrassed by her outburst. "That's what they say, anyway," she whispered.

"Who says?" he asked, trying to sound nonchalant.

She stared at her glass, turning it around on the Formica bar top. "Liliane."

"Liliane Poncet?" he asked, lowering his voice.

"We had an aperitif together a couple of nights ago."

"She knew M Lesage."

"Yes, they acted together years ago, and were a romantic couple."

Sandra's old-fashioned language touched Verlaque. "What did Mme Poncet say about him?"

She leaned in. "She said he couldn't act, and that he got his roles by . . ." She looked around and whispered, "The casting couch."

"I thought that was for male producers to seduce female actors?" Verlaque said.

"Apparently it can work the other way, too. Although I'm sure not as frequently."

Verlaque looked sideways at her. "Were they on good terms?" he asked. "During your rehearsals?"

"Gauthier wasn't nice to Liliane, that's for sure. But Liliane didn't hold a grudge, at least that's how it seemed to me. She was very gracious about his teasing and insults. But that's how a star behaves, isn't it? Classy."

"Mme Poncet," Verlaque said, holding out his hand. "It's an honor."

"I prefer mademoiselle," Liliane said, shaking his hand and sitting down across from him at a small table.

Verlaque smiled. "I think the last film of yours I saw was *Return to Burgundy*. I saw it with my late mother."

He was thankful that a quick search earlier on his cell phone had given him a list of the actress's latest films. He added the bit about his mother for emotional weight, with the strategy that they would now, if Liliane wanted to begin with some chitchat, talk about his mother and not about *Return to Burgundy*, which he had never seen. He had also never in his life watched a film with his mother. Nor his father.

"That was a female sort of film," she said. "Did your mother enjoy it?"

"Very much," he said, smiling. He checked himself and erased the smile, adding, "Despite her ill health." Liliane tilted her head to one side and sighed. Verlaque thought he was almost as good an actor as she was. He decided to change the subject before he got into trouble. "You knew Gauthier Lesage from way back, I understand."

"We were in a musical together, in Paris," she said. "About twenty-five years ago. Gauthier was fresh out of university. He was from Lyon, a posh industrialist's family. His father opposed Gauthier's idea of becoming an actor. The poor father."

"Why the poor father?"

"Both Gauthier and his sister were a disappointment."

"He told you a great deal about his family," Verlaque suggested.

"Why yes. We *were* close." She sighed. "I was older than him, and in between marriages." She coughed and drank some coffee. "Well, almost in between marriages. Technically I was still married to Stéphane."

"Stéphane?"

"Stéphane Breton, my second husband."

"Oh, I see." He certainly hadn't kept track of Liliane Poncet's career, or her husbands. "Was Stéphane Breton aware of your . . . relationship . . . with Gauthier Lesage?"

"Oh yes, he was livid. I left him not long after."

"And when did you stop seeing M Lesage?"

"The play didn't last long, a few weeks," she replied. "Gauthier and I went out together for another six weeks or so. Then he dropped me for a much younger actress. Well, one his age, and one whose father was directing a film Gauthier wanted to be in."

"No hard feelings?"

She shrugged. "In this business? No."

"And had you seen each other since rehearsals for this play began?"

"At a few parties, but I kept my distance." Liliane straightened her back, sitting erect and proud.

"Do you have any idea what happened to M Lesage? His current state of mind?"

"Why? What are you saying? Was it suicide? I thought he was murdered."

Verlaque quickly answered, "It was murder, Mlle Poncet."

Liliane's head dropped, her chin resting in the hollow of her collarbone. Her shoulders began to rise and fall and she sobbed, but no tears fell.

Chapter Fourteen

❧

Friday, August 11

Bruno Paulik heard the crying from down below and shifted in his seat. Emile Leclerc came up the stairs, carrying two cups of coffee. "I thought you might need one of these," he said, placing the mugs on the table. He sat down.

"Thank you," Paulik said. "That was very thoughtful," he added, truthfully, as he was in great need of a late-morning coffee.

"I'm used to serving people," Emile said with no hint of distaste or self-pity. "I own the butcher shop on the rue Espariat with my brothers."

Paulik smiled. "That's where I've seen you."

"I don't have my apron on now."

"That's it. Out of context." Paulik thought Emile looked slightly uncomfortable. "I'll begin with the obvious, for our records. Where were you late Wednesday night?"

Emile shrugged. "We got home from the rehearsal quite late. My wife was already asleep. I went out to our terrace and had a couple of smokes and a whiskey. I needed to cool off."

"What from?"

Emile paused. "From rehearsal. It's tough, acting."

"Did you know Gauthier Lesage?" he asked.

"No," Emile answered. "Well, just here, during the few practices he came to."

"He didn't come to your butcher shop?" Paulik asked, smiling again.

"No, he was a vegetarian and made a big deal about it. In fact, that's one of the only things I can tell you about him. He stuck to himself."

Paulik looked at the file that had just been updated and passed to him by a colleague. "Even though you lived on the same street?"

"Really? The rue Aude?" Emile asked. "That's news to me. What number?"

Paulik looked down at his list. "He was north of you, number twenty-eight."

"I had no idea." He sighed heavily and said, "Listen, you should know something."

"Go on."

Emile took a deep breath and then said, "At one of the rehearsals Gauthier was being especially cruel to Liliane, and I told him to shut up."

"What did M Lesage say?"

"Some nonsense about Liliane's lovers and husbands."

"And what did you say?"

"I told him to sit down and eat his cake," Emile said.

Paulik tried not to grin over the cake part. "Was he intimidated by you?"

Emile looked down, as if embarrassed. "Yes," he quietly said. "At any rate, Gauthier sat down and shut up." Emile crossed his arms and Paulik saw that they were thicker by half than his own. Paulik's wife, Hélène, called him a gentle giant. In the Luberon, where Paulik grew up, there were other boys his size, and they quickly fell into two groups: the gentle giants like him, who walked away from fights; and those who began the fights, falsely encouraged by their own towering presence and physical intimidation. This second group relished the fights, and they were often thick in the head. He wondered which side of the fence Emile Leclerc sat on.

Liliane Poncet was accompanied home by a young male police officer, her arm gallantly slipped through his as if she were leading him down the street and not the other way around. Verlaque watched, amazed at how just one minute ago Liliane had been so quiet and deep in thought.

"Mlle Singer?" he asked as he turned away from the doorway and followed Anouk to the lounge.

"Yes?" she asked, turning around.

"Could we speak now?"

"All right," she replied slowly, evidently uneasy. She accidentally dropped a rag she'd been carrying and Verlaque bent down and retrieved it, handing it back to her. "Thanks," she mumbled.

He looked at her. He had to agree with Bruno Paulik: Anouk Singer wasn't exactly the kind of woman a film star like Gauthier Lesage would go for. Her hair was unkempt and slightly greasy, her skin blotchy, and her clothes ill-fitting. But most of all she had a faraway, dazed look in her eyes, as if she was constantly taken by surprise by the world. They sat down on the sofas as Anouk played with the rag, rubbing it between her fingers. Verlaque looked at the wall behind her, which had been temporarily set up as the bar until the police had finished with the real one. A small shelf was lined with mismatched wineglasses and a few almost empty bottles of alcohol. Next to the shelf hung a series of framed photographs. One caught his eye, especially the signature at the bottom. He blinked, not sure he was reading it right.

"I was on a cruise ship," Anouk explained, watching him. "We did the halftime entertainment, me and another dancer. Between the bigger acts." She blushed.

Verlaque turned to look at the woman now sitting beside him. It took all his will not to look back at the scantily clad, extremely fit young woman in the photograph. He gulped. "So, that's you. That must have been tough, working on cruise ships, always far from home." He had no idea if that was true, but he couldn't think of anything else to say, never having been on one.

"Nah!" she answered with a wave of her hand. "I loved it!"

Verlaque asked, "Did you know Gauthier Lesage during that time?"

"After," she said. "The cruise ship was sold to a Norwegian company that wanted to specialize in nature trips, so we lost our jobs. But at the same time I saw an ad for a casting for a musical in Paris, so I decided to return."

"To dry land," Verlaque said, smiling.

"Yes. And I got the part, so I was thrilled. A dancer in the chorus, but my real love is acting."

"And M Lesage was in this play, too?"

"Yes," Anouk replied. "As was Liliane."

"Mlle Poncet?"

"Yes," Anouk said. "She had the lead role."

"Did you three hang around together then?" Verlaque imagined joking around off-stage, then drinks in a smoky Parisian bar afterward.

Anouk laughed. "Are you kidding? I was in the *chorus*."

"So, no."

"They didn't know I existed. Well, certainly not Liliane."

"But perhaps Gauthier Lesage?"

Anouk blushed and played with her rag. "There were a few moments . . ."

"Yes?"

"When I thought Gauthier was smiling at me."

"But you didn't speak?"

"No. After the play ended its run, I didn't see him again, nor Liliane, until this summer, here in Aix."

"Where did you advertise the play?" Verlaque asked. "For the casting? Weren't you surprised to get two well-known actors auditioning? No offense, I'm sure your theater is top-notch."

"No offense taken," Anouk said. "I would have been surprised, but last year I read an article in *Theater Today* that said film actors are returning to the theater, especially small, intimate ones like mine. It's good for their public image."

"But to have both Liliane Poncet and M Lesage here for the same play?"

Anouk shrugged. "It's a mysterious business. The strangest things can happen."

"Where do you place your ads?"

"Oh, right, sorry. On a website specialized in jobs in the arts. It's free."

"I assume that M Lesage has an agent."

"Um, yes, he does. She's also Liliane's agent. Julie Santelli, in Paris." She took her cell phone from her back pocket and scrolled through the contact list. When she got to "S," she stopped and showed Verlaque Julie Santelli's phone number, which he immediately added to his contacts.

"One final thing," he said. "That musical in Paris. Did everyone know Liliane and Gauthier were having an affair?"

Anouk winced. "Yes, it was obvious."

Verlaque asked, "Did Mlle Poncet's husband at the time, Stéphane Breton, ever come by?"

She stared at the judge, then swallowed. "Yes."

"Was there a scene?"

"Yes," she said.

"Did Breton threaten them?"

"He threw some of the props around the stage. The director was furious. Breton yelled that one day he would get his revenge." She paused. "It sounds very theatrical, doesn't it? But that's what he said."

Paulik looked with surprise at his cell phone and Verlaque's reply to his lunch invitation: *pas disponible, désolé*. It was rare that Antoine Verlaque turned down lunch, but perhaps because he'd been in Paris he was now behind on paperwork. Paulik shrugged and walked out of the theater, deciding to just buy a sandwich at a nearby boulangerie.

Verlaque watched the commissioner pause in the street and then turn right. Sighing with relief, he checked his phone for messages, but there were none. He left the building, turning in the opposite direction as Paulik. On rue Duperrier, he heard the sounds of children laughing and screaming from behind a stone wall. He saw that it was the neighborhood's elementary school and his heart started beating more quickly. Zigzagging through the narrow streets, he worked his way across the four-lane Sextius. The street always seemed to be full of double-parked cars, leaving only one lane in the middle for both directions of traffic to squeeze through. It reminded him of Rome, and Madrid.

Once on rue Lieutaud, he realized he hadn't looked up the chapel's address. He assumed it would be big enough to find easily, or well marked, or both, but once he got to the bottom of the street he realized that he must have walked right by it. Doubling back, he paid more attention this time and found it halfway up the block, with not very large wooden doors and a cast-iron marker put up by the city explaining the chapel's historical significance.

He stopped to read the plaque but after a few lines the words began to bleed together. He couldn't concentrate. He walked in, anxious. It took a few minutes for his eyes to adjust to the darkness, and he welcomed the coolness of the thick stone walls. It was humid, but cold. The scene of Christ's death was higher than he had imagined, built into a niche behind the altar upon a group of very large stacked rocks. He didn't like the rocks; they were too brutal, and the statues were unfortunately painted in the garish colors he knew had been common in the Middle Ages. He squinted, trying to pick out details in the faces: moles on cheeks, double chins, broken noses.

"Lovely detail, don't you think?" a voice said behind him.

Verlaque swung around and faced a middle-aged priest. "Yes," he replied, half lying. He turned back to look at the figures who held Christ's dead body.

"The sculptor was Jean Guiramand."

Verlaque raised an eyebrow. "Sorry, the name's lost on me."

"It shouldn't be," the priest said. "Guiramand sculpted the cathedral's doors."

"The same guy? So he was from Aix?"

"Mais non!" the priest exclaimed, as if reprimanding Verlaque for his stupidity. "Toulon!"

Verlaque tried not to laugh, as Toulon wasn't that far from Aix. He was about to tell the priest how much he liked Toulon when his cell phone began to vibrate. "Excuse me," he said. He turned around and ran out of the chapel into the bright light of the street, fumbling for his phone. He saw the caller ID and yelled into the phone, "Marine!" Two tattooed youth walked by him and smirked. "Marine," he said again, more quietly this time.

"Antoine!" his wife said. "What a relief!"

"Where are you?" he asked. He tried to control his breathing. "You weren't at home last night."

"At my parents' house. You saw. I left a note."

"What note?" His breathing became slower and more regular. So there was an explanation. The sun began to beat down on him and he found shelter under the tiny metal awning of a doorway.

"Zut alors," she said. "You didn't see it. I left you a note, as there was obviously a problem with your cell phone. I put it on the kitchen counter, next to where you always plug in your phone."

"Ah, I plugged my phone by the bedside last night, in case you called."

"*You* could have called *me* last night," Marine said.

Verlaque gulped. "I thought you were angry with me."

"No, I was *worried*," Marine said. "Anyway, maman exhausted me complaining about the government so I was in bed by 9:30. But why didn't you return my calls in Paris?"

"My phone was out of battery," he said. "And I plugged it in as soon as I got on the TGV, then fell fast asleep."

"Well, we can clear all of this up when you get home tonight. Papa said there would be a logical explanation. I have to go, sorry. Lunch is on the table." She hung up and Verlaque's heart sang for joy. He would explain everything this evening: seeing his father and Rebecca, running into Emily and talking about her family and their youth, and then drinking far too much with the Hedgehog.

Verlaque hung up and texted Paulik, asking where he was eating lunch.

Paulik replied: *A sandwich at the boulangerie on the corner of Sextius and Cordeliers.* A second text immediately followed: *It's not very good.*

I'll be right there, Verlaque texted back.

Chapter Fifteen

❧

Friday, August 11

By the time Verlaque arrived at the boulangerie, Paulik had finished his sandwich and was on the phone, listening to someone talk. Verlaque ordered a jambon-beurre, thinking they couldn't really mess up a ham sandwich. He took a bite and decided otherwise. Not enough ham and too much butter, unsalted.

Paulik got off the phone and said, "That was Cohen. She's finished examining the particles of fabric." He looked casually around, but they were alone in the place except for the staff, standing idly behind the counter chatting with one another. No surprise, thought Verlaque, since it was probably the worse boulangerie in Aix. "The fabric under his fingernails," Paulik continued.

"Yes?"

"Silk. Probably from a scarf of some kind. Multicolored."

"So the killer brought it with them."

"Or was wearing it," Paulik suggested.

"Or . . ."

"Got it upstairs."

Verlaque said, "Exactly. In that overstuffed wardrobe area."

"It would take some time to run up there," Paulik pointed out.

"Unless they began their visit upstairs."

"Or the murderer was up there, alone, before Lesage arrived."

"Maybe they had a key," Verlaque suggested, taking another disappointing bite of his sandwich.

"Or came in that tiny window," Paulik said. "So a small man, or a woman, and they were wearing that scarf. I have a cousin who wears a scarf every day, year-round."

Verlaque raised an eyebrow. Paulik hadn't shared any cousin stories in a while, and Verlaque had surprisingly missed them. "And?" he asked.

"He never gets sick," Paulik said. "He's sure it's because the scarf protects his throat."

"It must be hot in the summer." Verlaque finished his lunch, crushing the sandwich paper and throwing it into a garbage can.

"He never gets hot or cold."

"Is he a real person?" Verlaque asked.

"He's from my mother's side of the family," Paulik said, tapping the side of his head. "They're all a bit touched."

Verlaque laughed. "Same with my family. Ready to go back?"

"Yes, we can compare notes about this morning."

They left, crossing Sextius and walking through the tiny streets back to the theater. "Anouk Singer was a dancer," Verlaque began.

"Really?" Paulik looked at the judge, surprised.

"She could get in that window. She'd still be coordinated."

"Perhaps," Paulik agreed, not sounding convinced.

"And she has a motive: jealousy. Anouk was in that World War Two musical with both the victim and Liliane Poncet. She was sweet on Gauthier Lesage, I think, but neither of the actors noticed her."

"Why the twenty-five-year wait?"

"Did Anouk make a pass at him and was rejected? Again? Did something else happen twenty-five years ago?"

They walked down the rue de la Paix and were about to turn left to head to the theater when a door opened. Sandra Gastaldi walked out of a building, locking the door behind her. "Oh!" she said. "Hello."

Verlaque looked up at the three-story building with light brown shutters. The top floor had window boxes with fresh flowers; he guessed that was her apartment. "You certainly live close to the theater," he said, smiling.

"Yes," she replied, a bit uneasy. "But close to my bank, too, where I work. Except this week, of course. We've been given permission to stay at home."

"Normal procedure," Paulik said. "You all went through a shocking experience." He didn't want to add that the actors would be needed for questioning at a moment's notice, too, so going to their day jobs posed an inconvenience. Getting them to leave their residences was easier than dealing with angry bosses.

Verlaque looked down the street as they began to walk together. "You must be able to see the theater from your apartment," he said.

"Yes, from almost every window," Sandra answered. "I used

to watch the audience leave the theater, when I was back at home after arranging the costumes. It was thrilling."

"And you haven't seen anything unusual lately?"

She paused. She didn't know what to tell him. He smiled often, but he was intimidating, too. He'd think her crazy if she told him about the woman dressed up in prewar clothes. It was probably a student from the Beaux-Arts, she quickly decided. Why hadn't she realized that before? They were always dressing up, and the school was nearby. "No," she answered.

"Or hear anything?" Paulik asked.

Sandra slowed down and the men followed suit. She sighed. Paulik said, "It could be important."

"When you work with such a small group," she said, "you quickly become friends." She hesitated and then continued, "So I don't want to sound like a traitor, or a snitch."

"You won't," Verlaque reassured her. "I promise."

"The other day, I overheard an argument. I was upstairs working on the costumes, and was about to walk down the stairs when I heard them arguing."

"Who was arguing?" Verlaque asked.

"Emile and Gauthier. Gauthier was accusing Emile of being a bully."

"And is he?" Verlaque asked.

Sandra stopped walking and faced him. "Emile? No way. Emile told Gauthier to stop being cruel to Liliane, but I already told your commissioner that. We all wanted to tell Gauthier to stop; it was only Emile who had the courage to do it."

"So Emile wasn't being a bully," Verlaque suggested. "In your opinion."

"No. But Gauthier was egging him on, saying how he wasn't afraid of a big butcher. Emile told him to stop, more than once." Sandra swallowed. "And then Gauthier said something awful."

"Go on."

"He told Emile, 'Did you ever notice how in most films the butcher is always a big simpleton?'"

"And what did Emile say?"

"Emile told Gauthier that he should be more careful, because if he lost his temper, Gauthier could get hurt. Emile said, 'You're this close.' I couldn't see them, but imagine that Emile was doing that gesture with your thumb and forefinger, you know, when you press them almost together but not quite touching."

Verlaque nodded. "Yes . . ."

Sandra sighed. "I feel bad, telling you this."

"You shouldn't," Verlaque said as they continued walking. The theater was just a few feet ahead. "Because what your story tells us is that Gauthier Lesage could have had many enemies if he treated everyone that way. I would say that M Leclerc handled himself with much restraint."

"Are you on your way to the theater?" Paulik asked Sandra.

"No, I'm going to do some shopping."

"Before you go," he said. "Does the theater's wardrobe have a collection of scarves?"

If the question surprised her, she didn't let on. "Oh, dozens of them. You can make a drastic change to a costume with a simple scarf."

Paulik asked, "Did any of the actors in this Pagnol play have a scarf to wear?"

She stopped walking again and looked at the commissioner. "Oh, you're asking these questions for a reason."

"Perhaps."

"I wore one, if you really want to know. I'm playing a bourgeois Marseillaise who comes to the village with her family. My husband Ludovic is also wearing a scarf, a small dandyish one; he's played by Emile. And . . . let me think . . . Mme Toffi wears one. She's the woman who wants to open a restaurant in the same village, to compete with Cigalon's."

"She's played by?"

"Liliane. Mme Poncet."

"Are any of the scarves silk?"

She thought. "A couple, maybe. Most of them are donated, or we buy them real cheap, so I would guess the majority are polyester. I'd have to touch them to know. I can't remember offhand." She looked at her watch.

"Thanks," Paulik answered. "We'll see you around, then."

Verlaque smiled and added, "Have a nice afternoon."

Sandra waved and walked away, turning left down a tiny street no wider than a yardstick. "She hesitated when we asked her if she'd seen anything unusual lately," Paulik said quietly.

"I noticed that, too," Verlaque replied. "But now I think that she hesitated on our question because she didn't *see* anything, but heard it instead."

"Perhaps."

"You're Mister Perhaps today."

"And you're all smiles." Paulik paused, looking at the judge, and added, "Compared to this morning."

Verlaque almost told his commissioner the Paris story right there: his surprise meeting with Emily, the cigars and delicious wine, then meeting up with the Hedgehog and the whiskey. The aching head the next morning, the impossibly dull meetings, the race back to his father's house to fetch his suitcase then sprint for the TGV, the dead cell phone, and falling asleep on the train and almost missing Aix. But he stayed quiet. He often thought that the Pauliks were the perfect family. He was about to ask after Hélène and Léa when his voice was drowned out by the noise they now heard at the end of the street: raised voices, strange clicking sounds, and the blast of a car horn. The judge and commissioner stopped, looked at each other, and then broke into a sprint.

As they got close to the theater they picked out the shapes of journalists holding cameras and microphones, their cars parked at the beginning of the street. A Monoprix delivery truck was stuck behind their double-parked cars, its driver enraged, yelling at anyone who made the mistake of glancing his way.

Standing in front of the theater's front door was Anouk, her right hip thrust forward, hands on her hips, and her head tilted back, her eyes bright. Verlaque swore under his breath: It was obvious to him that she was enjoying her two minutes in the limelight. "Next question!" she shouted.

Paulik walked up to a young police officer who was standing to Anouk's right. "What's going on here?" he yelled.

"I didn't let them in the theater, sir!" the officer answered.

"I'm to thank you for that?" Paulik asked, enraged.

"Mlle Singer," a female journalist called out, "will your play be canceled?"

"I certainly hope not," Anouk answered, removing her smile now in order to look severe. "The show must go on!"

"You have our support!" someone called out.

Ten minutes later the street was calm. Verlaque gave the journalists the bare minimum of information and Paulik dealt with the delivery driver and some curious onlookers. But the real clearing away was thanks to Pauline Singer, who led her daughter away, chastising her. Verlaque heard the elder Singer say, "You've always been so desperate to be seen and heard!" and Anouk whimper, apologize, mumble something about Gauthier, and then break down. He didn't think he'd ever seen a middle-aged person be scolded by their elderly parents.

"We have two women crying over the deceased," Verlaque whispered as he and the commissioner leaned against a stone window ledge outside the theater. "Is it possible to kill someone you claim to love?" he asked. "Because I think that Anouk loved Gauthier, even if he didn't know she existed."

"Strong emotions, love and hate. It's all about passion, isn't it?" Paulik suggested. "So I'd say yes. But he didn't even know who she was, if she's telling the truth."

"She gave me his agent's name. I'll call her and set up an appointment."

Paulik looked at his boss. "She'll be in Paris."

"Yeah, and I was just there. And with Marine about to deliver . . . I don't want to go back." He looked at Paulik and raised his eyebrows.

"I hate going to Paris!"

"You can be up and back in a day."

Paulik laughed despite himself. "You always say that."

Verlaque said, "And the good news is, she's also Liliane Poncet's agent."

"Swell."

"I take it Gauthier Lesage's apartment is being examined?"

"Yes, Flamant is there now with a team. Twenty-eight rue Aude, the same street that Emile Leclerc lives on."

Verlaque said, "That's a small street. Perhaps they continued their argument closer to home."

"I'll have the officers ask the neighbors if they've heard anything."

Verlaque lowered his voice and said, "I think it's someone here, in this theater."

"Me, too. There are too many coincidences, and too many grudges, old and new."

"We have those with keys; the three actors with scarves, although anyone could wear a scarf, but in this heat it's a bit crazy, despite what your cousin thinks; and those who are small and limber enough to fit through the window in the storage room. He or she would have to be strong enough to fight Lesage, too."

"Or angry enough. We can eliminate the two kids," Paulik said. "And Mme and M Singer. They'll be on our B-list."

"And I don't see a motive for either the lighting guy or the handyman."

"We'll put Abdul Khattabi and Gérard Richet at the bottom of our A-list."

"What about the costume woman?" Verlaque asked.

"Sandra Gastaldi? She can go next to them on the A-list,"

Paulik said. "But . . ." He paused, biting his lip. "She's holding something back. It could be a hunch she has, or something she saw or heard that she's embarrassed about."

"Yes," Verlaque said, turning around and resting his elbows on the ledge so he could survey the empty street. "I think she's protecting someone, and my guess is Anouk Singer."

Verlaque couldn't remember a time when he had walked so quickly to their apartment. He zigzagged around limping tourists who were beaten down by the heat. They always seemed to stop right in his way as they scanned the bar terraces in hopes of finding an available table. He tried to be patient—they brought money into Aix, and, he had to admit, diversity and happiness, as they seemed to come from all corners of the world, spoke various languages, and were inevitably completely enthused and charmed by his small city. He forced himself to slow down in the middle of the grand square in front of the Hôtel de Ville, partly to catch his breath, partly to cool down, and partly to watch and appreciate the summer evening. Every single café and bar table was taken, a spritz—a cocktail new to Aix—on almost every table. The drink of the summer, he noted, but it always tasted better in Venice. The bright orange cocktail livened up what was already a jolly scene, especially in this pretty square lined with pastel-colored eighteenth-century buildings.

He was about to move on when an elderly Scottish couple stopped next to him, the woman complaining of fatigue and sore feet. Her sandals were too tight, apparently. Verlaque noticed a young couple at a table, the girl putting on a last bit of lipstick as her boyfriend leaned back, reached into his pocket, and pulled out a few coins to leave as a tip on the table. The telltale signs they would vacate their table in a few seconds.

"There," Verlaque said in English to the Scots, gesturing with his shoulder. "A table is opening up. Would you like it?"

The woman had time only to nod and smile and Verlaque was gone. He strode across the square and stopped at the table, asking the young couple if they were leaving. Receiving an answer in the affirmative, he motioned with his hand to the Scots, and they shuffled across the square. The young couple got up and left. Immediately there were two other couples—both French—on top of Verlaque, asking for the table. "It's reserved," he said.

The younger couples mumbled in frustration and left, the Scots finally arriving after what Verlaque thought was an eternity. "Here you go," he said, pulling out a chair for the old woman.

"Thank you so much," she said, almost collapsing into the wicker chair.

"You've been very kind," her husband said as he shook Verlaque's hand.

"Staying faithful to the old friendship between our two countries," Verlaque mumbled, not sure how to accept their praise, as what he had done would have been totally out of character for him in his younger days. It was something Marine would have done, but not him.

"Indeed!" the old man said. "I don't know what your day job is, but if you ever lose it, you'd be a great waiter!" He chuckled and sat down, his wife throwing him a look of embarrassment. Verlaque faked a laugh, gently bowed, and left, smiling at the thought of his day job.

He picked up the pace, tempted to buy ingredients for a spritz, but he didn't, as Marine couldn't drink alcohol. And anyway, he had drunk enough in Paris to last a while.

Finally home, he took the stairs up to their fourth-floor apartment two at a time and flung open the door, calling for Marine.

"Here!" she replied. "In the kitchen!" He could hear her making something and the clinking of ice cubes in a glass. He ran.

"Marine!" he said as she swung around to face him, her stomach looking even bigger than it had two days previously.

"My darling boy," she said as she held out her arms. He wrapped himself in them and buried his head in the side of her neck, staying there until she gently pried him away. "You scared me," she said quietly. "Not answering your cell phone."

"It wasn't intentional."

"I know," she said, looking grave. "But you know the first thing I thought of. . . ."

Verlaque gulped, not wanting her to say "another woman," as he had spent half the evening—but only drinking champagne!—with someone he had once been terribly in love with.

"A terrorist attack," Marine finished.

He kissed her. "I stupidly left my charger at my father's, and then drank far too much alcohol at that little hidden cigar bar I read about in the eighth."

She laughed. "You made up for lost time. These past nine months you've hardly had a drop. My father even guessed what you were up to: He said that you were having your last wild evening before the baby is born." She turned around to continue making whatever she had started when he came home. "Who were you with?"

He noticed a change in her voice, as if she were pretending to be nonchalant. He took a deep breath. "Two people," he answered. "First, Emily Watford."

Marine didn't turn around but he saw her back, for a split second, stiffen. "Lady Emily," she finally said as she cut an orange into slices.

"We smoked cigars and drank champagne and talked about the old days." He paused. "Marine," he said. "Turn around, please."

She turned around and he went on. "Nothing happened. I love you and only you. Emily and I only talked, in a room full of other people. But being with Emily made me realize something, finally."

"What?" Marine whispered.

"That it is possible to be happy in a family. It's not a cliché. All of my happy memories of the Watfords and Durrington Hall came back. We will have a beautiful family, the three of us, full of love. We will make our child feel loved and full of confidence each time they walk out the door." He stopped, choked up, unable to go on.

Marine kissed him and then pulled away, looking at her husband. "Who was the second person?"

"The Hedgehog!"

Marine looked at him blankly, until she slapped her forehead and began to laugh. "Axel Hérisson!"

"The only person in France with such an unfortunate surname, although it hasn't hampered his career in any way. He lives in a flashy condo near the Champs."

"Oh dear," Marine said, echoing most French people's dislike of that street. "I always figured he'd do well. Financially, at least. Is he still in law?"

"Finance."

Marine grinned as if she had a secret, and she let out a little giggle.

"What is it?" Verlaque asked.

"Axel and I slept together," she replied. "When we were students."

"Ah! The truth comes out!" He stared at his wife in disbelief. She never revealed her past amours.

She laughed again. "It was just once, after a party. We were both very tipsy, and embarrassed afterward. He'd always just been a friend to me. The hedgehog of our little group."

"Funny that you knew him in law school, and me at my first job in Paris. The Hedgehog and I worked side by side for two years."

"Well, continue your story," Marine said.

Verlaque went on, wishing he had something cold to drink, but Marine seemed to have abandoned whatever she had been concocting at the kitchen counter. "After Emily left the bar, Axel showed up, and we drank far too much whiskey, closing down the bar and continuing at his place until I fell asleep on the sofa and woke up with a pounding head and was almost late for my meeting. Which was a complete waste of time, by the way. And then on the train I charged my phone and saw your messages and panicked when you hung up."

"Oh! I'm sorry about that. I was a little angry, yes, but also my mother kept interrupting me with questions every time I tried to sneak away and call you. She was doing a crossword."

"A crossword!" Verlaque cried out, raising his arms in the air in mock frustration. "We had a near-marital breakdown over your mother's crossword! And to think that someone was murdered in a little theater here in Aix, and Florence Bonnet is wreaking havoc because of her crossword!"

"Murder? Theater?"

"Yeah, the Théâtre Vendôme."

"Le Vendôme!"

"You know it?"

"I went to dance class there when I was a kid!"

Verlaque said, "Please don't tell me your mother sings at Saint-Jean-de-Malte with Mme Singer."

"No, silly, the Singers are Jewish. Anyway, who died? It's horrible."

"One of the actors, a well-known character actor in television, I'm told," he said. "Gauthier Lesage."

Marine shrugged. "The name rings a bell. But I can't tell you much about him. Our local movie star buff will be able to fill you in on some juicy details, though."

"Sylvie," Verlaque said. Sylvie Grassi always had a way to tell stories about people he really didn't care about but make them extremely funny.

"Oh! *Zut*!"

"What is it?"

Marine turned around and faced her project on the counter. "My ice cubes have melted." She reached over to the refrigerator, opened the top door, and pulled out another tray of ice cubes from the freezer.

"What are you making?"

"Just a second," she replied.

Verlaque leaned against the opposite counter, content to watch her back and arms moving. Did Marine's natural grace come from

the Singers' dance school? Small world. He heard the same clinking sound and saw a flash of bright orange. She swung around.
"Ta-da!" she said, handing him a bright orange drink.

"A spritz!"

"I made a nonalcoholic variation for myself. It's mostly orange
juice." They toasted each other.

"You can't believe how much I was thinking of these drinks
this afternoon," Verlaque said. "Everyone in Aix is drinking them."

"I noticed that, too, when Papa dropped me off."

"How are you feeling?"

Marine instinctively rubbed her stomach. "Good. But getting
impatient. Three more weeks to go, if the dates are right."

He set his drink down and hugged her. They stood like that
for a few minutes until Marine's ringing cell phone caused them
to pull apart. She looked at the phone. "It's Sylvie," she said. "I'd
better take it; she's already left two messages."

"Go ahead," Verlaque said. "Ask her about Gauthier Lesage—
but don't give her any details," he quickly added, grabbing his
cocktail. Marine smiled and gave him a thumbs-up. He walked
upstairs to their office and out onto the terrace, relieved and happy
to be home. He took a sip of the spritz and realized that whenever
he thought of home it was this apartment, not the country house.
He knew that Marine felt the same way.

Chapter Sixteen

❧

Saturday, August 12

Gauthier Lesage's apartment was bright—it was always worth it, thought Verlaque, to have to climb up a few flights in order to have sunny rooms. Two large windows looked out onto the street. The furniture didn't surprise him—black leather armchairs, lots of stainless steel and the color gray. If Lesage had a car, Verlaque guessed it would be a BMW. The cool colors didn't help cool down the apartment—it was already stuffy and warm despite the fact that it was just after 9:00. He was tempted to open the windows but he knew, because of the search going on, he couldn't.

"The bedroom is through here," Paulik said, gesturing to an open door just off the living room. Two uniformed officers, carefully documenting and inspecting the apartment, stepped aside to let them pass. Verlaque nodded and followed the commissioner into a large bedroom. The double bed was unmade—was Lesage just messy, or had he planned to make his bed but didn't get the chance? Two more windows faced the street, and opposite those was a contemporary glass desk. Above the desk were dozens of photographs and magazine clippings taped to the wall. Paulik was already standing in front of it, his head moving up and down and back and forth. Verlaque walked over to the collage. After a few seconds he said, "It's all about Gauthier Lesage."

"Yes," Paulik replied. "His entire career on one wall."

Verlaque estimated the collage was about four feet across and three feet high, starting above the desk. Judging by the glossy colorful pages, the clippings seemed to have come out of various celebrity magazines.

Paulik stared at the photographs and clippings. He pointed to a small color photo. "That's Gauthier. Younger."

"Yes, with his arm around a very happy-looking, also younger, Liliane Poncet."

"In the middle of the collage."

"Anything else in the apartment?" Verlaque asked.

"Nothing," Paulik answered. "Follow me."

They walked back through the living room and Paulik opened a new cheap wooden door that led into the kitchen, also new and cheap. *Wouldn't a somewhat well-known actor be able to afford a better apartment?* Verlaque wondered. But it was the commissioner who said aloud what Verlaque had been thinking: "We've gathered up all of Lesage's paperwork and bills, and someone is going over it. He might have been in a bad way, financially, looking at this place. It's like someone decorated it on the cheap, trying to make it look like some fancy bachelor pad."

Verlaque nodded. "That would explain his accepting a role in a local amateur theater."

"The kitchen looks like he only used it for mixing drinks and making coffee. There are empty Nespresso capsules in the garbage. That's about it," Paulik said. "Oh, there's one last thing. The student who lives across the hall heard a loud argument coming from this apartment on Wednesday night, the night Lesage died. By the time he fumbled with unlocking his apartment door and turning on the hall light, the yelling had stopped. He heard Lesage's apartment door bang shut."

"Did he see anything?"

"A flash of a high heel going down the stairs."

"High heels?" Verlaque asked. "Are you joking? Was the student able to elaborate?"

"Not much. He'd been sleeping and tripped over his bicycle on the way to open his door."

"And he's sure of the high heels?" Verlaque asked, rubbing his chin.

"So he says," Paulik answered. "Although he *had* been sleeping, and admitted that he'd had a few beers at the Le Brigand."

"How many?"

"Four."

"Big lad?"

"Tiny."

Verlaque grunted. "Not much of a witness. What did he say about Lesage? Did he know him?"

"He met him out in the hallway only a couple of times," Paulik said. "Lesage barely spoke to him. The student rarely heard him in his apartment, but sometimes could hear music. French crooners from the sixties and seventies. But the student did have something interesting to add to his report."

"Oh?"

"One time he was outside, further up the rue Aude, and he saw Lesage arguing with Liliane Poncet."

"Would this kid know who Liliane Poncet is?"

"I asked that, too. His grandmother is a big fan. Has all her movies."

"Despite all the photographs in the collage, somehow your eye is drawn to the middle."

"To Lesage with Liliane Poncet."

"Yes."

"We'll question her again," Paulik decided. "In the meantime, all of the paperwork we found here in this desk is being examined. He rented this place from a real estate agency on the Cours Mirabeau."

Verlaque glanced around the apartment. "It's not the swanky kind of place I'd expect a somewhat well-known actor to rent," he said. "With a student across the hall and an old retired couple downstairs."

"I agree. I'll talk to the realtor about it, and call Lesage's agent in Paris."

"Care for lunch?" Verlaque asked.

"Yes. Somewhere air-conditioned, if possible," Paulik said. He smiled, relieved that his boss was back to normal. He didn't want to eat alone again in Aix's worst boulangerie.

On the walk back to the Palais de Justice, both men regretted their choice of restaurant, which was large and charmless, part of a new hotel complex on the northern end of the ring road. Its saving grace had been the air-conditioning. The service was slow, the waitstaff having to serve diners inside and weary tourists sitting, for some reason neither man understood, outside at small tables by the pool. It was almost 40°C! But Verlaque and Paulik enjoyed—relished, even—glasses of cool white wine and the fish of the day, which mercifully hadn't been overcooked, even if the vegetables had.

Once back at the Palais de Justice they found the officer who was going over Gauthier Lesage's paperwork. A half-eaten egg sandwich sat beside the keyboard and Verlaque apologized for disturbing his lunch. The officer waved it off. "No problem," he said. "I don't mind eating at my desk. It's air-conditioned in here."

"Find out anything interesting?" Paulik asked.

"Yep. I've already spoken to the realtor who rented Lesage's apartment to him. Lesage has been there for eleven months and is two months behind on rent. The realtor is furious." The officer pointed to a stack of envelopes with the letterhead of one of the bigger realtors on the cours. "And," he went on, pointing to another stack, which looked like bank statements to Verlaque, "he was in debt at the bank. Not by much, a couple hundred each month. But still. I'm just about to go through the computer records on him. I'm curious to see if he left any other traces. Real estate, perhaps. Car loans. That kind of thing. Oh, and Officer Goulin tracked down Lesage's sister."

"Excellent," Verlaque said. "Is she still in Brittany?"

"Yes, Morgat, in the Finistère. She's divorced and has gone back to using the name Lesage. Two local gendarmes have gone to her house to give her the news. Sophie . . . I mean, Officer Goulin . . . is in contact with them if you need more information."

"Thank you," Paulik said. "We won't keep you any longer." He turned to Verlaque. "We need to question Liliane Poncet again."

"Let's pay her a visit," Verlaque answered.

"Sir? Commissioner Paulik?" a voice sounded. They turned around to see Alain Flamant, a senior officer, hovering in the doorway.

"Yes, Flamant?"

"Could you spare a few minutes? I'm with a couple, M et Mme Tasset. They're looking for their daughter."

"Can't you deal with it?" Paulik asked.

"I tried, but they insist on speaking to you. She's been missing for over a year."

"You go, Commissioner," Verlaque said. "I have a stack of paperwork in my office that I've been avoiding. Come by when you're finished."

"All right," Paulik said. "I won't be long."

Liliane Poncet lived in the Mazarin, just a few doors away from the fountain of the Quatre-Dauphins. Neither man was surprised by this. Their walk had been mostly in silence until they reached the fountain, and they stopped to pay homage to the four carved dolphins.

Verlaque looked at the fountain's surprisingly clean blue water. "How did it go with those parents?" he asked. "I can't imagine having a missing child."

Paulik set his right leg on the fountain's edge and leaned on it. "I couldn't help them much more than Flamant could. He'd gone through all the usual checks and come up with nothing. Their daughter, Victoire Tasset, is twenty-three years old, so she's no longer a minor. They're from Paris."

"Why did they come to us, if they're from Paris?" Verlaque

asked, thinking of his own family. How would he deal with the family baggage with his own child?

"They have a vacation house here, in the country, not far from yours."

"I don't know the name Tasset."

"That's not surprising. They let it drop more than once that Aix is only one of their homes. They had a villa in Greece, but that was too far, so now they spend a few weeks of the year at a new house in Corsica. That's when they're not at their chalet in Megève skiing. As one does."

Verlaque smiled. Bruno Paulik, a farm boy from the Luberon, rarely railed against wealth and privilege. Verlaque tried to remember if he had called his parents very much his first year away at university. Twice, maybe. This girl was probably going through what he had.

They left the fountain and walked down the rue Cardinale, stopping at number 29. Paulik rang the buzzer marked "LP" and Verlaque sent a quick text message to Marine. He was starting to get nervous about the baby. What had he been thinking, going to Paris for two days? What if Marine had gone into labor?

Verlaque heard Liliane Poncet's voice on the intercom, saying, "Third floor." Marine texted back, saying she was fine but tired and was going to have a nap.

"Is everything okay?" Paulik asked, looking at the judge.

"Yes, I was just checking in with Marine. She's exhausted."

"Yep, I remember that. Hélène was exhausted, and I was edgy." A buzzer sounded and the elaborately carved wooden door clicked open.

A tall door was open when they got to the top of the stairs, and Liliane Poncet was standing in it, barely half the door's height. Her colorful clothes were in sharp contrast to the elegant building: The walls, even in the hallway, were decorated with white plaster carvings in the shapes of leaves and fruit. "Come in," she said graciously, standing aside for the two men. "Coffee?"

"Please," they answered almost in unison.

"I'll just be a minute," she said. "Please, sit down."

Paulik sat down, perched on the edge of a delicate armchair upholstered in a floral pattern. Verlaque walked around, pretending to admire the view from the tall windows but at the same time examining the room's furniture and objects. Like the hallway, the interiors were very old-fashioned and feminine. He disliked it— too many pinks and pale blues.

"Voilà!" Liliane announced as she walked back into the living room carrying an elaborate gold tray with three demitasses and a sugar bowl. She set the tray on a small coffee table and sat down opposite Paulik. "Judge Verlaque!" she called out. "Come and have your coffee."

Verlaque smiled and moved away from the window, oddly enjoying being scolded. He sat down on a small stiff sofa—eighteenth century, he guessed—and when he reached for his coffee he noticed that Liliane was wearing high heels. He tried to remember if she'd been wearing heels at the theater when he'd first met her. It seemed old-fashioned for someone her age; Marine's mother had taken to wearing running shoes all day long. Stealing his eyes away from her feet, he took his coffee and thanked her.

"Nice place you have here," Paulik said, gazing around the room. Verlaque watched his commissioner, always impressed by his Columbo-style innocent routine.

"Oh, the furnishings are dreadful," Liliane replied. "They're not mine. I'm renting it fully furnished."

"When did you move to Aix?" Verlaque asked.

"Two years ago, almost exactly."

"Why did you move here?"

"My health," Liliane explained. "Paris is too humid, and too polluted. I lived here when I was young, too, before we moved to Paris. I've kept my apartment in Paris, naturally."

"Is this the first play you've done in Aix?" Verlaque asked.

"I've done one play in Marseille and one in Toulon. But this was to be the first in Aix." Liliane shrugged. "Despite the opera festival and the famous dance company here, there isn't much of a theater scene in Aix. I was surprised by that."

"And you must have been surprised to see Gauthier Lesage at Anouk Singer's theater," Verlaque suggested. He took a sip of coffee and watched her.

"Of course I was."

"Mlle Poncet," Paulik began, "was Gauthier Lesage harassing you in any way?"

Liliane bit her lip and reached for her coffee cup.

Paulik continued, "You were seen in downtown Aix, arguing."

She sighed. "He wanted money. Same old thing!"

"Did he say what for?" Paulik asked.

"No, and I didn't ask him. I said no, by the way. It was only a thousand euros, but it's the principle. I knew it wouldn't help him."

"Why's that?"

"Because he always needed money. It was a problem all his life. He'd earn it and spend it. Except now, he doesn't earn that much."

"Didn't you feel sorry for him?" Verlaque asked, remembering how she had sobbed at the news of Lesage's murder.

"Yes, but tough love was needed." She got up and began pacing the room. "Or so I thought." She rubbed her eyes. "Do you think I should have helped him?" Verlaque watched Liliane as she dabbed the corners of her eyes with a tissue. Was she acting? He couldn't tell.

She went on, "He and his sister Clara were cut out of the father's will, you know."

Paulik nodded. "Were there other siblings?" he asked.

"No. Just the two of them." She frowned and then walked back to the chair she had been sitting in.

"You told me at the theater that you didn't really know Gauthier," Paulik said. "What did you mean?"

"Oh, I don't know what I meant. I was upset."

"Did he have secrets?" Paulik asked.

"Don't we all?"

Verlaque shifted on the uncomfortable sofa. He could have guessed that would be her reply. It was beginning to sound like a theater piece to him. "Did you have contact with him, outside this Pagnol play?"

"No. Well, except for that one time he asked me for money."

"Had you been at his apartment?" Verlaque asked.

"I beg your pardon?"

"The witness saw you both on the rue Aude," Verlaque explained. "That's where M Lesage lived."

"Ah, I understand your question," she said. She got up and walked slowly to the window, looked out, then turned around. "I happened to be walking up the rue Aude, to go to the flower market. I had no idea he lived on that street."

"Right," Verlaque said, nodding. "But didn't you find it odd that he ended up here, in Aix?"

She bristled, just for a second. What did Gauthier Lesage have on her? "I can lay no claims on Aix," she said. "Everyone wants to come here, especially Parisians."

"And you didn't find it odd that he auditioned for the Pagnol play?"

"No. Again, it's a free world. Besides, he must have needed the money. Anouk can't pay us very much, but it would have helped Gauthier. And as I said, there really isn't much theater in Aix."

"And why did *you* want to do the play?" Verlaque asked.

"I love Pagnol," Liliane answered—very quickly, Verlaque thought. She walked over to a low freestanding bookshelf and pointed to a row of paperbacks, skimming her hand along a dozen or so books. "All Pagnol. These are my books, by the way, not the apartment owner's. One of my first stage plays was a Pagnol. I played Manon in *Manon des Sources* when I was eighteen." She pulled at her skirt coyly. "Maybe I thought I'd come full circle. Who knows how many more plays I'll have the energy to do?"

"You seem to be in great shape," Verlaque said, smiling. He stood up and Paulik did the same.

"Oh, I exercise every day!" She did a little shuffle of her feet.

"Thank you for your time, Mlle Poncet," Paulik said.

She walked them to the door and opened it, said goodbye, and closed it.

The men walked down the stairs, and outside along the rue

Cardinale, in silence. They stopped again at the fountain, protected by the shade of one of the four ancient chestnut trees that sat on each corner of the square. The shade was wonderful, and the sound of the fountain's tinkling water made one think that the air was cooler than it actually was. Paulik was the first to speak. "She's lying."

"I agree," Verlaque said, pulling out a Partagas D No. 4 and snipping the end off with a small cigar cutter he always kept in his jacket pocket. He lit the cigar and Paulik waited—he was used to this ritual—until the judge took a few puffs of the cigar to get the combustion going. "I think Lesage was after more than just some quick cash."

"And she doesn't want to tell us—or can't."

"She's in good shape for her age."

Paulik smiled. "She could have got through that little window at the theater."

"Yes, she could have. But we don't have a motive."

"Was Lesage blackmailing her? She might have something to hide. And did you notice her shoes?"

Verlaque laughed. "High heels."

A group of teens began a water fight at the fountain, dipping their hands into the water and splashing one another, and the men moved on, heading toward the cours. Verlaque walked and smoked and Paulik looked from side to side along the street. He finally said, "There are even more real estate offices on this street than there were last week."

"I'm sure you're right."

"All the same," Paulik said as he skipped off the narrow

sidewalk into the street to allow a mother pushing a stroller to pass. He hopped back up onto the sidewalk, next to Verlaque. "Liliane Poncet is a pretty good liar."

"I was impressed." Verlaque puffed on his cigar. He grinned and chuckled to himself.

"What's so funny?"

"Well, I've been getting some good practice in at lying, too. Yesterday I told Liliane how much I loved her in *Return to Burgundy*, but I've never even seen it. I think I delivered an Oscar-worthy performance." Verlaque smiled as he walked.

"Really?" Paulik said, also grinning. "What did she say?"

"She thanked me, and said it was a very feminine film, to which I agreed. Not bad, eh?"

"It was on television last week."

"What a coincidence. I wish I'd have seen it."

Paulik once again had to hop down into the street, this time to allow an elderly gentleman to pass. He hopped back up on the sidewalk once the man had passed. "Yeah, it's too bad you missed it," he said. "As Liliane Poncet isn't in it."

Chapter Seventeen

❧

Saturday, August 12

Paulik was still grinning when they arrived at the Palais de
Justice. They stopped at the bottom of the steps of the court-
house and Verlaque said, "You go on up. I'm going to get another
coffee in the square and finish my cigar."

"Sure thing," Paulik said. He turned to head up the stairs but
stopped when Verlaque called after him.

"Why do you think she lied about the film?" Verlaque asked.

Paulik walked down three steps to join the judge. "Either she
couldn't be bothered to rectify your mistake," he said, "or she simply enjoyed tricking you. Or, third possibility," he said, pausing.
"It was some kind of silent contract she was making with you."

"Explain."

"Maybe she wanted to see how well you could lie. And . . . if
you could lie, then *she* could lie, too. As if you were giving her
permission."

Verlaque mumbled *merde* and turned around and headed across the square to the Café Le Verdun. Paulik walked up the stairs and into the vast inner courtyard of the palais, where he walked quickly, trying to avoid chatting with colleagues. He waved across the courtyard at the police force's medical doctor, with whom he'd just had his yearly check-up, and then ran up the stairs to the second-floor offices, where he knew that Sophie Goulin and Alain Flamant were working on the Lesage case. When he walked into their cramped office he saw that Flamant was on the telephone. Goulin greeted Paulik with a wave of her pen in the air. "I just got off the phone with Clara Lesage," she said.

"How was it?"

"Not a lot of grieving or love for her brother," Goulin said. "Although she did ask about a will. She's broke, she says. She lost her secretary job at the Morgat town hall."

"When did they last see each other?"

"Their mother's funeral in Lyon, five years ago. Their father died before that."

Alain Flamant hung up and swung his chair around to face the other two. "That was Gauthier Lesage's bank manager in Paris," he said. "The bank manager is new, but he was looking at his computer screen as we spoke and he told me that there have been regular deposits into Lesage's account this year."

"When do they start?"

"He's looking into it," Flamant said. "It might go far back. Like I said, he's new and sounded a bit flustered. They come once a month, on the fifth, and the source of the deposits is unnamed, just another bank account—Parisian, the manager confirmed, given the codes. He's emailing me drafts of Lesage's bank statements."

"We think Lesage may have been blackmailing someone," Paulik said. "Possibly Liliane Poncet. Officer Goulin, do you think the deposits could have come from a family member?"

Goulin shook her head. "Very unlikely. They sounded like they hated each other. Unless there was a trust set up for him. But the sister has nothing, so that would hardly be fair."

"And the trust account would come from Lyon, we'd assume," Flamant added.

Paulik asked, "How much are the deposits?"

"About five hundred euros each time," Flamant said. "Not a whole lot."

"But enough to keep your head above water," Goulin said. "If you're having money problems, that much a month would really help."

Paulik sat down, rubbing his forehead. He looked up at Sophie Goulin and asked, "Did you call Clara Lesage on her cell phone?"

"No," Sophie replied. "It was her landline, in Morgat."

"Oh, okay." He went back to rubbing his forehead.

"Did you think she might not be in Britanny?" Goulin asked.

"It was a thought," Paulik said. "I was thinking of my cousins, the kids of my Aunt Celeste and Uncle Jean-Luc, and their two sons."

Sophie looked across the desk at Alain, who raised an eyebrow. They loved Bruno Paulik's family stories. Paulik continued, "When Uncle Jean-Luc died, a few years after Celeste, he left more money to the elder son. The younger was enraged, and they're still not talking. It's been five or six years now."

"You don't think that Clara Lesage would come all the way

down here from Brittany to kill her brother?" Sophie asked, bewildered.

Paulik sighed. "It sounds outrageous, doesn't it? But my parents told me that a few months ago they were invited to dinner at the younger son's house. They accepted, not wanting to choose sides. Well, right in the middle of dinner the elder brother shows up, knowing that my parents were there. He wanted to make amends."

"Thinking that your parents would be a sort of buffer," Flamant suggested.

"Exactly."

"So what happened?" Goulin asked, on the edge of her seat.

"They had a fistfight!" Paulik said, almost shouting. "My poor old pa had to break it up. He's almost eighty!"

"Wow," Goulin mumbled, looking at Flamant, whose mouth was gaping open.

"It's what my mom said after," Paulik said, "that really struck me. That the younger brother, or maybe even both of them, who knows, really *hated* each other. She could see it, and feel it."

"I can understand what your mother said," Sophie said. "About the hate. Because whom do you know so well? Your spouse, and your siblings. So you feel doubly deceived. You're so disappointed. Crushed. And that disappointment and confusion turn into rage."

"Yeah, look how many nasty divorces there are out there," Flamant added. He swung his chair around to face the computer and started to type. "There's a direct flight from Marseille to Brest. At least there used to be."

"Ryanair," Goulin said, pulling her chair beside his. "We were thinking of going to Brittany this summer, to escape the heat."

Paulik got up and walked to the door. "Check all the flights, and try to find out what her married name was. She may have flown under that."

"Right," Goulin said.

"Even with a possible motive, we still need some proof," Paulik said. "I'll visit Dr. Cohen on my way home, to see if she can tell us anything more."

On his way home Verlaque stopped in at a pasta shop and bought a tray of fresh ravioli for two, stuffed with ricotta and artichokes. "Just serve it with melted butter and fresh sage, if you have that," the seller told him.

"I think we do have sage," he said, "on the terrace. And butter instead of olive oil?"

"*Sì!*"

He thought they still had some Parmesan from their last weekend trip to Liguria, but he bought some more just in case. He lingered over the wines—there was a good selection from Piedmont—but didn't buy any. It wouldn't be fair to Marine. Besides, maybe on the terrace he could sneak a little glass of grappa. Marine didn't care for it much anyway.

When he got home Marine was standing in the living room with one hand on her stomach and the other holding her cell phone. "Is everything all right?" he asked, setting the bag of food down on the sofa.

"I had the most horrible stomach pain about twenty minutes ago," she said. "I had to sit down and do that deep breathing we've been practicing."

Verlaque nodded, biting his lower lip, as he really hadn't been helping much in that department. "That sounds bad. And now?"

"Nothing since that one. I just got off the phone with my doctor. It took me a while to get through. She said that if that's the only contraction I've had, then not to worry. They need to come quicker and closer together."

"That's what the book said," Verlaque said, lying. He hadn't read much of it.

Marine smiled. "She said this is pre-labor, and it can last a few days, or even a week or two."

Verlaque began unpacking the groceries. "So we have time to eat!" he said.

"I'm starving."

"It has cooled off a bit, so go and sit on the terrace, and I'll bring the food up on a tray."

"Thank you!" Marine said, walking over and kissing him.

"Do we have sage?"

"Yes, on the terrace."

"I'll come with you, then," he said. "I'll carry a first load up." The terrace was off the mezzanine that served as their office. The views were wonderful, but it was inconvenient walking up and down the stairs with food and drink.

"Do you want a glass of wine first?"

"Well, maybe I'll have a little glass of white."

"To help you snip the sage," Marine said. "That's quite a job."

"Very funny."

Once on the terrace Marine rested on a chaise longue as Verlaque poured her a glass of sparkling water. He took his glass of wine over to the edge of the terrace and looked out at the sky. It was the golden hour, lighting the exterior walls of their apartment a brilliant orange. From their terrace he could see dozens of roof-tops, the cathedral's octagonal tower, and a small bit of the grand square just south of the cathedral. He heard the *clunk clunk clunk* of a skateboard, and people laughing. He turned around to see Marine, her eyes closed and face pointed up toward the sun. She opened her eyes and said, "How's work? Any progress?"

"As I was walking home I bumped into Bruno," he said. He told Marine about Paulik's theory of Clara Lesage.

Marine listened, her eyes still closed. "I don't see it," she said when he had finished. "Kill her *brother?*"

"I don't see it either," he said. He took his sage clippings and went downstairs to cook the ravioli, which was ready in just a few minutes. He wondered why they didn't eat it more often. He tossed together a green salad, thankful that Marine had already washed the greens and wrapped them in a tea towel. Making the dressing was easy, he had always thought, compared to washing the greens. Placing the plates on a large tray, he carried it back up to the terrace and they sat down to eat, enjoying the fading light and sounds of the streets below.

"I'm wiped," Marine said after they had each eaten a peach for dessert.

"You go ahead to bed," Verlaque said. "I'll clear up and be with you soon."

"Thank you," she said, carefully folding her linen napkin so that it was ready to reuse for the next meal.

As Antoine Verlaque was clearing up the terrace, Sandra Gastaldi was sipping an herbal tea in her small kitchen, smiling at her guest. She was happy to have company, and relieved that he had seemed to enjoy her lasagna. "More tea?" she asked, lifting the teapot in his direction.

"Sure, one more cup," Jean-Marc said.

"And have a cookie. They're store-bought, but I think quite good." She swallowed, wishing she'd had time to bake them herself. He smiled politely and she relaxed, feeling comfortable. He was posh but not a snob, and the fact that he was gay—she was fairly certain of this—removed any potential romantic awkwardness.

"No, thank you," Jean-Marc answered. He was worried about the amount of preservatives in the cookies. "Thank you for the excellent dinner," he went on. "I often eat alone."

"Oh, me, too! I have to force myself to cook a proper hot meal sometimes."

"Thank goodness for—"

"Picard!"

"Exactly!" They laughed, and shared a few tips from buying food at France's premier deluxe frozen food company.

"It's so quiet," Jean-Marc said. "You can't even hear the cars driving down Sextius." He saw Sandra glance at her watch, and he decided to quickly finish his tea and say goodbye.

She promptly got up and stood beside the open window. "Sometimes all I hear are cats," she said, looking out. She turned to Jean-Marc and motioned for him to join her. "I bought this place because I can see down two streets," she said. She pointed down the rue du 11 Novembre. "All the way to the theater."

Jean-Marc looked down the street, dark now but bathed in a dull golden light thanks to the streetlamps. "I looked long and hard for an apartment with the living areas looking onto a street like this," he said. "You did well to find this. Well, Sandra, thank you so much for dinner—" A door banged shut, and they both jolted. A woman, dressed in a vintage suit and hat, came out of the theater. Sandra put her hand on Jean-Marc's shoulder. Neither could move. The woman lunged forward, as if racing out the door, and walked so quickly that she was gone in a flash.

"Did you see that?" Jean-Marc asked. "She looked like Greta Garbo. That vintage suit . . ."

"I can't believe it."

"Should we tail her?" he asked excitedly.

"She'll be long gone," Sandra said. "And we're hardly sleuths, the two of us." She sat down at the table, stunned. Jean-Marc stayed at the window, leaning out as far as he could, looking up and down the street. "Was she really in our theater?" Sandra asked. Her face was white. "Is it possible?"

Jean-Marc brought his upper body back into the room and leaned against the wall, his hands behind his back. "Maybe she came from a neighboring building, and from far away it just looked like the theater's door."

"Do you really think so?"

"No, I'm just trying to convince myself we didn't see it." He stared at his feet for a bit, then asked, "Do you think it was Anouk?"

Sandra looked up. "Nah. I don't want to sound mean, but Anouk isn't that chic. Plus, I've known her for so long, I'd be able to tell."

"Yes, I suppose you're right."

Sandra picked her nails. "I have a confession."

Jean-Marc sat down opposite her. He grabbed one of the cookies and moved it nervously from hand to hand. "What is it?"

"I've seen this Greta Garbo person before."

"Me, too."

"You're joking!" Sandra said, jumping up. "That's why we're kindred spirits."

Jean-Marc laughed. He liked Sandra. He felt good around her. "Where did you see her?"

"Near here, farther down, before the theater. And you?"

"Closer to my place on the rue Papassaudi. It was just after we began the rehearsals."

"So it's connected to the play. She is, I mean."

"You're the one who's sleuthing now, Sandra!" He took a bite of the cookie. As he feared, it tasted artificial, but he was too polite to set it down. "I saw her grave once," he said.

"Whose?

"Greta Garbo's. In Stockholm, on a small hill. There's a bench, that's all."

"*Gala*!" Sandra cried.

"What are you talking about?"

She ran to her small living room, Jean-Marc right behind her, tossing the cookie in the garbage on his way. She said, "The article! I forgot all about it. When I was having an aperitif with Liliane on the Cours Mirabeau, she reminded me of an article about one of her ex-husbands in *Gala*. I meant to look it up, but with all the excitement at the theater I forgot. Last night I found the right issue." Her face reddened. "My mother collected these. I don't have the heart to throw them out."

"My mother collected rich husbands," Jean-Marc said, sitting down on the sofa.

Sandra laughed and opened the now vintage magazine.

"The colors and fonts are so garish," he said, shaking his head. "And it wasn't that long ago."

"Styles change so quickly, don't they? Now I remember this issue, seeing the spreads." They laughed at the clothing and the sexist ads. She flipped quickly through the pages. She stopped, tapping a photograph with her finger. "Here's what I was looking for, after the Belmondo article."

Chapter Eighteen

❧

Sunday, August 13

Just after 8:00 in the morning, Verlaque hung up his cell phone and turned on the espresso maker. "Everything okay?" a sleepy Marine asked, rubbing her eyes as she walked into the kitchen. "It's early."

"That was Bruno," Verlaque said. "There's been an accident at the theater."

"Oh no! Again? What happened?"

"Liliane Poncet this time," he replied. "She's been rushed off to the hospital. Anouk Singer found her at the bottom of the stairs early this morning. Bruno doesn't know yet if she fell, or was pushed."

Marine sat down. "Will she be all right?"

"I hope so," he said, downing his coffee and setting the cup in the sink. "I'm sorry I don't have time for breakfast with you. Did you sleep well? Any more contractions?"

"Nothing," she replied, smiling. "I'll let you know, I promise."

It took Verlaque fifteen minutes to walk across town, including the time spent buying a croissant to eat on the way. When he arrived at the theater he carefully brushed the crumbs from his mouth and his shirt.

Paulik was in the lounge, sitting with Anouk and her parents. Verlaque wished them a good morning and sat down. "What happened this morning, Mlle Singer?" he asked.

Anouk dried her reddened eyes and said, "I came very early, just before seven. I'm not a good sleeper."

"That's always been true about Anouk!" Mme Singer cut in, a little too quickly and loudly, Verlaque thought.

Anouk shot her mother an annoyed look and went on. "I wanted to go through some paperwork upstairs in the office but decided to make myself a coffee first." She took a breath. "But when I went down the stairs, I saw Liliane right away, lying there. She wasn't moving."

"Did you touch her?"

"No! I ran back up the stairs to get my cell phone out of my purse, and I called Emergency."

"Did you see anyone?"

Anouk shook her head. "I used my keys to open the front door. I didn't notice anything unusual."

"And now I'd like to ask you how you got in," Verlaque said. "Your keys were taken during the first day of the police investigation."

She gulped. "I had a spare set."

"I guessed as much," he said.

"And Mlle Poncet had keys?" Paulik asked.

Her face went white. "I had a third set."

"Anouk is always losing her keys," Mme Singer chimed in. "So one day Léo went out and had a bunch of extra sets made."

Anouk cried, "Oh dear! What have I done?!"

Paulik and Verlaque exchanged looks. Paulik asked, "Mlle Singer, why did you give Liliane Poncet a key to the theater?"

"She said she needed to practice on the stage, alone," Anouk said, catching her breath between sobs.

Paulik sighed. "You gave M Lesage a set of keys for the very same reason."

"Is that normal practice?" Verlaque asked. "For actors to practice alone onstage?"

"Well, no," Anouk replied.

Verlaque saw the look of disappointment on the elder Singers' faces. "Mme and M Singer," Verlaque said. "Why don't you go and rest? It's early, and Mlle Singer will be needed here for another few hours."

Léo Singer got to his feet and helped his wife get up from what was a very soft and old sofa. They shook Verlaque's and Paulik's hands, as if they had been colleagues, or friends. Léo looked sadly around at the room and said, "We poured our heart and soul out into this place. Ran it as a very profitable dance school for twenty-five years."

Verlaque smiled. "I know. My wife came here as a girl."

"Is that so?" Léo said. But he didn't ask who Verlaque's wife was. Verlaque thought later that perhaps the elder Singer had been too shocked and fatigued to bother about the name of yet another student. Thousands of youngsters must have passed through, back in the day of the dance school. He and Pauline shuffled away, accompanied by a young officer who had been observant enough to see they may need some assistance walking home.

Verlaque leaned forward, his elbows poised on his knees. "Mlle Singer, could you please tell us what happened all those years ago in Paris? Why did both Liliane Poncet and Gauthier Lesage show up here, at your theater? And don't tell me they did it for publicity."

Anouk began to sob. "I don't know!"

"You can speak freely now," Verlaque said. "Your parents have gone."

"Liliane was my idol!" she said, crying.

"What have you said to Anouk?" a female voice yelled from behind Verlaque. He turned around to see Sandra Gastaldi rush in, throwing her purse on the floor and wrapping her arms around Anouk.

"Mlle Gastaldi," Verlaque said as calmly as he could. "There has already been one murder on this premises, and now Liliane Poncet is in the hospital after an accident here last night."

Sandra put a hand to her mouth. "Last night?"

Anouk blew her nose. "I found her, Sandra! Lying at the bottom of the stairs."

"How is she?" Sandra asked, trembling.

Paulik replied, "She's fighting for her life."

"Is there a possibility that Mlle Poncet was here alone, and just fell?" Sandra asked.

"No," Paulik replied. "There was a struggle."

"What kind of brute would . . ." Anouk said, her voice trailing off.

"I have something to tell you," Sandra said, wringing her hands.

"Go on," Paulik said, not surprised. He'd thought that she was holding something back when they had walked down the street together.

"Last night," she said. "This sounds crazy, but we saw a woman dressed up. It's the second time I've seen her."

"We?"

"Oh, I invited Jean-Marc over for dinner. He's in the play, too."

"Yes, I know. Go on."

"We saw her late last night."

"Dressed up?"

"Vintage, late nineteen-thirties, early nineteen-forties, judging by the bell-shaped hat and padded shoulders."

"Did you notice the time?" Verlaque asked.

"Midnight," she said. "I checked my stove clock."

"Why didn't you call the police?"

"We weren't sure," she said, sighing. "From the view of my windows, it looked like she could have been leaving a neighbor's. She was almost running."

"So you didn't actually see her leave the theater?" Paulik asked.

"We started doubting ourselves," Sandra said. "But now I'm sure she left the theater." She reached into her purse and took a faded clipping out of it, handing it to Paulik. "I remembered this, too, from years ago." She tried to laugh. "My mother kept clippings of her favorite stars."

Paulik took the clipping, looked at it, then handed it to Verlaque, who put his reading glasses on. "An actress dressed in period costume?" he ventured. "A film set during the war, perhaps."

Paulik leaned over to have a second look. "Liliane Poncet."

"Yes," Sandra said. "The *West Side Story* musical. Same outfit as the woman last night."

"It doesn't make sense," Paulik said. "Liliane was in the theater, unconscious."

"I know," Sandra said. "But both Jean-Marc and I saw this woman—we're calling her Greta Garbo—at other times in Aix, around the theater. Ever since we started the play rehearsals."

Verlaque and Paulik exchanged looks. Verlaque guiltily realized that he had a missed call from Jean-Marc and hadn't returned it.

Sandra went on, "We think that Liliane was dressing up, following Gauthier around."

The commissioner and the judge kept silent. Neither of them liked the idea that Sandra and Jean-Marc—especially Jean-Marc, who as a courtroom lawyer should know better—were developing their own hypotheses for the crimes.

Verlaque turned off his espresso maker and handed a cup to Paulik. "Thanks," Paulik said, taking a sip. "One coffee wasn't enough this morning."

Sophie Goulin came to the office door, which was open, and knocked gently on the doorframe.

"Come in, Officer Goulin," Verlaque said. "Coffee?"

"No, thank you," she answered, putting a file on his desk. "The file, so far, on Liliane Poncet. Inside are two separate files of her ex-husbands."

"Can you give us a briefing?" Verlaque asked. He gestured for her to sit down.

"Yes. Her first husband, a screenwriter, Guy Minoux, died very young in a car accident, alone and broke. The second husband is Stéphane Breton, still alive. He wasn't in the theater business—he's an artist who's had a number of small businesses, none of them making any money. A series of bankruptcies. It says here that his last address is Greece."

"He's a guru?" Verlaque asked, looking at the page on Breton.

Sophie replied, "It says *healer*, sir."

"Any photos?" Paulik asked.

Goulin coughed and reached into the file, pulling out two photographs and spreading them across the desk. One, a black-and-white with a young bride and groom standing on the steps of a small church. "Liliane and Guy Minoux," Sophie said. They then looked at the second photo, this one in color, Liliane and Stéphane Breton wearing almost identical white jumpsuits. "Unfortunate, that seventies fashion," Verlaque said.

"And listen to this about Stéphane Breton," Paulik said, reading another of the documents from Liliane's file. "That ex-husband in Greece. Apparently he threatened Gauthier Lesage at the end of that *West Side Story* play, in front of the entire cast and crew. He found out about their affair."

Verlaque said, "But that was so long ago."

"True. If Breton were angry he would have done something long ago. It's almost ten," Paulik answered, looking at his watch. "I'm going to jump on a train for Paris to visit that talent agent. I want to tell her in person about Liliane."

"Good luck," Verlaque said as Paulik was leaving the office. "Sorry about your Sunday."

Paulik stopped at the door. "The girls were fast asleep when I left," he said. "And today they're invited to a friend of Hélène's to go swimming. Ciao."

Verlaque sat down and called Jean-Marc.

"Bonjour, Antoine," Jean-Marc said when he picked up.

"*Salut*, Columbo."

"Oh dear," Jean-Marc said. "You spoke with Sandra."

Verlaque filled Jean-Marc in on Liliane's fall and told him that he had spoken with Anouk, her parents, and Sandra, all of whom seemed to be protecting Anouk. "And what's with the amateur detective work?" he asked. "You and Sandra saw a woman leaving the theater in a vintage outfit that perfectly matches what Liliane wore in that musical they did in Paris?"

"We both thought it was Liliane," Jean-Marc replied. "The woman was petite, and even walked like Liliane."

"She was gone in a flash. . . ."

"What if it was Liliane? And she met Gauthier at the theater, surprised him, and strangled him?"

Verlaque closed his eyes, knowing that Liliane could have fit through the window, and that Gauthier had been taken by surprise, strangled from behind. He also thought about the student who lived across from Gauthier, who heard an argument on Wednesday night and saw a woman leaving. "And last night?" he asked. "You saw this woman leave the theater."

"She might have come back," Jean-Marc suggested. "I went home shortly after, and I would imagine Sandra went to bed."

"But Liliane is now unconscious."

"She threw herself down the stairs in guilty remorse. What was she wearing when they found her?"

Verlaque held his phone out from his face, staring at it in disbelief.

"You don't know, do you?"

"No," Verlaque answered. "But I'll find out right away."

"The scene of the crime," Jean-Marc continued.

"I have to go now," Verlaque said. "Let me know when you get back to earth." He hung up, frustrated with his dear friend. At least it wasn't Marine's mother this time, imagining that she could solve the crime with the astute assistance of her elderly cronies.

Chapter Nineteen

❧

Sunday, August 13

Bruno Paulik jumped off the Line 1 Metro at the Louvre-Rivoli stop. After hundreds of trips to Paris, mostly for police work, he was now used to the Metro and its long corridors. Early for his appointment with Julie Santelli, he walked slowly, surprised at how many people were on the Metro even though it was Sunday. He looked at the cinema posters lining the walls, picking out films for him and Hélène to see alone, and others suitable for the whole family. The concerts and plays were enticing, too, but those he wouldn't have access to in the south. Climbing the stairs, he emerged on the rue de Rivoli with its lovely arcade and touristy souvenir shops. The agency was one block up, on the rue Saint-Honoré, and he walked toward it, thankful he didn't need to pull out his dog-eared map, which his teenage daughter, Léa, thought was the biggest joke in the world.

In a few minutes he stopped at a sleekly renovated building.

No one was around, as it was a Sunday, and of course the doors were locked, so he sat down on a bench to wait for Ms. Santelli. When he saw a thin woman in a short leather jacket, blue jeans, and high-heeled boots walking toward him, he quickly got to his feet. "Julie Santelli," she said, shaking his hand. "Thank you for coming all this way, Commissioner."

She punched a code into the alarm system and then unlocked the glass doors. "We'll take the elevator up to the fifth floor. We'll be more comfortable in my office than down here in the lobby."

"Fine," Paulik said. They rode the elevator in silence, as it was obvious to Paulik that neither one of them wanted to talk about Liliane's attack before they were sitting down, tête-à-tête. After inserting a code into another alarm system and unlocking yet another set of glass doors, they were finally inside the agency. "Would you like something to drink?" she asked, her voice flat as if already drained of emotion. "Tea? Coffee?"

"Nothing, thank you."

He followed her into her office, its walls covered in black-and-white photographs of film stars. Some Paulik knew, some he didn't. But he did recognize Liliane Poncet's portrait. He sat down opposite Ms. Santelli.

She said, "I heard about Gauthier when I was on holiday. I would have contacted you sooner."

"We're doing everything we can—"

She cut in, "How is Liliane taking it?"

Paulik was surprised she didn't ask more about Gauthier Lesage's murder, so he asked, "Why did both Gauthier and Liliane want to take part in this Pagnol play?"

"Liliane told me she loved Pagnol," Ms. Santelli replied. "And she was living in Aix, so it was a convenient career move."

"Career move?" he asked. "Au Théâtre Vendome?"

"Come, come, Commissioner," she said. She laughed. "You sound like a Parisian."

Heaven forbid, thought Paulik. "I'm a lover of good theater, even if I'm from the south."

"Pagnol is good theater."

"I know," he answered, annoyed. He loved Pagnol. "But the Singers' theater seats maybe seventy people."

"Other actors are doing the same thing. We're copying the British. I did tell her to do only one play a year in a small theater. Besides, her life in Paris is very hectic, and Aix is calm. She grew up there."

"And Gauthier Lesage?" he asked. "Why did he come to Aix?"

Here she paused too long. Paulik was about to speak when Ms. Santelli finally answered. "Unlike Liliane, I wasn't convinced that doing a Pagnol play in Aix was a good move for Gauthier."

"Why not?"

"Money," she replied flatly. "He needed it. Even an insurance commercial on the radio pays better than a small theater. Plus, with ads you're done with work in a day and a half."

"But he was determined to do the play?"

"Yes," she replied, sighing. "He was desperate to get to Aix. He'd had a little vacation and was in good shape. Sea and sun, you know. So I gave up arguing and told him to do it. To be honest, I think he was still hooked on Liliane. It was pathetic, really. You know they dated a very long time ago?"

"Yes." Paulik paused and crossed his legs, and the agent picked up on his body language.

"What is it, Commissioner? Have you caught Gauthier's murderer?"

"No," he said. "And last night Mlle Poncet was attacked."

"What?!" Julie Santelli was on her feet, quickly walking around her desk to him. He shot up out of his chair and she grabbed his arms, shaking him. He planted his feet firmly on the carpeted floor and stood still. "Is she all right?! Our Liliane! Poor Liliane!"

"She's in the hospital, in intensive care." He added, immediately regretting the cliché, "She's in good hands."

Julie Santelli collapsed on a small sofa and put her head in her hands.

"Can I get you anything?" Paulik asked.

"Yes, my cigs. They're on my desk. It isn't allowed anymore, in the offices."

"This is a special situation," he said, handing her the pack along with a small lighter. He sat across from her, a low coffee table between them. "Do you know why anyone would want to attack either M Lesage or Mlle Poncet?"

She sat back, thinking and smoking, her hand shaking. "No, I don't. I'd only be guessing, and I don't want to make someone appear guilty if they're not."

"What about her ex-husband?" Paulik asked.

"Highly doubtful. I don't think they've spoken in decades. But," she said, taking a drag on her cigarette, "I know someone who might know." She leaned forward and wrote down a name and an address, handing it to him.

It had been years since Paulik had wandered the cobblestone streets of Montmartre. Léa must have been five or six, he thought. He'd forgotten how unlike central Paris, especially down by the river, this hilly neighborhood was. It felt like a village—a village in a city, dotted with small squares and fountains, with the famous hundreds of steps leading up to the church. He looked at the address on the piece of paper Julie Santelli had handed him: 7 rue Tardieu. It wasn't far, and he wouldn't have to climb the steps.

When he arrived at the building he stood back and looked up at it, something he had always done, even before he became a police officer. It was a solid stone building from the turn of the twentieth century, in good shape, with flowers in the window boxes. Down below was a design shop selling colorful household goods, and across the street was a bar whose terrace was already packed and noisy in the late afternoon. He felt sorry for the neighbors. He rang the buzzer labeled "C Falzon" and waited for the doors to click open, in the meantime mentally downgrading Montmartre. What was the point of charming streets if you couldn't sleep at night?

"Commissioner," Mme Falzon said as she opened her third-floor door. A small dog yelped from behind her. She stepped back slightly when she saw the wide-shouldered bald man standing in the hallway. He showed his photo ID and she smiled, stepping aside. "Please, come in."

Paulik walked in and almost tripped over the yelping little dog. "Coco!" Mme Falzon scolded. "Go to the sofa!" Paulik took a few more steps into the living room but had to stop; the small room, no bigger than a bedroom, was so packed full of objects he didn't know where to stand. Mme Falzon quickly removed a stack of books from a wooden chair and pulled it to where Paulik stood. She shook his hand. "Corinne Falzon. Coffee? Tea?" she asked.

"No, thank you," he answered. He actually did want a coffee, but he saw that her "kitchen" was in fact a kitchenette in the corner of the room: a small sink, two electric burners, a microwave on a shelf, and a small refrigerator below. Beside the microwave were two plates and two bowls, and two mugs hung from hooks below the shelf. He'd heard of people living in these kinds of apartments in Paris but had never seen it with his own eyes. Student digs in Aix, sure, but those were meant for a semester or two, until the student moved on to share a bigger place with friends. Here, Mme Falzon seemed to have her whole life in fifteen square meters: the sagging sofa, which he now realized might be her bed; the walls covered in small paintings, mostly mediocre romantic cityscapes; photographs; film posters, some of them autographed. Every horizontal surface was covered with *objets*: trophies, small porcelain vases with a few strands of dried flowers, more framed photographs.

She sat down opposite, sharing the sofa with Coco, who took up more space than the diminutive Mme Falzon. To his surprise, she shook a finger at him. "Shame on you," she said.

"I beg your pardon?"

"You took a long time to call on me."

He blinked, scarcely believing that he was being scolded. "The crimes did take place in Provence, over eight hundred kilometers away," he said. He then added, "Madame."

"Crimes, plural? I thought just Gauthier was attacked?"

He cleared his throat and told Mme Falzon of Liliane's attack. She listened carefully, and for a few minutes they sat in silence. Mme Falzon finally spoke. "And the attacker? It's the same person?"

"Yet to be determined," he answered. "But I would say so, yes."

"So would I. If you want my unprofessional opinion."

"Did either of them have enemies? I was told you knew them both very well, back in the day."

She held her head high and made a clicking noise with her mouth. "Back in the day was a long time ago. But no matter," she said. "Take a look around you."

He glanced at the walls and then noticed that many of the film posters were of Liliane. "Mlle Poncet's agent told me that you were great friends with Liliane Poncet," he said.

She crossed her fingers. "We were like this. Inseparable in the early days."

"Were you an actress?"

She laughed. "I ran the *tabac* counter at the local brasserie in Pigalle, where they all came after shows."

"They all?" he asked.

"The actors! Stars!" She looked around at the memorabilia and sighed. "Those were the good old days." She leaned over the tiny coffee table and said, "You can't believe the price of an apartment here now. Even Pigalle is considered chic!"

He nodded sympathetically, wholly understanding why someone her age would be scandalized by the price per meter of Parisian real estate. He was, too. "Were you still in contact with Liliane Poncet?"

"Yes," she replied. "She would visit me here from time to time, even after she became famous and rich and moved to the Left Bank. Of course, I hadn't seen her since she moved to Aix."

Paulik nodded, feeling sorry for Corinne Falzon. Did anyone visit her?

"Fans were always bothering Liliane in the street," she went on, her eyes getting smaller with fatigue. "They were polite, mind you, but I was always worried that there might be one who was a bit crazy, who would try to harm Liliane, like that New Yorker who murdered the Beatle with the long hair."

Paulik nodded, thinking that had John Lennon lived, he might be the same age as Corinne Falzon. But she seemed so old and out of touch.

"Of course, none of the fans ended up being frightening, not the way some men were . . ." she said, her voice trailing off at the end dreamily.

"Could you elaborate?" he asked. "Who do you mean?"

"Coco!" she cried. The dog barked as people passed by in the street below the window. "Ah, the old Pigalle days."

"Yes, was there someone from those old days who threatened Liliane and/or Gauthier?"

Corinne Falzon didn't reply but instead got down, slowly, on her hands and knees. Paulik looked on perplexed, wondering if he should help.

"They're right here, don't worry," she said, reaching under the sofa. "Found them, Père Daniel."

"I'm a commissioner, not a priest," he said, helping her to her feet. "From Aix. Bruno Paulik."

"I know! That's why I want you to have these." She handed

Paulik a dozen or so thin black notebooks. He took them, bewildered, and thanked her.

She said, "This may look like a small apartment, but under this sofa I have saved all of my letters and agendas over the years, safely put away in flat boxes." She got up and picked up a black Moleskine notebook off her nightstand. "Here," she said, handing it to him. "The last one. I'd already got it out when you called. I have others, when you need them."

"Thank you, this will do for now," Paulik said. He quickly flipped through one. It was full of notes, dates, and theater and film stubs, all clearly organized, the notes in her elegant hand written with a fountain pen. "These are impressive," he said, although, he thought to himself, useless. Just a minute ago she had forgotten who he was. "You certainly were busy."

She smiled sheepishly, pointing at the books. "I didn't go to *all* those plays and concerts. My friends—the brasserie's customers— would give the stubs to me." His heart sank. Of course she couldn't have gone to many plays on her salary. "You'll guard those with your life, won't you *mon père?*"

Paulik tried to smile. He didn't bother correcting her this time. "I'll bring them back to you personally."

"Before you go, if you wouldn't mind pouring me a little whiskey," she said, pointing with a long thin finger toward the kitchenette. "This news about Liliane is upsetting."

Paulik nodded and found a glass and the bottle, almost finished. He picked up a stained tea towel and tried to wipe the grime off the glass before pouring. "Don't bother with that," she said. "A few germs won't kill me!"

He handed her the whiskey and she sat back on the sofa, her feet dangling like a little girl's. He said goodbye but she already seemed to have forgotten him. Across the street he bought a bottle of water from a corner shop and paid for a carrier bag for the black notebooks.

On the train he sat back, exhausted by the city, frustrated that Julie Santelli hadn't given him more information, and saddened for old Mme Falzon, still living the heyday of Pigalle in her scattered mind. He drank half the water, then began looking through the first of the notebooks. The front page was dated 1972–73 and the book was full of ticket stubs, a few small color photographs of movie stars he didn't know, and clipped articles folded two or three times from the bottom so they didn't take up much room in the book. He eyes began to close, so he blinked a few times and looked at his cell phone. There was a message from Sophie Goulin: *We've had a call from Abdul Khattabi, one of the actors. He'd like to speak with us tomorrow morning.* Paulik texted back *Fine* and put his phone away. He closed his eyes, giving in to the rhythmic motion of the train.

Chapter Twenty

﹡

Monday, August 14

Abdul Khattabi was already in the waiting room when Sophie Goulin, who herself was early, arrived at the office. She offered him coffee and he declined, but he asked for a tea. She made a pot for the two of them and found an empty office to talk in, texting Paulik with the room number. Five minutes later he was there. They exchanged pleasantries for two or three minutes, chatting about the heat and Abdul's job as custodian at the university.

"What brings you here today, M Khattabi?" Paulik asked.

"It took me a while to build up the courage," Khattabi said. "I spoke to my wife about it many times. I feel guilty, even now."

"Go on," Paulik said, hardly daring to breathe.

"I've worked at the theater a long time. Ten years or so. And I love all my fellow coworkers, and actors. But I feel I have to tell you some things about the theater, because someone is dead." He took in a big breath. "Even if none of us liked Gauthier."

"Take your time, M Khattabi," Paulik said.

"Phew. Okay." He straightened his back and took a deep breath. "Gauthier and Emile. They had a fight."

Paulik nodded, knowing about the argument that Sandra had reported. Was this going to be new information?

Khattabi went on, "Emile told Gauthier to show more respect to Liliane, during one of our rehearsals."

"Yes, we heard of that."

"Well, later that day I overheard Gauthier say something terrible to Emile, about butchers in plays and films always being big dumb guys."

Paulik nodded. "We were told about that, too."

Abdul Khattabi's shoulders fell in relief. "Did Emile tell you?"

"No." Paulik now wondered why Emile hadn't shared that information. "Sandra did."

"Oh, I did see her hiding in the wings. I wasn't sure if she heard or not." He picked at his jeans and Sophie leaned over the table and poured out more tea. He thanked her and continued, "There's more. That evening, when we were finished, I was walking down the street on the way to my bus stop and I saw Emile. And Gauthier."

"I see."

"They were arguing, and a streetlight was burned out so I was able to move close to them and listen. I was worried about them. They both have tempers. I have five kids, so I'm a good listener."

Paulik nodded. "What did they say?"

"Emile said that if Gauthier was a real man, they could fight it out right there and then. He said that Gauthier was a washed-up television star with no talent and big teeth."

Paulik looked down at the grains on the wooden table, trying not to smile.

Sophie saved him. "Did they fight?"

"Gauthier said something I didn't hear and Emile shoved him up against a wall. I was about to run forward, as Emile had his hands around Gauthier's throat."

Paulik and Sophie Goulin exchanged looks.

Khattabi said, "Gauthier started muttering with fear and Emile released him, so I stayed hidden. His body fell forward like a sack of potatoes. Gauthier told Emile to come to the theater later that evening. They could hash things out and be friends."

"What did Emile say?"

"He said that Gauthier was crazy, they'd never be friends."

Paulik asked, "What night was it?"

Khattabi hung his head. "The night Gauthier was killed and put in that storage room. That's why my wife said I had to come today."

"Thank you, M Khattabi, for telling us this," Paulik said. "If you could stay here a little longer, and repeat what you just told us, Officer Goulin will tape it for our records."

"Will you need to use it?" Khattabi asked with worry.

"Hopefully not," Paulik answered truthfully.

It took no time for Paulik to walk to the Boucherie Leclerc. When he arrived there was a line out the door, with five or six customers waiting in the street, shuffling back and forth with impatience. "Pardonnez-moi," Paulik said as he moved around the crowd toward the front door.

"Hey there!" a customer yelled. "Think because you're a big tough guy you can jump the queue?!"

"No," Paulik said, pulling his badge out of his pocket. "It's because I'm a police officer."

An elderly lady put her foot in Paulik's way, taping her cane on the cobblestones. "Just because you're *un flic* doesn't mean you can have your pork chops ahead of us!"

Paulik sighed. "Madame, I'm not here to shop, I'm here on police business." He shoved his way through the open door and saw the wide shoulders of Emile straightaway, the butcher cutting a large piece of beef and chatting with a customer. Emile looked up and saw the commissioner, just as tall and wide as he was. He took off his apron, handing it to one of his brothers. "We can go out back," he said to Paulik. "There's a small courtyard."

Paulik followed Emile, feeling the curious eyes of the Leclerc brothers and their clients on his back. "Mind if I smoke?" Emile asked once they were outside. "My wife doesn't know."

"Go ahead." Paulik saw a full ashtray and figured this was where Emile, and possibly his brothers, all smoked in secret.

Once Emile lit up, Paulik asked, "Could you elaborate on the argument you had with Gauthier Lesage, outside the theater on the night of his murder?"

Emile blew out smoke and set down his cigarette. "Someone saw."

"Yes. I remember you telling me that when you got home you had a whiskey to cool down. You said it was from the acting."

"Gauthier pestered me on the way home," Emile said. "He was on my heels, not letting up. I finally couldn't stand it anymore and shoved him against a wall."

"Anything else?"

"Well," he said, hesitating. "Yeah, well, I kind of put my hands on his throat. But not for very long. I let go."

"Did you go back to the theater that night?" Paulik asked. "Like he suggested?"

Emile looked surprised. "Wow, that person heard everything. Of course I didn't. I was exhausted."

"Can you prove it?"

He shrugged. "You can ask my wife, but she's a heavy sleeper; I've always been jealous of that. She's wiped out every night." His hand lightly trembled as he picked up his cigarette.

"Thank you, M Leclerc. Sorry to have bothered you at work. I'll see myself out." He turned around and added, "Please tell your wife I will be wanting to speak with her more about that night."

"I'll tell her. There's one last thing. I don't know if this is important, and it may seem like snitching to you now, but I did see Gauthier outside of Liliane's apartment on the rue Cardinale. It was this spring, before we began our play rehearsals."

Paulik stopped. "Go on."

"Only I didn't know it was Liliane's address until now," Emile explained. "It said in the papers that she lives on the rue Cardinale. I recognized Gauthier right away, from those stupid television shows he does."

"What was he doing?"

"Well, at the time I didn't think anything of it. He was chatting up a female postal worker, who handed him what must have been a registered letter because he signed for it."

"You're right, that is odd, as Gauthier lives on your street."

"Which I honestly didn't know until you told me a few days ago," Emile said. "Anyway, I could hear them laughing. Do you think that he signed off on a registered letter that was destined for Liliane?"

"It appears so. We'll look into it," Paulik said, not wanting to commit. It was clear to him that Emile hated Gauthier, but enough to make up this story? "Can you remember exactly when it was? I'll have to trace the letter."

Emile stubbed out his cigarette and pulled out his cell phone. "That should be easy, as I'm never in the Mazarin," he said as he looked at his phone. "Here it is. I delivered a big order of meat and cold cuts for a party at number ten, rue Cardinale. Our delivery kid called in sick that day, and the client was frazzled. It was Tuesday, April eighteenth."

Out on the rue Espariat Paulik texted Alain Flamant and Sophie Goulin and gave them a condensed version of Emile's story, asking them to check in with the postal office to try to track the registered letter. He sighed, thinking of the red tape nightmare and ineptitude of the postal service. He then texted Verlaque and suggested lunch at the Italian place. They met up halfway. "I keep feeling every good meal that I eat these days may be my last," Verlaque said as they walked across the square.

"Before the baby, I hope is what you mean," Paulik answered.

"Exactly. After that we won't be eating or sleeping, from what I've read."

"Ah, it isn't that bad," Paulik said, feeling guilty about the lie.

A woman walked by pushing a baby stroller. Inside a tiny infant wailed. Verlaque looked at his commissioner with a raised eyebrow. "And that noise!" he said, wincing. "What do you do with that?"

"That's why they make that noise," Paulik said as they turned down a side street. "To get you to *do* something. Hopefully to pick them up. With Léa it was almost always because she wanted to nurse some more." He chuckled at the memory. "They're not faking it, you know. They're not acting."

"Like Liliane Poncet? Or Anouk Singer? Who else has been skirting the truth?"

"Sandra Gastaldi took ages to tell us about seeing the costumed woman. How could she not think that important?"

Verlaque nodded. "Well, Jean-Marc didn't tell me right away, either. He said he thought it was silly. And it is, when you think of it. Aix is the city of art and music, don't forget. Probably an actress or musician, or some affected art student."

"Coming from the *theater*?"

"*Maybe* they came out of the theater," Verlaque said. "Neither Jean-Marc nor Sandra were one hundred percent sure." Paulik filled him on Emile's fight with Gauthier. "What do you think about their fight?" Verlaque asked.

"That Emile has trouble controlling his temper, that's about it," Paulik said. "But I'm going to speak to his wife and ask a few more questions, just to be sure."

"Do you know what Liliane Poncet was wearing when she had her accident?"

"Not a vintage suit," Paulik replied. "I thought the same thing."

They arrived at the restaurant and were greeted by the owner, who was thrilled to see them, although he preferred when the judge came with his striking and kind wife. "Your table by the window is ready," he said, gesturing with the palm of his hand toward the table. "An aperitif?"

"Yes," the men said in unison.

"And I'll bring you both a daily starter and then the main dish? Keep it a surprise?"

"That's perfect," Verlaque said, sighing. "I can't decide on anything right now."

"The judge is about to become a father," Paulik said, grinning as he sat down and unfolded his napkin and placed it on his lap.

"So I heard," the restaurateur replied. "My congratulations. In that case, I'll bring you an extra treat or two, since once the baby arrives I won't be seeing much of you." He walked away laughing and Verlaque glared at Paulik.

"He's exaggerating," Paulik said, trying to look nonchalant.

"Some homemade tapenade," a waitress said, setting down the dip, bright green, made with green olives. With it she placed a shallow bowl of razor-thin slices of toast and two low-cut crystal glasses filled with some kind of dark red liquid.

"Campari?" Verlaque asked.

"A Negroni," she answered. "My boss thought you needed something stronger today."

"Thanks," Verlaque said, lifting his glass to toast with the commissioner.

"Cheers," Paulik said. "Don't worry, we may be able to get in a few more lunches before Junior arrives." He laughed, spreading some of the dip onto a piece of toast, and then decided to change the subject before his boss angered, or got even glummer. "When we get back I'll get the team to start checking every hotel in downtown Aix. I have a feeling that we will find that Stéphane Breton has checked into one of them."

"I'm not sure. Why wait twenty-five years?" Verlaque said.

"He could be renting an Airbnb, too," Paulik said. "That would be more confidential. I'm not sure what kind of background checks they do."

Verlaque sighed. "There must be hundreds of those in Aix. And now that Liliane is in the hospital, he could be gone." He took a sip of the Negroni, which was strong and bitter, just as he liked it. Marine liked Negronis, too. He tried not to feel guilty. He set down the drink, thinking of his wife. "It could be a woman," he said. "That student across from Gauthier's apartment saw a high heel heading down the stairs."

Paulik looked up, battling with a piece of toast that broke as he tried to spread too much tapenade on it.

Verlaque continued, fascinated by Paulik's handling of the thin toast with his huge hands. "Did Liliane attack Gauthier, then someone else attacked her? She's athletic, and wears high heels. . . ."

"Like Stéphane Breton?"

"I see you're a little obsessed at the moment. Did he just discover something about them recently? That set him over the top? Is that what you're thinking? And who would know?"

"Anouk," Paulik suggested.

"Ah yes, the admirer."

The owner walked by to check on their drinks, eyeing the almost empty glasses with a smile. As he walked away, Paulik lowered his voice and said, "She's a gushing schoolgirl with a failing theater, occupying a building that must cost a fortune to run, even if her parents paid it off long ago."

"Anouk." Verlaque sat back and stared at the commissioner. "Anouk is a perfect suspect," he said. "She may hate both Liliane and Gauthier, Gauthier for ignoring her and Liliane for stealing Gauthier away. But how does murder suddenly make you rich?"

"We haven't figured that one out yet. But the costumes," Paulik said. He leaned forward. "She must have loads of vintage outfits. And she was in that *West Side Story* play."

"Have her followed."

Paulik grabbed his cell phone and went outside. The restaurateur came to the table. "Is the commissioner unhappy?"

"Not at all," Verlaque said. "So, what's next?"

"Should I bring the entrée now?"

"Yes, yes," Verlaque said. "Bruno will be right back." He checked his cell phone and saw that Marine had texted him, saying she was having lunch with Sylvie and then they were going swimming. He smiled, relieved she was eating and getting exercise.

Paulik returned and said, "Done," just as the restaurateur arrived carrying two bowls of steaming long macaroni-shaped pasta.

"Busiate from Trapani," he said, setting down the bowls.

"Feeling in a Sicilian mood?" Verlaque asked.

"My new girlfriend," he replied, setting his hand over his heart.

"Is she in the kitchen?" Paulik asked, tucking his napkin under his shirt collar.

"No, she's at my place. But her aunt is in the kitchen!"

Verlaque looked at Paulik with a raised eyebrow. The poor aunt, he thought. "So what do we have here?" he asked.

"Busiate, auntie-style. She forms the pasta with a bamboo

skewer, and in the olive oil sauce she adds one garlic clove per person, some tomato and basil, and almonds and pine nuts."

"So it's like a Genovese pesto, but not nearly as green," Verlaque said.

"More delicate," the owner said. "I'll bring you a glass of wine."

Paulik rubbed his hands together and they both began to eat, commenting on how perfectly cooked the fresh pasta was. The waitress came back with two wineglasses and poured in a rust-colored wine. "From Mont Etna," she said. "It's volcanic, so lighter than most reds. It will go well with this pasta."

They toasted each other and as Verlaque tasted the wine he looked around the room, taking in the framed posters of various Italian islands. He snickered at one of the images, which looked alarmingly like a Greek white-walled village, not one of Italy. He pointed it out to Paulik, who agreed. "It's the blue trim," Paulik said. "That blue-and-white combo always reminds me of Greece." He bowed his head, bringing his attention back to the bowl of pasta.

Chapter Twenty-one

✦

Monday, August 14

Anouk Singer stood at the Monoprix cosmetics counter and carefully studied the lipsticks. After ten minutes she rubbed the colorful red and pink stripes off the back of her hand with a tissue and finally chose one. She then took the escalator downstairs to the food hall and bought a bag of salad mix, some goat's cheese, and a bottle of wine, carrying it back upstairs with her in a net bag, out into the bright hot street.

Two customers behind her was Alain Flamant, dressed not in police uniform but in chino shorts and an OM soccer shirt. He was relieved that Anouk wasn't going back to the cosmetics area, even if it was scorching hot outside.

Unlike in Monoprix, Flamant had no excuse for going inside an ultrafeminine dress shop located on a pedestrian street perpendicular to the Cours Mirabeau, so he waited across the street, pretending to look at overpriced bathing trunks in the window of a menswear shop, when Anouk entered. Out of the corner of his eye he could see her walking through the store, draping various items over her arm. She spoke to a saleswoman, who took the clothes and disappeared into the back of the shop, Anouk following her. The changing rooms, he guessed. He turned his eyes back to the bathing suits, most of them covered in colorful tropical flowers. His own bathing suit was navy blue, purchased on sale at Monoprix, he mused.

A few minutes later Anouk walked out of the dress shop, carrying two large expensive-looking shopping bags in her right hand and the food bag in her left. She walked slowly now because of the bags, and Alain followed about twenty feet behind, losing himself in the crowd. Anouk was tall for a Frenchwoman, which made things easier. He could see her reddish hair popping up now and again. She walked south along the cours, toward the Rotonde fountain, and he relaxed a little, knowing that now, given her shopping, she'd be heading toward home. But then she surprised him by going into one of the banks on the giant Place Jeanne d'Arc. He sat on a bench outside and waited, his eye on the bank's glass doors.

"Sure is hot," a voice said in English.

Flamant looked to his right and realized he was sharing the bench with a tall middle-aged man wearing a baseball cap. Flamant, always regretting that his English was so poor, nodded and tried to smile. The tourist smiled and pointed to Flamant's shirt. "OM fan? They're not very good, are they?" he asked, feigning to jab Alain's rib, laughing. "No offense."

Flamant looked straight ahead, not wanting to take his eyes off the bank.

"Okay then," the tourist said. "Sorry for living. Sheesh." He looked around the square and began humming a song, and Flamant was relieved when a woman of about the same age wearing a flowered sundress arrived.

"Has Earl been bothering you?" she asked Flamant.

Alain looked at her and smiled, shrugging.

"He's deaf," Earl said. "I hope you didn't buy another Provençal tablecloth."

"Don't be silly," she said, shifting her parcels.

Her husband stood up and tried to grab one of the bags and she resisted, laughing. "Stop it, Earl! You didn't want to go shopping, so you get what you deserve!"

"You bought more linens printed with those bugs!" Earl said. "The ones making the annoying screeching racket!"

"They're called *cigales*, Earl!"

As they argued over the shopping bags, they blocked Flamant's view. He quickly got up, accidently bumping into the woman, who dropped her purse and the shopping bags. "Sorry!" he said in English. He ran to the bank.

Standing at the self-service counter, he looked around the bank but couldn't see Anouk. Thinking she might be meeting with a banking specialist, he walked around the counter and down a carpeted hallway, glancing through the glass partitions into each office. Since it was August, only three of the offices were being used, and Anouk Singer wasn't in any of them.

"Can I help you, sir?" a young employee asked him.

Flamant turned around, sighed, and reached for his badge, showing it to the youth. "I *was* looking for someone, but seem to have lost her."

Back at the Palais de Justice Verlaque and Paulik found Sophie Goulin at her desk. "Come into my office," Verlaque suggested. "We'll have a session."

"Right, sir," Goulin said, grabbing a pen and stack of papers.

Once in Verlaque's office they sat at his round glass conference table, a pitcher of water and three glasses before them.

"Stéphane Breton, Liliane's second husband?" Paulik asked Goulin. "Did you find him on his island?"

"He lives in Patras. We found his meditation center, but not him."

"Aha," Paulik said. "Somehow I'm not surprised."

"Where is he?" Verlaque asked, looking out the window at the cloudless blue sky.

"He's here, I can feel it," Paulik said.

"They don't know, precisely," Sophie answered. "He's been gone for a week. But . . . the person I spoke to, Sharila, said that's not unusual. He left her a note that he was going to walk up into the hills and meditate. Do some yoga."

"What? In a cave?" Paulik asked. "Right!"

"That's what she said. . . ."

"And I suppose he doesn't take his cell phone."

"I asked that," Goulin replied in all seriousness. "He takes nothing, not even water. There are natural springs up there. He fasts."

"Anything else?"

"No, I had to hang up," Goulin answered. "Sharila was trying to sell me on the benefits of fasting. I go crazy if I skip even one meal. But we're checking outgoing flights from Greece, in case he was lying to Sharila, or she's lying to protect him."

"Good. Stéphane Breton's marriage was upset by Gauthier, so he has a motive," Verlaque said. "But once again, why wait so long? And why should Breton care about Liliane after all these years?"

"Ego?" Paulik suggested.

"Can you give me the name and dates of that play they were all involved with?" Goulin asked.

"I have it written down in my office," Paulik replied. "I'll email them to you. In the meantime, while you're checking on flights, check on the ferries leaving Patras for France and Italy as well."

"Right," Goulin said.

"And Sophie," Paulik said, "I was going to visit Emile Leclerc's wife at their apartment on the rue Aude, but I'd prefer you do it, as a female officer. He has a temper, and if he's been violent with her, she might talk to you about it."

"No problem. And I've been talking with the director of the post office. They're looking up that registered letter to see where it came from. He's also promised to send me the names of three or four possible employees who deliver on the rue Cardinale. I'd like to chat with them myself."

"Only three or four?" Paulik asked.

"The Mazarin is a desired route," she explained.

"Right," Paulik said, remembering Verlaque's words that in Aix, it all came down to real estate. "Good work, thank you." His cell phone rang and he answered it, listening to the caller speak. He hung up. "Merde."

"What is it?" Verlaque asked.

"Flamant lost Anouk Singer." Paulik let his head fall onto the desk.

"Nice T-shirt," Paulik said when Alain Flamant walked into his office.

"As if I don't feel bad enough!" Flamant said, collapsing into a chair, pulling his OM T-shirt out from his chest, as it was sticking to him.

"What happened?" Paulik asked.

"I got distracted in front of a bank she went into and lost her."

"Distracted?"

"A Yank couple were arguing about *cigales*," Flamant said.

"Americans, Flamant," Paulik said. "We need their tourist dollars."

"Anyway, they blocked my view so I didn't see Anouk leave. By the time I looked for her in the bank, she was gone. I ran to her theater, and apartment, but she wasn't at either."

"Do you want a glass of water? You look exhausted."

"Please."

Paulik went out to the hallway to the watercooler and brought his officer a glass of water. Flamant gulped it down, thinking water had never tasted so good.

"What did Anouk do this afternoon?" Paulik asked.

"She went to Monoprix, then bought some clothes."

"Can you be more precise?"

Flamant rubbed his head. He had a wicked headache. "At Monoprix, she bought lipstick. I couldn't see what color."

Paulik grinned and Flamant continued, "Then, downstairs in the food hall she bought cheese, a bag of salad greens, and wine."

"Sounds like dinner."

"Possibly dinner for two," Flamant said. "It was a whole bottle, and they sell half bottles at Monoprix."

"I think she enjoys her tipple."

"Oh. Then she bought some fancy clothes at a dress shop around the corner. Italian, I think."

Paulik raised his eyebrows at "I think." Flamant wasn't looking too good, and it slightly worried him. The officer's stomach made a loud rumbling noise and Paulik pretended not to notice.

Flamant went on, "I waited across the street, pretending to be enamored by bathing suits that cost over one hundred euros each."

"And then the bank?"

"Yes, the HSBC by the Rotonde."

Paulik nodded, thankful Flamant seemed to remember at least the name of the bank. "Why don't you go home now, and take a rest? It's hot to be tailing someone."

Flamant slowly rose to his feet, wiping his sweating forehead with a crumpled tissue he pulled out of his pocket. He nodded, made for the door, and then collapsed.

That evening Verlaque felt frustrated and glum. He'd had a call from Aix's chief prosecutor, who yelled down the phone that he wanted some suspects, and a trial, as soon as possible. Yves Roussel then let it slip he was anxious to have the trial before his annual two-week cruise in Corsica, which was coming up at the end of the month.

Verlaque opened the door to the apartment and walked in, plugging his cell phone in and setting it on the kitchen counter. He found Marine in their bedroom, reading, with her feet propped up on a pillow. She smiled and blew him a kiss. "Isn't it hot today?" she asked.

"Yes, one of the officers even fainted from the heat while tailing Anouk Singer," Verlaque replied, sitting on the edge of the bed. "Although just before I left this evening I found out that he had food poisoning, too. In Bruno's office. Apparently it wasn't a pretty sight."

Marine groaned. "The poor man. Any progress at the theater?"

"None, and Yves Roussel is in a tizzy that we haven't brought in anyone yet. Our suspects all seem to be missing, including Anouk Singer."

Marine propped herself up higher. "Anouk? A suspect?" She snorted.

Verlaque went on to tell her of Alain Flamant's report, and the fact that Anouk was the only person at the theater who had a history with Liliane and Gauthier. "How did both of those actors, quite famous I'm told, end up at her tiny theater? I think she arranged it all. Plus," he said, taking off his shoes and letting them drop to the floor, "we had her story about where she advertised for the actors' auditions for the play checked. She told me it was a cultural website, but they told our officer she didn't post any sort of ad in the past year."

Marine dismissed him with a wave of the hand. "That's Anouk! She was always super flighty! She just can't remember where she posted the audition, if she did at all. I always see her call-to-audition posters around town, taped to shop windows."

"You Aixois always stick together," Verlaque said, stripping down to his boxers. "I'm going to have a shower."

"Enjoy it." Marine went back to her book but set it down after a few minutes, musing over her husband's report. She couldn't imagine the awkward Anouk Singer killing anyone. What about one of the actors? It seemed to her that actors were hot-tempered, jealous creatures. Or was that a myth?

She could hear the shower water was off, and Antoine was in their dressing room, opening and closing drawers. He came back into the bedroom wearing shorts and a pink linen shirt. "You look lovely," she said.

"Trying to make up?" he teased. "For not believing my hypothesis?"

"I shouldn't have laughed," she said, taking his hand. "Sit down and tell me more about what Anouk did today, when she was followed by the poor officer who fell ill."

Verlaque sat down next to her, propping himself up with his elbow. "She went to Monoprix—"

"Highly suspect!"

"Are you going to listen?"

Marine smiled. "Go on. I won't interrupt anymore."

"Where she bought lipstick, a bottle of wine, cheese, and salad."

"Okay, so far so good. Completely normal."

"And then she went around the corner to a dress shop and bought some clothes. Flamant can't remember the name of the shop, but he thought it was pricey."

"Can Anouk afford expensive clothes?"

"You see!" Verlaque sat up. "Not from what I can tell, she can't. Too bad Flamant couldn't remember the shop's name."

"Any details?"

"Well, he thought it was Italian, and it was across the street from some expensive men's bathing suits."

Marine put her fingers to her temples. "Got it. Marina Rinaldi. Yes, very pricey Italian clothes. Plus sizes. Does that sound right?"

"Yes, given her body shape. You know she used to be a dancer on a ship?"

"I'd heard that. I think she wanted to get away from her parents. They were hard on her, I always felt."

Verlaque didn't like this observation. It worried him. But he didn't let on. "And then she went to the bank, after which Flamant lost her."

Marine twitched her nose. "Bank, dinner, expensive clothes, and makeup. Hum." She looked sideways at Verlaque.

"A date," he said. He began pacing the room.

"Possibly." Marine heaved herself out of bed, holding her distended stomach. "Although that said, women always fancy themselves up for a rendezvous with a girlfriend. I do with Sylvie."

"Really?"

"It's a pride thing. And Anouk didn't go home?"

"She didn't answer the door when Flamant rang, no."

"So she may have gone straight to her friend's house. To show her the clothes, then have dinner."

"That's a girl thing, too?"

"Certainly," Marine answered, walking down the hallway toward the kitchen. Verlaque followed. "But not at all a thing you'd do with someone you're attracted to, or having a date with," she continued, holding her index finger in the air. "You'd go home and put on the new dress first."

"Aha, got you!" Verlaque said, opening the fridge to get some cold water. "How do you know it's a dress?"

"In this heat?" Marine asked, smiling.

Chapter Twenty-two

❧

Tuesday, August 15

Verlaque somehow felt immediately relaxed and calm when he crossed the Cours Mirabeau and walked into the Mazarin neighborhood. He sometimes regretted not buying an apartment here, but he had been anxious to buy when he first arrived in Aix, and didn't know the town as well as he did now. Since moving to the city he'd read almost obsessively about its history. He couldn't remember the name of the architect in charge of designing this new neighborhood in the mid-seventeenth century, but Verlaque didn't envy him. He'd been given the task by the Archbishop Mazarin, who'd bought the orchards from the Knights of Malta. The Archbishop wanted the latest in urban planning, elegant enough to compete with the best streets in Paris. And so his chosen architect wisely created straight streets, making them wider than in the old town, and gave the intersections focal points, like fountains or trees.

Walking down the rue Cardinale, Verlaque looked at the giant red doors of Saint-Jean-de-Malte at the end of the street. The square in front of the church housed a stone fountain, its carved Maltese cross visible from where he was standing. He picked up the pace, hoping to get to Liliane Poncet's apartment before he saw anyone he knew, especially Marine's mother, who was one of a handful of women who ran in and out of the church all day long making sure that the suave and intellectual Dominican brothers had every need met. He smiled, imagining that perhaps the priests wanted nothing more than to sit quietly in their well-tended garden beside the church and read books, a cigarette in hand.

He arrived at number 29, enjoying his imaginary scene, rang the bell, and was let in. When he walked into the apartment, Sophie Goulin was sitting at an ornate wooden desk reading, as if she lived there. As he got closer he saw that she was going over papers in a large pink binder, like the ones his father had always kept financial records in, a different color for each year. Verlaque now did the same. He wondered if he'd teach his child to continue this tradition. Would he work on labeling the sections every year, with the child's help, as his father had done? It was one of the only things they had done together, but his younger brother quickly took over the role of assistant clerk, as Sébastien enjoyed detailed work, and more important, he absolutely loved money.

"Hello," Verlaque said, pulling up a chair. "Find anything?"

"I think so," Goulin said, pushing the binder along the desk so that he could see. She turned the page to a bank statement and pointed to a column. "Liliane Poncet makes deposits into an account every month, the same amount that Gauthier Lesage was receiving. I'm sure the account number will match up. I was just about to call Flamant to check."

"Is Flamant feeling better?"

"Yes, thank you."

"Good. And I'm sure you're right about the bank account," he said, "but I don't know why. Why give an old flame money? They weren't even together that long."

"He might have had something on her?"

"Yes, but normally blackmailers want more and more. The rates keep going up."

Goulin said, "Until they're stopped."

"If Liliane attacked Gauthier, then why was she attacked? That means we're looking at two different attackers."

"It's possible," Goulin answered.

The door buzzed and she got up and went into the hallway to answer it. Verlaque could hear Paulik's voice on the intercom, and in under a minute the commissioner was in the room with them.

Paulik wiped his brow and Verlaque noticed that he looked pale.

"Let's sit down," Verlaque said. "This apartment is stifling."

"I'll open the windows," Goulin said. Verlaque silently thanked her; she also must have noticed the commissioner's drained face.

"Is it the heat?" Verlaque asked Paulik.

"No, Yves Roussel."

The front door's intercom rang and Goulin buzzed in the visitors. She came back into the room accompanied by two young uniformed officers. Introductions were made and the older-looking of the two, a woman with her hair pulled back into an immaculate bun, said, "We've just covered the neighborhood door-to-door. Between the two of us we have two hits, one each."

"Hits?" Paulik asked.

The female officer explained, "We each met a neighbor who saw someone dressed in a vintage costume, at night, around here." It was obvious that they had decided beforehand that she would do the talking. Her younger, male associate stood rigidly beside her, staring straight ahead.

"They're sure?"

"Yes. And the neighbor across the hall saw Gauthier Lesage leaving this apartment, late at night. He thought he heard Liliane and Gauthier arguing."

Verlaque asked, "He recognized Lesage?"

"Oh yes, from game shows."

"I see."

"Thank you," Paulik said.

"I'll go back to the offices with you," Goulin said to the officers. "There are some files there I need, and I have to harass the post office director, who still hasn't called me back about that registered letter."

Paulik said, "I'm going to leave, too. I'll call Stéphane Breton again. Maybe I can get his assistant to crack. Roussel is buzzing around like a mosquito."

Once alone in the apartment Verlaque walked around, taking it in. He snickered at the brightly colored Provençal landscapes and frilly furnishings. He stopped at the row of Pagnol books and picked up *Jean de Florette*, his favorite. He thumbed through it and carefully put it back, not wanting to damage it. He heard laughter from outside and went over to the window and leaned out, watching two little girls—he guessed they were both about five—play in the garden below. There were three small trees in the garden, and dangling from each one were CDs, swinging in the breeze. The girls ran between the branches, hitting the CDs as they went, making the shiny silver discs spin. He didn't know what the discs were there for, but he imagined they had a purpose. To attract the sun down into what he imagined was a dark garden. Or to dissuade birds? Perhaps they were fruit trees.

He closed the window and left, careful to lock up behind him. He was thankful to get out into the fresh air. There was a little yellow scooter parked beside the ground floor flat's door and he smiled, thinking of the girls in the garden. He dialed Marine to check on her as he walked along the rue Cardinale to head back to the Palais de Justice.

"Hey," Marine said, picking up on the first ring.

"How are you?" he asked.

"I'm fine," she said. "Sylvie's here."

"I won't keep you, then."

"But I did have another contraction."

He stopped walking and had to apologize to the person behind him who almost ran into him. "Are you all right?"

"Yes, yes. A false alarm. Sylvie said the same thing happened to her and she went to the clinic far too early. They sent her home. But I feel better with her here."

"I can come home."

"No, no. You have a murder to solve. But . . ."

"Yes?"

"I was thinking about Marina Rinaldi."

"The dress shop?"

"Yes," she replied. "Maybe Anouk was buying clothes for someone else?"

"A man?"

"It's possible. But you said your wandering woman wears vintage clothes."

"That's what people have said, yes. But she could change her wardrobe, I suppose."

"Well, it was just a thought."

"I'll try to get home early," he said. "Please thank Sylvie for me."

Verlaque walked down a hallway at the Palais de Justice, impressed by all the activity. Through a glass partition he could see Yves Roussel also watching the scene, his arms folded across his chest. He was scowling the way he usually did, except for when his soccer team, the OM, was on a winning streak; on those days, he walked around the Palais de Justice cracking jokes with anyone unlucky enough to be near him.

Sophie Goulin sat in front of a computer. She suddenly let out a whooping yelp and waved a piece of paper in her hand. "The accounts match up," she said. Verlaque walked over. "Liliane Poncet was sending Gauthier that money, every month."

"Let's get someone to the hospital to ask her," Verlaque ordered. "Maybe she's awake."

"The commissioner is on his way," Goulin said. "The hospital called; Liliane opened her eyes this morning. Tomorrow morning I'm off to meet with Claire Leclerc, Emile's wife. She assured me that Emile won't be there; he's going to visit a farm."

"Good luck, and thank you. Has anyone found Anouk Singer yet?" Verlaque asked, looking around the room.

"I was just about to go round to her place," Alain Flamant said.

A younger officer, standing beside Flamant, mimed vomiting and fainting. Flamant laughed good-naturedly. Verlaque said, "It isn't as hot today, Alain." Everyone laughed and Verlaque was slightly ill at ease, as he hadn't meant it as a joke.

Bruno Paulik hated hospitals. He had, he knew, an irrational fear of them, as if they were places to go to die instead of get well. He'd seen his father's parents, alive and well and working hard on the family farm, go to the hospital in Avignon for what seemed to be minor ailments, never to come out again. The Aix hospital was no better: the same putrid smells, the same rude staff, and you needed the equivalent of a detailed Michelin map to find your way around.

When he got to Liliane Poncet's room a nurse was standing by her bedside, tucking in the crisp white sheets. Paulik introduced himself and showed his badge. "She woke up this morning," the nurse said. "But she's asleep again."

"Any chance she'll wake up again?"

"You're welcome to wait," the nurse said.

Paulik looked at Liliane and saw that half her face was very swollen and covered in bruises. Bandages surrounded her head; it reminded him of those turbans that Hollywood actresses wore in old films. "That's the side she fell on," the nurse explained, seeing Paulik's stare. He wondered if his mouth had been open, or if he had looked shocked by Liliane's appearance. He looked down at the film star, suddenly very sad for her. Alone, in a hospital in Aix. He reached out and took her hand.

"They can feel that," the nurse said. "The patients in this state, I mean. Even when I'm busy I try to take their hand at least once a day."

Paulik looked at the nurse. She was tall and thin, her skin jet-black.

"She's awake," she suddenly said.

Paulik looked down and realized he was still holding Liliane's hand. He let go. She was staring straight ahead. It was difficult to tell if she could see very far, or even make out their appearances. She slowly licked her lips, as one does when about to speak. Instinctively both Paulik and the nurse bent from the waist to get closer to her. Liliane's eyes closed again, and they straightened their backs, disappointed. They were about to leave the room when she spoke.

"Guy . . ." she said.

"Pardon, Mlle Poncet?" Paulik asked, walking quickly back to the bedside.

Liliane said, "I'm sorry, Guy," before her head fell to one side—the side of her face not bruised—and she closed her eyes. Paulik watched, relieved, as her chest began to rhythmically rise and fall beneath the white sheets.

Chapter Twenty-three

❧

Wednesday, August 16

Sophie Goulin sat at a small round kitchen table across from Claire Leclerc. Their apartment, while small, was comfortably furnished with a mixture of new and inexpensive antique furniture. There were real paintings on the walls, and some black-and-white photography. But what held Sophie's attention, while Claire poured them two glasses of cold water, was an oval-shaped mosaic hanging above the stove, made up of shards of colorful broken plates. The image—Sophie had to squint to be sure—was a red steak, surrounded by fragments of different shades of green ceramic. Visually, it was one of the more striking pieces of art Sophie had seen in some time.

"You don't have to like it," Claire Leclerc said, motioning with her shoulder to the mosaic. "Not everyone likes a piece of prime rib looking down at them while they're having breakfast."

"Au contraire," Sophie said. "I love it. The style is called *pique-assiette*, right?"

"Yes. Stealer of plates. The thief in this case is me, the artist Emile. I buy antique porcelain at the flea market. Most people want complete sets, so single plates sell for almost nothing."

Sophie smiled, enjoying the way Mme Leclerc spoke. "Are the green pieces are a table? Or a plate?"

"A green checkered tablecloth that we have."

"Your husband is talented," Sophie said, turning away from the mosaic. "One of the city's favorite butchers, an actor, and an artist."

"It helps him, having an outlet."

Sophie watched Claire Leclerc, who took a sip of water and carefully set her glass down. She looked at Sophie, without blinking or flinching. "An outlet from what?" Sophie finally asked.

"His temper. That's why you're here, isn't it?"

Sophie nodded. "Are you all right?" she asked.

"Of course. Oh, I see what you mean. Of course I'm all right. Emile's never laid a hand on me." She held up her hand. "I swear."

"Can I believe you, thief of plates?"

Claire Leclerc managed a small laugh. "Yes, you can. Emile gets angry at other men. Men who harass him. When he was small, he was bigger than all the other boys in his class. Bigger than even the boys two years ahead. But he was slow at school, especially math. You know how important mathematics is in this country, in our schools."

"Don't I know it," Sophie answered. "My younger son is having real problems at school."

Claire sighed. "And when Emile was about nine years old, Mme Leclerc, his mother—she ran the till at the butcher shop— ran off with a neighbor who ran a fabric store on the same street. It was a scandal, and Emile was teased."

"I see. The poor kids. Did Mme Leclerc stay with this man?"

Claire smiled. "Yes. But it was a woman, not a man. They live in Paris now. They're in their late seventies now, still campaigning for gay rights."

Sophie thought, *Good for you, ladies.* But she felt for the Leclerc brothers, too. They were just children when Mme Leclerc left. "Does Emile get into fights?"

"Not anymore," Claire said. "And he's never had a record. I assume you checked the police files after M Lesage's murder. He's clean."

"Yes, we checked everyone's record."

"Emile was frightened when he got home that night after he was questioned by the commissioner," Claire said. "He said that Lesage was teasing him. They had a few run-ins, once inside the theater and once in the street."

"He told you about that."

"Of course."

Sophie finished her water and set down her glass. "Can you tell me if your husband was with you on the night of Tuesday, August eighth?"

"I was already asleep when he got home," she replied. "Emile is worried about that, too. I do remember him getting into bed, but I can't say what time it was. I rolled over and fell back asleep. Sometimes he smokes cigarettes out on the terrace. He thinks I don't know."

"And the night of Friday, August eleventh?"

"That night I remember better, as we watched a television program together that finishes quite late."

"Can you tell me what program it was?" Sophie asked, looking at her notepad, her pen ready.

Claire Leclerc let out a tiny moan. "It's a little embarrassing."

Sophie looked up from her notepad. "No need to worry," she said. "I've seen and heard everything."

Claire coughed. *"L'amour Dans le Pré."*

Sophie wrote down the title and would check the times back in her office. She thought it started at 9:00 p.m. but couldn't be sure. She hated reality television, and the idea of having to watch a program about farmers inviting women to their farms in hopes of finding true love made her stomach turn. "I can explain," Claire went on. "It's because of Emile's work, as a butcher. He feels connected to those farmers."

Sophie smiled. "As I said, no need to explain."

"I teach French literature, so I do feel the need to explain. It's quite sweet, really; some of the farmers are really lonely, and they just haven't had time to meet the right woman."

"Maybe I'll give it a try," Sophie said, lying. "And after the show?"

"We stayed up late, especially for me. We each had a glass of Calvados out on the terrace, and laughed and talked about the show. It's silly, really. Then went to bed well after midnight. I woke up around three a.m. to use the bathroom, and Emile was beside me, snoring away."

Sophie thanked her and gathered her things to leave. On her way out she took another look at Emile's *pique-assiette*. It really was lovely. Could someone who created art, and acted, and who had a loving intelligent wife also be a killer?

Paulik entered the large, open office where Sophie Goulin was seated at a desk. "Are you free?" he asked her.

"Yes," she replied, looking up from her computer. "I just got back from speaking with Claire Leclerc." She filled him in and gave him her honest assessment: that Emile was innocent, his wife telling the truth.

Paulik listened to Sophie's explanation. "I think you're right," he said. "This goes back further than the theater troupe performing *Cigalon*. At the hospital Liliane was awake only for a few seconds. But she said *Guy*. Liliane didn't have any children, right?"

"That's correct." Sophie swung her chair to face a table behind her desk and grabbed a file. She opened it and read the first page. "Liliane had two brothers, both deceased," she said. "They grew up in Nantes."

"What are their names?"

Sophie read the document. "Neither are Guy," she said. "Wait a minute. Guy Minoux."

"Ah! Liliane's first husband, right?"

"Yes, the one who died young in a car accident."

"She said she was sorry," Paulik said.

"Perhaps she said Guy's name but the sorry was for someone else," Sophie said. "When my grandfather was dying his thoughts were all disjointed, and he was mixing up everyone."

Paulik nodded but didn't say anything. His experience had been very different: When his own grandfather was dying his thoughts were crystal clear and included minute details of his life and those around him.

Sophie went on, "I did find the name and number of the director from that musical that Liliane, Anouk, and Gauthier were doing in Paris twenty-five years ago. I'll call him this afternoon."

"Great, thanks. We need to talk with more people who knew Liliane and Gauthier back then. Anyone you can think of."

Her cell phone rang. Reaching across her desk, she grabbed it and answered. She began speaking, and motioned for Paulik to stay. She nodded, listening, took a few notes, and thanked the caller. "Finally! That was the post office," she said, hanging up. "There was indeed a registered letter delivered that day in April, for Liliane Poncet. It was signed for, but the signature is illegible."

"Forged by Gauthier Lesage, you mean?"

"Yes, he must have used his charm on the delivery woman." Sophie looked at her piece of paper. "Her name is Thérèse Borgetto. I'm going to call her in."

"Where was the letter from?"

"Luxembourg, a company called MDM."

"Sounds fake," Paulik said.

"Yes, it does, doesn't it?"

Marine was happy to be out of the house, and although she was thankful for Sylvie's attention, she was also relieved that Sylvie had rushed off for an appointment, finally leaving her in peace. While Marine was entertained by Sylvie's dramatic account of the birth of her daughter, Charlotte, her storytelling was often an embellished, highly dramatized version of the rather dull events.

Marine wanted to run one last errand before the baby decided it was time to enter the world. She and Verlaque had decided to put their country house on the market, and she had booked an appointment with an old school girlfriend, Annette, who ran a busy realty agency in the Mazarin.

At the bottom of the rue Aude Marine paused, staring at the elegant proportions of the Place d'Albertas, with its pebbled court-yard and delicate tulip-shaped fountain. The massive double doors clicked open behind her and she moved over to allow a long, sleek Jaguar to pass through and into the secret courtyard of the Hôtel d'Albertas, whose mansion had views of the square. She remembered her mother telling her that the marquis who built the mansion was knifed to death while eating dinner with his family, just after raising a toast to his wife. She hoped that the Jaguar's owner didn't come to the same end. So much beauty, thought Marine, and yet so much violence and heartache had touched Aix. She shook the bad thoughts out of her head and walked on.

By the time Marine arrived at the Cours Mirabeau, she was tired and thirsty. She saw an empty table on the terrace of Le Mazarin Café and sat down, waving to the waiter Frédéric as she did. He smiled and walked over, ignoring a table of tourists who were also trying to get his attention. Normally Marine would have felt guilty or sorry for the tourists, but today she didn't care. "Bonjour, Frédéric. Un Perrier," she said, smiling.

"Still no baby?" Frédéric asked, smiling as he looked at her stomach.

"It's taking ages!" she complained happily, rubbing her belly.

"I'm going to bring you something to snack on," he said, turning to go. "And you will eat every single bite."

Marine thanked him and sat back, enjoying watching people walk back and forth along the cours in the dappled sunlight. In no time she had seen four or five acquaintances, but she was too tired to make conversation and answer pregnancy questions, so she tried to hide her face in the shade, reading the slim volume of Jacques Prévert poems she had brought with her. As she turned a page she happened to look up and see Anouk Singer hurrying along, a small binder tucked under her arm. Anouk stumbled, tripping over a cobblestone, but recovered her balance with a flushed face and carried on with a determined—grim, even—look.

Frédéric returned, setting down a bottle of mineral water and an oval plate arranged with four small tin bowls that contained, as he had instructed the kitchen staff, "Healthy snacks, fit for a princess." One bowl contained curried chickpeas, always on the aperitif menu at the café; another contained popcorn, which Frédéric had hesitated upon, thinking it may be too greasy; the third was a bowl of black olives soaked with cumin seeds; and the fourth was filled with miniature pretzels. "The pretzels look like airplane food," Frédéric apologized. "I'm sorry. But it was that or potato chips." Marine thanked him profusely.

Half an hour later she left the café, leaving a small tip on the table and waving to Frédéric. She crossed the cours, feeling better and more energetic. As she walked down the rue Mistral she lingered, taking her time, as she was a few minutes early.

She stopped when she saw Anouk leaving her friend's realty office, the binder still clutched under her arm. Anouk looked harried and distracted. She turned left down the rue Mazarine, disappearing out of sight, and Marine carried on, wondering what Anouk had been up to.

"This is very troublesome, very troublesome indeed!" Yves Roussel yelped, his voice rising and cracking at the end of the sentence. Verlaque tried not to stare at the prosecutor, whom he thought even shorter than the last time they'd met. Once or twice Verlaque caught Paulik's expression, which was one of boredom mixed with exasperation.

"Stéphane Breton threatened both victims, sir," Paulik explained. "And he has no alibi for Gauthier Lesage's death."

"Says who?" Jean-Paul Breton asked, his face red. "My brother was meditating and fasting in a cave!"

Verlaque sighed. "He could have been anywhere that week."

"He's a professional, and his assistant vouched for him!"

"Sharila," Paulik said, scratching his head. "I think that's her name. Or is it Shangri-la?"

Breton scowled and then turned his back on Paulik. "And who says that Stéphane threatened Liliane and Gauthier?"

"It was in front of the cast and crew," Verlaque said.

"*West Side Story*?" Roussel asked, his voice again shrill. "This play, this play, it was twenty-five years ago, was it not?"

"Affirmative," Paulik answered.

"Stéphane's assistant also reported one of your officers calling her repeatedly, asking questions!" Jean-Paul Breton said, his voice now rising just like Yves Roussel's.

"It's normal routine in a murder inquiry," Verlaque replied dryly. "Especially given the fact that your brother was married to Liliane Poncet, and was a rival of Gauthier Lesage's."

Jean-Paul Breton snorted with contempt. "A rival? I've got to hand it to you, Yves. Your magistrate and commissioner are talented at pulling out needles from haystacks that have been long ago buried, and who knows who planted this needle!"

Roussel threw up his arms in exaggerated helplessness. Paulik looked across the room at Verlaque and rolled his eyes.

"My brother is in Greece," Breton continued. "Running a successful business. When you so cruelly accused him of being here, in Aix, he could have called a lawyer. But he called me, his brother."

Verlaque didn't point out the fact that Jean-Paul Breton *was* a lawyer, well known for getting high-profile criminals shortened prison sentences. He took in the Marseillais politician: expensive suit but ill-cut; too-long grayish hair slicked back, hiding a bald patch; and a number of corded colorful bracelets on his left wrist, the type that Verlaque thought looked fine on surfers and awful on middle-aged overweight men wearing baggy suits.

"Well, if that's all, we have to get back to work," Verlaque said, standing up. Paulik followed suit.

"No more accusations until you have proof," Roussel said. Verlaque and Paulik raced out of the office. Roussel opened the door and rushed up to them in the hallway, shaking his finger. "Next time you accuse someone of murder," he whispered loudly, "make bloody sure he or she is guilty." He returned to his office to console the politician, thankful he'd planned ahead—he had a bottle of pastis ready.

When they got back to Paulik's office Sophie Goulin and Alain Flamant were sitting across from each other at Goulin's desk, their faces solemn. "What's wrong with you two?" Paulik asked. "We were the ones getting a dressing-down by Roussel, not you."

"The hospital called," Goulin said. "Mlle Poncet died this afternoon from her head wounds."

Paulik said, "Oh, no. That's awful."

Verlaque sat down, deflated. He pulled out his phone to check on Marine. He was superstitious and didn't want any more bad news, but the only message was a text saying that she was having a mineral water at the Mazarin Café and that she loved him.

Paulik rubbed his forehead. "I'll go back to the hospital and talk to people there," he said. "Would you mind calling Ms Santelli?"

"Mlle Poncet's agent?" Verlaque asked, getting up again. "No problem. She should be notified right away." Walking through the succession of drab hallways, he thought about the case. What connected Liliane to Gauthier, if they were no longer lovers? But maybe they were? The neighbor saw Gauthier leaving Liliane's apartment late at night. And why had Liliane kept in touch with Gauthier all these years when she could have so easily ditched him? She even sent him money once a month.

He shut the door to his office and sat down, taking a deep breath before dialing Julie Santelli's number.

"Judge Verlaque," she said when she answered. "What can I do for you?"

"Hello, Ms. Santelli," he replied. "I'm afraid I have very bad news." He told her of Liliane's death and listened while Ms. Santelli wept and blew her nose. "Do you have someone with you?"

"Yes, my assistant is here," she replied. He heard her ask the assistant for a glass of water and an aspirin.

"Should I call back?"

"I'll be all right," she said. He waited, and soon heard the assistant's voice and the sound of Julie drinking.

After another minute, she asked, "Do you have any leads?"

"No," he answered honestly. "Can you tell me why Liliane stayed in touch with Gauthier all this time?"

"Liliane was a softy," she said. "She had a lot of money, and he didn't. I think it was as simple as that. If you need a tip, you should speak to Stéphane Breton, Liliane's second husband. I didn't say anything to your commissioner when he was in Paris, because I didn't want to throw out accusations, but now I'm ready." Verlaque listened, wishing she had. She continued, "Stéphane is nasty. Plus he threatened both Gauthier and Liliane, a long time ago."

"Yes, we are aware of that," he said, remembering the scene in Roussel's office. "Anouk Singer was a dancer in that play and told us about it."

"Anouk Singer? Never heard of her."

Verlaque got up and began pacing the room, hoping he didn't look too much like Yves Roussel. "Thank you, Ms. Santelli," he said. "And again, I'm sorry."

"Thank you."

"I have one last question."

"Yes?"

"Just before Mlle Poncet died, she mentioned *Guy* to my commissioner."

"Guy? That doesn't make sense."

"Liliane's first husband," Verlaque said.

"I know who Guy is," Ms. Santelli replied with a loud sigh.

"But why think of him at that moment? He died very young, before she was even famous."

Marine sat in the realty office, relieved. There was no rush to sell their country house. Houses like that were always in demand. "Talk about it more with Antoine," her friend Annette suggested. "With the proceeds you could buy a much larger apartment downtown. However, those don't come on the market very often, so if you find one, we may have to pounce on it."

Annette got up to retrieve some brochures of real estate for sale, leaving Marine to look around at the glossy photographs of old stone houses graced with olive trees and long fashionable swimming pools just like theirs. Why hadn't it worked for them? They were downtown creatures, she supposed.

Annette returned with the brochures and handed them to Marine. "Good luck with the baby," she said. "I had heard you were expecting."

Marine laughed. "Word gets around."

"Especially in Aix. It's still a small town in many ways."

"It sure is," Marine replied. "In fact, coming in here I ran into Anouk Singer. I used to go to dance school at the Singers', as did half of Aix. You did, too, right?"

"I did! So did my little brother. He was much better than me, and went on to study dance at the conservatoire."

"Anouk sure didn't look good," Marine said, trying to get Annette back on track. She frowned, hoping that her worried face and voice would lead to some answers.

Luckily, Annette seemed to be in a gossiping mood. She leaned in and whispered, "She wants to sell the building. It's too hard keeping the theater afloat, and she has someone who's interested in buying. Big multipurpose spaces downtown are rare."

"Oh, then that's good news," Marine said. She put on her sad face again. "But then why did Anouk look so worried?"

"Her parents," Annette said, lowering her voice again. "They don't know." She picked up a cell phone, puzzled. "*Zut*," she said. "Anouk forgot her phone. She was very distracted."

"I can take it to her."

"Not in your condition!"

Marine laughed. "The theater is on the way home. Sort of. Don't worry, I won't say anything about the sale."

A young realtor came hurrying over. "The apartment on the Cours Mirabeau is leaking water from the upstairs neighbor's bathtub, and we're about to show it in fifteen minutes!" he said, his arms flailing. "To Parisians who've just arrived on the train!"

Annette jumped up. "I have to go! Let me know if it's a girl or a boy, Marine!"

"Will do!" Marine said. Her friend and the harried assistant left, grabbing another employee to help them clean up the flooded flat. Marine gathered up her things and put Anouk's cell phone in her purse.

Chapter Twenty-four

﹌

Wednesday, August 16

Mlle Gastaldi," Verlaque said as he hung up the phone. Sandra Gastaldi was standing at his office door, with Bruno Paulik. "Please come in, both of you."

Paulik held out a chair for Sandra and she sat down opposite Verlaque. Paulik sat next to her. "Mlle Gastaldi is worried about Anouk Singer," he said.

"I see," Verlaque said. He wasn't surprised; they'd been distracted by Stéphane Breton and Emile Leclerc. So distracted that they had ignored Anouk Singer and her best friend, Sandra. "Why are you concerned, mademoiselle?"

Sandra took a breath and began, "Anouk came over for dinner on Sunday night." Paulik and Verlaque exchanged looks: That's where she'd been when Flamant lost sight of her. "She brought some wine and cheese, it was so sweet."

"And she wanted to show you some clothes she just bought," Verlaque suggested, remembering Marine's theory.

Sandra looked up, shocked. "How in the world did you know that?"

Verlaque glanced at Paulik, hoping the commissioner was impressed, too. Verlaque went smugly on, "I even know where Mlle Singer bought her clothes. Marino Rinaldi."

"*Marina*," Sandra corrected. "Yes, two dresses on sale; otherwise that shop's too expensive. Anyway, Anouk goes shopping when she's distressed, so I was concerned."

"How was she behaving, exactly?" Paulik asked.

"Well, even more skittish than usual. She drank too much and hardly ate; I had her sleep on the sofa because I was so worried about her. She was mumbling."

"What about?"

"It was nonsense; I could only understand bits and pieces. *The stupid play.* She said she was in trouble," Sandra said, choking up. She drew a breath and continued, "And she kept apologizing to her parents."

Verlaque's back tightened, as did his stomach muscles. He thought of Marine. She'd been right about the dress. Did Anouk kill Gauthier and Liliane for the publicity? But how could that help if the play was canceled? For future productions? Or was she jealous of them, and their fling twenty-five years ago? Or was there something they had completely missed? "Why didn't you keep her at your place?" he asked, conscious of the fact that he sounded angry. "Why did you let her go?"

"I'm sorry, I meant to keep her at my place," Sandra explained, sniffing and wringing her hands. "But Anouk got up in the early morning and left while I was still asleep."

"You did well to come, Mlle Gastaldi," Paulik said, shooting the judge a reproachful look. "I'll have an officer walk you home."

"Thank you," she said.

Verlaque half got up and nodded, then sat back down again. Paulik took Sandra by the arm and they left, and Verlaque quickly texted Marine to see where she was. Perhaps she was still meeting with the realtor; they'd been friends at high school, he recalled.

Paulik came back and sat down opposite. "You were a bit rough," he said. "She was terrified."

Verlaque ran his fingers through his hair. "This case is slipping away from us."

Paulik said, "We're getting close. Let's send someone over to the theater to see if Anouk's there. In fact, I'll go over there myself." He got up but turned to say, "By the way, I phoned the director of that play twenty-five years ago."

"The *West Side Story* set during the war?"

"Yes, that one," Paulik said, smirking. "Officer Goulin found me his name and number. He remembered the night when Stéphane threatened Liliane and Gauthier in the theater."

"And?"

"He said it was pathetic. Stéphane was so drunk he was almost incoherent. And he said that Gauthier just ran around the stage, afraid that his hair and clothes might get messed up."

"Is Anouk lying?" Verlaque said, rubbing his eyes.

"I'd better go try to find her."

"Me, too," Verlaque said, relieved that Paulik was the one going to chase down the raving lunatic. He wanted to get home as quickly as possible and wrap his arms around Marine.

Marine couldn't believe how good she felt. She hadn't had this much energy in months. She grinned, remembering Sylvie's labor story, which Marine had heard a thousand times—of how Sylvie had so much energy the day before she went into labor that she had actually agreed to go sailing in Marseille with friends. Marine didn't think she could do *that*, and she also didn't think she'd be going into labor anytime soon. The contractions had disappeared. She only wished she'd asked to use the bathroom at the realty office; she already had to pee again. She felt for Anouk's cell phone in her purse, glad to be doing a good deed. And she'd be able to use the theater's bathroom. It was closer than her apartment.

When she got to the theater she pulled at the glass entrance door. It was locked. She cupped her hands, peering through the glass, but couldn't make anything out in the dark hallway. Suddenly a face, wild-looking, appeared on the other side of the glass door. Marine jumped back. "Oh, Anouk!" she said, laughing. "You frightened me."

Anouk opened the door. "Are you all right?" Marine asked. Anouk's eyes were red, her skin blotchy, and her hair a tangled mess. "Do you remember me?" Marine asked.

Anouk nodded and ushered Marine in, locking the door behind them. She walked down the hallway and Marine followed. "I remember your mother," Anouk finally said. "She was bossy. And I remember you. You were nice to me."

"I was a lousy ballerina!" Marine replied, trying to sound

jovial. "Anyway, I came because you forgot your cell phone at the realtor's. I was their next client." Marine reached into her purse and gave Anouk the phone.

Anouk grumbled a thank-you. "Want something? Some rosé?"

"I could really use your bathroom," Marine said, surprised to be offered wine given her obvious very pregnant condition. "Then I'll be off." She really wanted to leave; the dark lounge gave her the creeps, and Anouk looked half-crazed. But the baby was pushing down on her bladder and it was beginning to hurt.

"The red door behind you," Anouk said.

Marine thanked her and hurried in. When she was done she washed her hands, hugely relieved and determined to leave right away. She opened the restroom door and Anouk stood there hovering. In her hands was a small knife.

Marine looked at the knife and felt weak. She rocked back and forth and caught herself by holding on to the door frame.

"I know why you're here," Anouk said. "You're married to that snooty judge, aren't you?"

"Yes, but I really only came to give you your phone."

"You're trying to find out things, to tell him."

"He's hardly told me anything about this case," Marine said truthfully.

"Husbands and wives share everything."

"Can we sit down, Anouk?" Marine said. "I don't feel well."

Anouk looked at Marine's stomach almost with surprise, as if she hadn't noticed it before. "I suppose," she said. "Over there." She gestured with the knife. "On the sofa."

"Thank you," Marine said. She sat down and her stomach contracted, and she moaned in pain.

"What's wrong? Are you faking it?"

"I'm afraid not, Anouk."

"You are!"

Marine drew a few deep breaths and tried not to think of the knife, still in Anouk's hand. The contraction rose up in her and she drew in a succession of quick breaths. When it was over she leaned back on the sofa, sweating.

"You're not faking it," Anouk said, realizing. She looked worried and helpless. Marine decided Anouk's tough act was just that—an act. But she still held a knife.

"I need to leave now, Anouk."

"I want you to tell your husband and the big policeman to stop coming here. It's bad publicity My parents are worried sick."

"The police are just doing their job," Marine said. "Two of your actors were attacked in the theater."

Anouk grimaced. "My parents have aged in these past ten days. I can see it."

"It will all be over soon, Anouk. You just need to tell the police everything you know."

"How was I supposed to know all of these horrible things would happen?" she complained. "Liliane came by the theater one day. She saw my posters around town announcing the auditions. She said she loved Pagnol. She signed up that day—she didn't need an audition, obviously."

"And Gauthier Lesage?" Marine asked. "Did you invite him?" She felt another contraction coming on and tried to focus on Anouk's face. She attempted to breathe deeply, but it came out more like pathetic panting.

"No, he came on his own. Liliane was surprised he was in Aix.

But I think she was still sweet on him." She sighed. "Who wouldn't be? He was so dreamy. . . ."

Another contraction hit and it threw Marine back against the sofa. She tried to breathe deeply, but it hurt so much she found herself gagging. She felt sick and wanted to vomit. The contraction finally finished, and she looked up to see Anouk leaning over her.

"Are you okay?" she asked.

Marine saw the knife sitting on the coffee table. She leaned back, relieved that it was no longer in Anouk's hand. "I need an ambulance."

"I'll call one." Anouk took her phone and dialed, her hands shaking.

"Clinique Etoile in Puyricard!" Marine shouted. She wished Anouk would go into another room to make the call, so that she could text Antoine. But Anouk watched Marine as she spoke into the phone.

"Here, I have water," she said once she hung up. She took a water bottle that had been sitting on the table. "It's probably been around here awhile. I hope you don't mind." She lifted the bottle carefully up to Marine's lips, her hands shaking slightly.

Marine smiled weakly and thanked her. The water tasted divine.

Anouk went on. "I just wanted people to come to my theater."

"Anouk," Marine said, panting. "You just threatened me with a knife."

"A knife?" She looked down at the sofa and saw the knife lying beside her. "I wasn't going to use it on you! You were nice to me all those years ago! Not like Gauthier." She began to cry again. "I've made a mess of everything . . . but I didn't hurt them."

Marine asked, "Do you know who did?" Anouk began talking, but Marine could only see her mouth moving; she couldn't hear the words. Anouk's face grew puzzled, then alarmed, and she stopped speaking. Marine fell onto her side, clutching her stomach. She realized she couldn't hear Anouk because she herself had been screaming.

When the contraction ended, Marine looked up and Anouk was gone. She closed her eyes, frightened but too tired to move. She tried to rest but soon heard a commotion—a banging sound, footsteps, and voices—and her body shuddered. Opening her eyes, she saw a man standing above her: bald with the most wonderful blue eyes and long dark lashes, just like Bruno Paulik. He asked her if she was all right and she realized it *was* Bruno.

Another man crouched down beside Bruno; he had curly blond hair and wore a uniform. She'd never seen him before. Squinting, she realized he was a paramedic. Together they helped her into a wheelchair.

"Let's get you to Etoile, Mlle Bonnet," the paramedic said. "Or the nuns will have my skin."

Chapter Twenty-five

❧

Thursday, August 17

The next morning Bruno Paulik tried to stay patient as he looked at the disheveled mess that was Anouk Singer. He hadn't slept well, nor had Hélène. Léa had knocked on their bedroom door three times asking if Marine and Antoine's baby was born yet. Judging by Anouk's appearance, she hadn't slept well, either, but who ever did in a holding cell?

"Let's start at the beginning," he said, trying not to sound weary, or angry. "You advertised the play, although not on that free culture website you said you had. They had no ads from you." Had Anouk kept Marine at the theater against her will? He would find out, and if Anouk had put Marine or the baby at risk there would be hell to pay. He laid his cell phone on the table that separated them; he was waiting for news from Verlaque, who was at the clinic. Anouk quietly sobbed, blowing her nose now and again.

"It started before that," she answered, her chest heaving as she tried to control her breath. "Liliane came into the theater one morning. I thought I was seeing things."

"And what did she want?"

"To talk about Pagnol. We talked all morning, and when she left I'd decided to put on *Cigalon*."

"Let's go further back now," Paulik said.

Anouk closed her eyes. "To Paris, you mean."

"That musical. Marine Bonnet spoke to me in the ambulance," he said. "What did you have on Liliane and Gauthier? What did you overhear?"

She closed her eyes again. He was tempted to tell her to stop the theatrics. Instead he glanced at his cell phone, but there were no messages. Hélène and Léa were at home, staying close to the phone, and he knew that Marine's friend Sylvie was already at the Clinique Etoile, probably chain-smoking in the garden and telling her life story to some orderly or nurse or, heaven forbid, one of the nuns who ran the clinic with great efficiency. He almost grinned. When Anouk began speaking, breaking his reverie, he flinched.

"They were talking in a hallway outside one of the dressing rooms," she said. "I didn't mean to listen in, but I froze, unable to move. They couldn't see me. I was in awe of them, you see."

"Go on."

Anouk continued, "Gauthier was crying. I couldn't see them, only hear them. Liliane told him she was tired of him. She was going back to her husband. Stéphane Breton."

"How did Gauthier take it?"

"He was sad at first, then he sounded angry," she replied. "She just laughed and told him to grow up, that Stéphane was one

hundred more times a man than he was. And then she said something else. . . ."

"Yes?"

"She said that Gauthier made her look bad, as he was a lousy
actor and would never have a career like hers. I couldn't move, or
they'd know I'd heard everything. I stayed hidden, behind some
props."

"Did you ever tell anyone this? Your parents?"

"My parents?" Anouk asked, surprised. "No way." She wiped
her tears away and said, "Gauthier then asked Liliane for money.
To keep quiet. About what, I still don't know. He didn't say, but
Liliane was so angry."

"Ah bon?"

"But he did say a few things," Anouk said. "Something about
how Liliane was able to buy such a fancy apartment near the Jardin
du Luxembourg. He said the fame and money shouldn't be hers.
She cheated someone."

Paulik made notes. "Was that the last time you saw them?" he
asked. "Or did you then have a relationship with Gauthier?"

"He'd never have noticed me. I'm so ashamed."

"This is a murder investigation, Mlle Singer. Are there other
things you've been lying about?" Paulik asked. "Like why you
wanted both Liliane and Gauthier here in the first place?"

She nodded. "They're so famous! I was thrilled when they
came!"

"Did you arrange that?"

"No," she said, surprised again. "How could I have?" She hung
her head and the tears fell. "I somehow imagined it was all my
doing, my genius."

Paulik waited, looking at his phone, willing it to buzz, but there were no messages. "Did you kill them?" he finally asked.

"No!" she said, sobbing. "I was with my parents those nights! I told you!"

"Your parents love you," he said.

"They would never lie to a policeman and judge."

"Did you set Liliane and Gauthier up? Did you arrange for them to go to the theater on the nights of their deaths to meet someone else?" he asked.

She shook her head and cried, "No!"

Paulik tried one more thing. "Marine also told me you said that Gauthier was cruel to you." He thought of Marine; she shouldn't have talked, she should have saved her energy. Once she was in the ambulance another contraction hit her hard and as soon as it was over she fell asleep, exhausted.

"He laughed at me," Anouk answered. "When he came to the first rehearsal he told me he only agreed to come to Aix so that he could get more money from Liliane. He said my theater was a joke, and I was a hag."

"Did you hate him?"

"Yes, but I didn't kill him!"

Paulik set his pen down, realizing that there might be some truth to Sandra and Jean-Marc's crazy idea that Liliane Poncet was the person walking around Aix dressed in a vintage suit.

Paulik knew he couldn't hold Anouk. She had an alibi for both murders, and although she had frightened Marine, Marine had been adamant she didn't want to press charges. "Anouk lives in a dream world," she said. When she was lifted into the ambulance she added, "If I'm not an awkward duckling, it's thanks to the Singers and their dance school." He nodded, knowing that he had never met anyone as graceful as Marine Bonnet.

As he walked down the hall to his office he looked at his phone; still no messages from the clinic. He realized he hadn't eaten and he turned around and left the building, deciding he'd go to the Italian restaurant where he had eaten lunch with Verlaque. It was 1:15 p.m.; hopefully the kitchen would still be open.

By the time he arrived it was 1:30, but the waitress greeted him with a smile and led him to a table, swiftly removing the second place setting when he said he was alone. He asked if there was any of the daily special left. "No," she answered, "but there's an excellent fillet of halibut with lemon and butter." Paulik, never a great fish eater, tried not to look too disappointed. She quickly added, "The fish is marinated for fifteen minutes in lemon juice, then quickly fried in butter. It's perfect on a hot day like today. And I can give you a little summer risotto on the side, made with green beans and zucchini."

"Okay," Paulik replied, smiling, happy about the cheesy starch. "And I'll start with one of those Negroni drinks."

When the Negroni arrived, accompanied by a small bowl of olives stuffed with almonds, he took a sip and wondered how it had taken him almost forty years to discover just how good bitter cocktails are. He supposed it was because his wife was a wine-maker, so they rarely drank hard liquor. He looked around at the posters on the wall and remembered how irritated Verlaque had been by the one Greek island poster among the other more obviously Italian ones. He took another sip, popped an olive in his mouth, and looked back at the Greek poster. Then he took his drink and phone outside the restaurant and quickly dialed Sophie Goulin.

"Let's talk to Stéphane Breton again," he said when he had Goulin on the line. "I don't care what Yves Roussel thinks."

"I don't, either, so I was just about to start in on that," she replied. He nodded, happy he had such an organized and competent officer. She went on, "He's back at the mediation center today after his break in the hills."

"I'm beginning to doubt that he's well rested."

"Me, too, but I didn't let on to his assistant. She sounds a little too enamored of him. There are two direct flights to Greece from Marseille, Athens and Chania, but he wasn't on them."

"Is Chania in Crete?"

"Yes," she said. "We're still checking the ferries."

"Okay, great, thanks," he said, hanging up. He took another sip and a couple walked by, speaking English. They saw his red drink and gave him a thumbs-up and a wink. He smiled and waved, slightly embarrassed. He went back into the restaurant and the owner came out from the kitchen and shook his hand.

"Where's your friend, the judge?" the owner asked.

"At the maternity clinic."

"What?! Any news?"

"No," answered Paulik. He held up the Negroni. "That's why I needed one of these."

"Good idea," the owner said. "I'll join you."

Paulik, pleased, sat back down. Within minutes the owner was sitting across from him, nervously making his way through a bowl of pistachios. "Gennaro," he said, shaking Paulik's hand again.

"Bruno."

Paulik's fish and risotto arrived and Gennaro made a gesture for him to eat. "You must have already eaten, before the lunch service?" Paulik asked.

"No, I usually eat after," Gennaro replied. "But I don't think I'll be able to eat a meal until we get the news." He looked at Paulik's plate and then at Paulik, saying, "But you go on. Please." Paulik cut into his tender halibut and guiltily put a piece in his mouth. Gennaro ate another pistachio, tossing the shell on the already high pile on the table. When the last customer paid their bill and left, he yelled across the room to the waitress. "Hey, Adriana! The judge and his wife are having their baby!"

She yelled back, "What?! And by the way, Gennaro, she's a law professor, not just his wife!"

Gennaro shrugged. "Come sit down and bring some more pistachios!"

A third Negroni landed on the table, along with Adriana, who pulled up a chair and collapsed into it. "I'm exhausted!"

"Your phone is beeping!" Gennaro said, looking at Paulik's phone.

"Oh! I'd put it on silent," Paulik said. "Because of the restaurant."

"Hurry and pick it up!"

"It's a text message," Paulik said. "With an image, I think." He read the message and smiled. His eyes welled up and he tried not to look at his new friends, their faces expectant, their elbows poised on the table. He said, "It's Antoine, I mean the judge. They are all fine. They have a girl." He was quite certain his voice cracked when he said *girl*, but Gennaro and Adriana only made cooing sounds and passed on words of congratulations for Verlaque. Paulik clicked on the image and waited for it to open. A baby girl appeared on the screen, fast asleep and wrapped in a yellow blanket in Verlaque's arms. "Rosa," Paulik said. "It says here her name is Rosa."

Gennaro stared at him. The waitress muttered something in Italian and downed her drink. "You're joking," Gennaro said.

"No," Paulik replied, showing him the text.

"That was her mother's name," Gennaro said as he looked at the smiling but teary-eyed Adriana.

Chapter Twenty-six

❧

Thursday, August 17

Sharila cringed as she heard her name being called across the garden. Well, "garden" was a bit of an exaggeration: Her boss had bought some dried-up cacti on sale at the local hardware store and arranged them haphazardly around their flagstone terrace, not even bothering to replace their plastic containers with ceramic planters. It now seemed that this was symbolic, the dried plants in their plastic pots. She was angry at herself for not believing or seeing it this past year.

"Sharila!" came the voice again, and she set down her pen and got up from her desk. "Ah, there you are," he said as she walked outside. She couldn't believe how hot it was. She'd never gotten used to it. "Do we have more clients signing up for the fall session?"

"Yes, four so far," she answered, shielding her eyes from the sun. She'd forgotten her sunglasses. Through her splayed fingers she could see his ridiculous outfit: baggy linen trousers and a white cotton shirt with a panama hat, and old worn-out espadrilles on his feet. He tried very hard to look like an expat entrepreneur living in a hot Mediterranean country, but he only looked silly and out of place. She hadn't thought that at the beginning; she had been in love with him then.

"And that policewoman?" he asked, trying to sound nonchalant. "Has she called back?"

"No," she said. "I made it quite clear that you'd been meditating up in the hills."

"Are you sure you didn't say anything else?"

"Of course I'm sure." She tried to control the mounting anger in her voice. "I even told her how good fasting is for the body."

"Well done," he said, giving her a peck on the cheek. She recoiled, remembering the life she'd given up, running away from her parents. Now she missed their terrace with its view of the Eiffel Tower; her parents, less so, but they'd make amends.

"Is that all?" she asked. "I have lots of work to do."

"Yes, yes," he answered dismissively with a wave of his hand.

When Paulik returned to the Palais de Justice he could only see the back of his officers' heads, hunched over computer screens. He knew they were working on the murder case, but he wanted to tell them the news of Rosa Verlaque. Or would it be Rosa Bonnet-Verlaque? He coughed and Sophie Goulin looked up. "It's torturous," she said, sighing. "One of the ferry companies is on strike."

One of the rookies looked up from his computer, a telephone receiver cradled between his shoulder and chin. "I've been on hold for ten minutes."

"But on the good news side, I've been able to track down this mysterious company from Luxembourg," Sophie said.

"MDM?" Paulik asked. "Is it real?"

"Indeed it is," she said, turning to her notes. "It's a mining company."

"In Luxembourg?"

She laughed. "Head office is in Luxembourg, for obvious tax reasons, but the mines are in the Americas, some in northern Canada, and the rest in Peru and Bolivia."

"Why in the world were they sending a registered letter to Liliane, and why did Gauthier intercept it? Assuming he did."

"That, unfortunately, I don't know. But I'd bet my life that he opened that letter on the stairs and didn't give it to her."

"I thought you said you had good news," Paulik said.

"Sorry if I got your hopes up," Sophie said. "When I asked questions about the stockholders, MDM said they'd only talk to Interpol. It's classified information. So, I've called Brussels and submitted a request."

"Fingers crossed Interpol is fast. Well then, I can tell you a piece of good news," Paulik said.

"Oh, please do," Sophie said.

"Judge Verlaque and Marine Bonnet had a baby girl this morning. Her name is Rosa."

A loud whoop went up throughout the room. An officer tapped his pen repeatedly against a ceramic mug.

"Oui? Je suis encore là!" the rookie said into the telephone receiver, giving Sophie Goulin a thumbs-up.

Sophie's computer beeped and she turned her chair around to

face it. "I just got an email from one of the ferry companies from Athens," she said. "They make daily trips via Patras to Brindisi and Bari."

"They're towns in Puglia, right?" Paulik asked.

"Right, in the heel." She turned back to her computer and read. "No sign of Stéphane Breton on either trip, all week. *Zut*. I've pulled up this map of all the ferry routes from Greece to Italy. Have a look." She turned her screen to face Paulik.

Paulik looked at the green, red, and blue dotted lines. Up and down they went, crisscrossing the Aegean Sea in multiple directions. "I had no idea there were so many," he said.

"There's Patras," Goulin said, pointing to it with her pencil. "It's a port on the mainland, northwest of Atheno."

"He could have taken any number of ferries," Paulik said. "They all seem to pass through Patras, then make their way up and down the Aegean. Split up the lines between you."

"Right."

"Did Breton's assistant say she'd call you when he got back to the center?"

"Yes, but I'm not sure I trust her. Her voice sounded odd, as if she were trying to sound like she loves him but actually despises him."

"He could have been standing there when she got your call," Paulik suggested.

"I thought of that, too," Goulin said. "I'll call back."

"Thanks," Paulik said. "I'll be in my office if you need me."

Paulik returned to his office, leaving the door open in case there was some information on Breton. He called the house, telling

Hélène and Léa the good news about the baby. He thought of calling Verlaque but didn't want to bother them yet. But just as he set his phone down, it rang.

"Antoine," he said, seeing the caller ID. "Thank you for the photograph. How are you all?"

"*Salut*, Bruno," Verlaque said. "Exhausted and deliriously happy."

"I'll bet. Marine had a tough go of it, didn't she?"

"Yes," Verlaque said, his voice shaken. "Bruno, there was a moment late last night, when I was . . . really frightened."

Paulik nodded and took a deep breath. He said, "They're so strong though, women. We've both played rugby, but I don't think it compares."

Verlaque laughed. "No, not with what I saw last night. Well, it's over now, and both Marine and Rosa are fast asleep. They'll be at Etoile for the week."

"Want me to come and pick you up?" Paulik offered. "You should get some sleep, as well."

"Nah, my car is here, thanks. Listen, there's one thing that's been bothering me, about that new Italian restaurant we like."

"Ah bon?" Paulik asked, confused.

"The poster of the Greek village . . ."

"Right." Paulik now understood. "Me, too. I'm tracing the steps this week of Stéphane Breton, flights and ferries to France."

"Excellent."

"I'm also going to call Julie Santelli in Paris. When I saw her in Paris she mentioned that Gauthier had been very relaxed. He'd been on a vacation before coming to Aix. Sea and sun, she said."

"Greece."

"Exactly."

Verlaque yawned and apologized. "I'd better get home to bed."

"Yes, you'll need energy for next week," Paulik said, hoping he wasn't worrying the judge with what was coming: the baby crying, both parents in tears, feeling helpless and inefficient, wondering how to comfort the baby . . . He cringed at the memories.

He was about to say goodbye and hang up when Verlaque spoke. "Bruno," he said, "does this feeling ever lessen?"

"Pardon?"

"That every time I look at Rosa I think my heart is going to burst."

"No, it never does."

The female police officer from France called again. "You've just missed my boss. He's in town, buying computer paper," Sharila replied. Buying office supplies was her job, but Sophie Goulin wouldn't know that. Sharila didn't want to risk her chance to leave this place. She had to put Goulin off as long as possible. Stéphane must think that she was doing her usual work for him—covering up, mostly, as she'd always done—because she'd decided that she'd leave tomorrow morning, early, on the first ferry.

"Ah, there you are," he said, suddenly standing behind her, his hands on her shoulders.

She flinched and quickly hung up. She couldn't remember if she'd closed the ferry schedule she'd been looking at on the computer. She looked at the screen and saw the color photograph of the sea, her screen saver. She sighed in relief.

"Who was that on the phone?" he asked, moving around her chair to stand in front of her.

"Oh, just a telemarketer," she said. "Once again trying to get us to switch internet companies."

"It seemed like a longer call than that," he said, peering down at her.

"They were persistent."

He looked at her, then moved away from the desk and walked to the door. "I'll be meditating down by the pool if you need me. Dinner at seven?"

"As always," she replied, turning back to the computer.

Paulik was beginning to dial the Parisian phone number when he saw Alain Flamant standing in the doorway. "Have a second, sir?" Flamant asked.

"No!"

"Sorry, it's the Tassets again."

"Wait a minute," Paulik said, hearing the other end ring once. Something was making him feel uneasy. Was it because the Tassets' daughter made him worry about his own daughter? And now Marine and Antoine's daughter as well? "Tell them I'll be with them in a second."

"Thanks."

On the third ring Julie Santelli answered. Paulik apologized for interrupting her once again. He promised to be quick.

Ms Santelli said, "I hope so. Two of my most important clients have been murdered in your city. One of France's most beloved actors."

"I offer my sincere condolences. We've been working around the clock, with extra personnel, to solve these crimes."

"Thank you," she said. "What can I do for you?"

"You told Judge Verlaque that M Lesage had been on vacation before moving to Aix. Can you remember where it was, and when? You mentioned sun and sea."

"Yes," she said. "I think he went to Greece. I'm not sure where, exactly." There was a pause as she opened a large black appointment book and flipped back through the months, stopping in spring. "Ah, here we are. He went from May seventh until May twenty-first. He mentioned Athens, now that I think of it, but that's maybe just where he flew to. Did you check the calls on his cell phone, and his computer?"

"Yes, and nothing has come up," he answered. Paulik didn't tell her that Gauthier, had he been meeting Stéphane Breton, would have used a throwaway cell phone and been careful not to leave any traces of a trip to Greece. He kept quiet, not wanting to alarm her.

But it was Julie Santelli who surprised the commissioner when she said, "No doubt Gauthier hid all that information."

"I beg your pardon?" Paulik asked. "Do you know why he went?"

"No, but Gauthier would do anything for money. I was his agent and I knew him better than anyone. Gauthier never paid for his own trips, and he didn't know anyone in Greece." She began to make hacking noises, a phlegm-filled smoker's cough.

"Does a mining company called MDM mean anything to you?" he asked.

"Nope."

He saw Mme Falzon's notebooks sitting on top of a filing cabinet. He walked over and took them down, putting them in his backpack, the telephone receiver balanced under his chin.

Julie Santelli stopped coughing and cleared her throat. "Stéphane Breton!" she said. "Greece . . . I didn't make the connection. They must have been together."

But Paulik had already hung up, as Mme Tasset was now standing in his office sobbing.

Paulik sat at his desk, across from M and Mme Tasset. Mme Tasset dried her tears and thanked Sophie Goulin for the tea. Paulik looked up and winked, thanking his officer, amazed that she'd found an actual teapot and two cups that were clean and not chipped. He looked at the middle-aged couple, trying not to judge them for their very Parisian, and expensive, attire: She was in a short linen dress with a big pearl necklace that even Bruno knew must have been expensive, and he wore linen pants and—despite the heat—a neatly pressed jacket over a pristine striped shirt. On his feet were shiny leather moccasins with those tassels Paulik couldn't stand and no socks. They were both very tanned.

"I'm sorry we barged in," M Tasset said. "But we're at our wit's end. You see, a friend of ours saw Victoire here, in Aix, two days ago."

"Did he speak to her?" Paulik asked.

"He tried to, but she ran into a crowd when she saw him. She was wearing a large hat, which she's never done before, and sunglasses, but she'd taken them off for a second, so he recognized her."

Paulik leaned forward, his elbows resting on the desk. He tried to speak softly. "Victoire is twenty-three."

Mme Tasset began to cry again and Paulik reassessed his harsh judgment of the couple. The woman collected herself and began to speak. "It's all my fault. Victoire left after her sister died.

I shouldn't have said those things. . . ." Her husband reached for her hand and held it. She went on, "I compared her to her sister. It wasn't fair of me, but I was grieving. . . ."

"All three of us," her husband said. "We were all grieving."

"I know," she replied, still crying. "We all miss Aurore."

Paulik passed a box of tissues across the desk. He sat and thought while the parents collected themselves. "Your country house, here in Aix, can you remind me where it is?"

They gave him a road name and rough directions between downtown Aix and their home. He nodded, noting that it wasn't far from Marine and Antoine's country house. When he used to come from the Luberon to Aix on his motorcycle, he'd take those back roads. He then realized something: Verlaque had told him about the girl named Aurore who had fallen outside their house, and how Marine had cared for her. Paulik had been sweet on an Aurore in junior high, so he remembered the name.

"Do you have a photograph of Victoire?" he asked.

"Of course," M Tasset said, fumbling for his cell phone. "I gave a printed photograph to your officer, as well."

"Okay, but for now I'd like to send the photograph to our magistrate."

"The examining magistrate?" M Tasset asked, his face full of worry. "What's wrong?"

Paulik held out his arm, palm facing out. "Not to worry. It's because he lives near you, and he might recognize her."

M Tasset shrugged, passing Paulik the phone. "I doubt it. I think Victoire has been wearing disguises."

Paulik felt a shiver run up his spine at the word *disguises*. He looked at the photograph and sent it to Verlaque with a short explanation attached. "While we're waiting, I'll go and fetch your file. Please help yourself to more tea."

"Thank you, Commissioner," Mme Tasset said. She managed a smile.

By the time Paulik returned with the file, he had a reply from Verlaque: *That's her, says Marine.* He paused, collecting his thoughts. They still didn't know where Victoire was, and he had before him two distraught parents who had already lost a child. A daughter. He took a deep breath and walked back into his office.

"Here's the file," he said.

"Has the magistrate replied?" Mme Tasset asked, her eyes red.

"Not yet," Paulik said. "Were they twins, your daughters?"

"Almost," M Tasset said. "A year apart, and very similar in looks."

Paulik nodded and promised to keep in touch. As soon as they left he called Sophie Goulin. "The Tassets had a house in Greece," he said. "Things are starting to connect. I think that Victoire Tasset met Stéphane Breton there. Check flights from Marseille to Greece, for a Victoire, or Aurore, Tasset. She may be using her deceased sister's passport."

"Do you think she's Sharila? I can't believe that I've been speaking to her all this time."

Chapter Twenty-seven

❧

Friday, August 18

Paulik arrived at the Palais de Justice a little late the next morning, as he had to drop Léa off at the conservatoire for a concert recital. He decided that he'd take the time to stand in line at Michaud and buy pastries for his team. They'd been working tirelessly the past few days. He'd finally taken Mme Falzon's notebooks home and read about half of them. By the time he got to the office it was almost 10:30 a.m.

"Hello, everyone," he said as he walked in, putting the red cardboard box of pastries on their central worktable. One of the junior officers saw the Michaud name and grinned.

"Interpol has come through for us," Sophie said. "Liliane Poncet received a letter that was mailed out to all stockholders back in April."

"Excellent!" Paulik said. "What was in the letter?"

"Good news for the stockholders, and why the company MDM

wouldn't tell me over the phone. One of their mines struck gold, so to speak."

"Like in the Westerns," Flamant said.

"Yes, and the stockholders are now rich," Sophie replied. "Liliane bought shares in the company back when she knew Gauthier."

"And I spoke to that postal worker, Thérèse Borgetto," Sophie went on. "It happened just as we imagined. She was tongue-tied when she saw Gauthier, the famous actor, and he gave her some song and dance of how he'd personally deliver the letter to Liliane, who was ill and couldn't walk down the stairs."

Paulik grunted. "And I suppose she's lost her job over this?"

"Yes," Sophie confirmed. "But Gauthier wouldn't have cared one bit about that." She was about to add something when her cell phone rang. She shrugged apologetically and answered it. "Allo!" She listened and then looked at Paulik and waved her finger in the air, then put it to her mouth. The room went silent. "Hello, Sharila. Yes, I can hear you." Sophie put the phone on speaker.

"Officer Goulin, I don't have long to speak. I'm at Charles de Gaulle, we just landed on the first plane out of Athens. I'm waiting for my bag."

"You're in Paris?" she asked, shocked. Sophie looked at Paulik. "Please, go on."

"I've left Greece. For good."

"Does M Breton know?"

"No, I snuck away very early this morning. He'll be furious, but I don't care. Oh, here come the bags on the baggage belt." She paused and went on, "I want to tell you that I'm willing to testify against him. He didn't go to the mountains to meditate last week, and I have the proof. He rented a car in Ancona, Italy. You can call them at the Avis office."

"Do you know why Gauthier Lesage was in Patras?"

"Stéphane offered him a free holiday, that's all I know. They spent their time whispering."

"That is such a help, Sharila," Sophie said.

"Victoire. My name is Victoire."

Sophie nodded at Paulik. "I didn't think Sharila was your real name. Thank you, Victoire. Can you tell us anything else? What were you doing in Aix?"

"Here's my bag!" she said. There was a muffled sound and a few seconds later she came back. "Please give me a few hours to be with my family. They just flew up from Aix. You can call me on this number. Oh, I can see them!" Sophie heard more muffled sounds, Victoire saying *Maman!* and loud crying.

"Victoire!" Sophie said. "Please don't go yet." The phone went dead and Sophie hung up.

"Well done," said Paulik.

Sophie shrugged. "I tried to get her to talk more. As you heard, Stéphane Breton rented a car in Ancona last week."

"That means he probably took a ferry there," a young officer said. "It's too small to have an airport." He looked at his computer screen. "Ah, Patras to Cephalonia to Corfu to Ancona in Italy. I see the route now."

"Get the Greek police in Patras on the line right away," Paulik ordered. "I'll take the call in my office." Paulik was too nervous to eat any of the pastries he'd bought. He'd have to speak English with the Greek commissioner, and his English was terrible.

Once Paulik had left the room, the young officer looked at the Michaud box. "Help yourself," Sophie said. She looked over toward his computer screen and gave him a raised eyebrow.

"It was the next ferry route I was going to check!" he said defensively. "The ferry company that goes to Bari *just* got back to me this morning, and of course there was no passenger named Breton."

"Okay," Sophie said. The officer wheeled himself on his chair over to the worktable and opened the Michaud box, smiling. Sophie was about to ask if there were any glazed brioches when Antoine Verlaque walked in, carrying an identical red box from Michaud.

"Oh, I see I'm not the first," he said.

There was much back patting and congratulating. When it was quiet Sophie told him, "The commissioner is on the phone right now to the Greek police in Patras."

"Patras?" Verlaque asked. "I think there's a wonderful ancient theater . . ." he said, his voice trailing away.

Sophie looked at the officer and he shrugged. *What's wrong with the judge?* they both wondered.

"I've got something to show you two," Verlaque said, pulling out his cell phone. "What's your name?" he asked the young officer.

"Kévin, sir."

"Kévin, and Sophie," Verlaque said. "Just look at these photos." He held his phone up so that they could see it. The photograph was of a sleeping baby. He scrolled to the next photo, also of the sleeping baby. "Did you see that?" he asked excitedly.

"What, exactly, sir?" Kévin asked.

Sophie gave Kévin a sharp look. He was too young to have friends with babies, she guessed.

"Didn't you see the difference in the two photos, Kévin?" Verlaque asked. "I'll show you again. Please concentrate this time." Kévin leaned in to get a closer look at the screen, his brow furrowed.

"Yes, I think I saw the difference," Kévin said, shooting Sophie a desperate look.

"Of course you did," Verlaque said, beaming. "In the first photo, Rosa's left arm is down at her side, and in the second photo her left arm is across her tummy."

Sophie flinched to hear the judge use a word like *tummy*.

"Rosa's super coordinated," Verlaque went on, still looking at the photograph as he walked toward the door. Paulik came out of his office and gave the judge the *bise* and offered his congratulations. Sophie and Kévin exchanged looks over the bise. Normally male associates shook hands; perhaps they were good friends? The two men spoke a few minutes over Rosa and her extraordinary talents, Marine's fatigue and joy, and then Paulik brought Verlaque up to speed on the case. He said, "The Greeks have been watching Stéphane Breton for some time. There have been complaints made from former clients to the local chamber of commerce, and they now have proof that Breton's been cheating on his taxes for years."

Verlaque snorted. "He's become Greek, not paying taxes!"

Paulik coughed, hoping the judge's comment wouldn't be taken too seriously by Sophie and Kévin. He also hoped that neither of them had Greek relatives. "They're on the way to pick Breton up."

"That's that, then," Verlaque said, rubbing his hands together.

"Well," Paulik began, "if it *was* Breton, we still have to determine how and why he killed Liliane Poncet and Gauthier Lesage."

"I'm sure you will!" Verlaque said, now at the door. "I'm off! Good luck with everything!" He gave a happy little wave and left.

Paulik looked blankly at his colleagues, wondering what he could say. *Perhaps I shouldn't make a big deal of Verlaque's flippancy,* he mused. *The Bonnet-Verlaque family has just changed, forever. Sophie probably understands; Kévin might in a few years' time.* "Let's get back to work," he finally said. "Hopefully Victoire Tasset will be able to shed more light."

Paulik sat at his desk reading Corinne Falzon's notebook. She had marked the page on May 19, the day Stéphane Breton threatened both Liliane and Gauthier. Mme Falzon cited the name of the brasserie, presumably the one where she ran the cigarette counter, for she had written in blue pen *I was working when Liliane came into the bar, terrified.* It was a long time ago, though, and Paulik knew it wouldn't hold up in court.

He turned the page and continued looking through the book, made up mostly of theater and cinema stubs and Corinne Falzon's comments on which actors and singers had bought cigarettes from her on various days. He didn't recognize the names for the most part; these were Montmartre actors, not the successful film stars who lived on the Left Bank. Except for Liliane.

He was beginning to read a review of the *West Side Story* musical when a color photograph fell out of the book. It had been cut from a magazine that had been inserted between the last page and the back cover. The photograph was of a present-day Liliane, smiling in front of a door painted glossy black. A bit of the building's golden stone wall was visible on the left, and the number 29. He took the clipping and quickly went back into the shared office where Sophie and Kévin worked. Showing them the photograph, he asked them if there was any chance they could find its source.

"It's Liliane Poncet," Paulik said. "I think in Aix, on the rue Cardinale."

"No problem," Kévin said, turning to his computer and typing. In a few seconds he turned his screen toward Paulik. "There it is," he said. "*Gala* magazine, an article about Liliane living in Aix."

"How did you do it so fast?" Paulik asked.

"I clicked on Google Images and typed the words *Liliane Poncet living in Aix*." Kévin looked at the photograph and said, "The caption says this photograph was taken of Liliane in downtown Aix, but it doesn't say where."

"I knew it was her apartment on the rue Cardinale because I've been there," Paulik said. "But if you don't know where she lives but want to find her, this photo would help."

"Right," Sophie Goulin said. "She's wealthy enough that you'd guess she would live in the Mazarin. Kévin, does the article say where she lives?"

Kévin had been reading the article on his screen. He turned to them and said, "It just says she loves living downtown."

Sophie said, "So you'd assume the Mazarin."

"Exactly," Paulik said. "And you'd start on the rue Cardinale. It wouldn't take you long to find this black door—"

"Which is an unusual color for Aix," Sophie cut in.

"Even if you didn't start with the rue Cardinale, it wouldn't take you long to find it," Kévin added. "There aren't even ten streets in the Mazarin."

"So someone like Breton could hang outside Liliane's door, waiting for her," Paulik said.

"Which is why we didn't see any traces of unusual phone calls on her cell phone or landline," Sophie suggested. "They could have just spoken in person."

"When did that *Gala* article come out?" Paulik asked.

"This March," Kévin said.

Paulik began pacing the room. "Breton sees the article and gets in touch with Gauthier, offering him a free vacation in May."

"And in Patras they plan on killing Liliane Poncet!" Kévin said excitedly.

"Because Liliane left him?" Paulik asked. "There has to be more. And what's in it for Gauthier?"

"At any rate," Kévin said, "Gauthier was double-crossed."

Sophie said, "Victoire told me Gauthier and Stephane whispered and schemed. No longer enemies, apparently. At least not in Greece."

"So why kill Gauthier?"

"Two different killers?" Kévin asked.

Paulik looked at the rookie. "You may be on to something."

"Anouk Singer?" Sophie suggested.

"Why?"

"Jealousy? Anouk told you she loved Gauthier, and neither he nor Liliane even recognized Anouk when they came to the theater. He laughed at her, and her theater."

Paulik was afraid that Sophie may be right. "Anouk Singer lives in a dream world," he said, quoting Marine. "But is she a murderer?"

"It was her theater, sir," Kévin said quietly. "Her pride and joy. Even her best friend said so, didn't she?"

Paulik excused himself and went back to his office. Opening Mme Falzon's notebook, he began rereading. He yawned, turning a page that was full of theater stubs. The next page had a small Polaroid of Mme Falzon sitting behind her cigarette counter. "Taken by GM many years ago," she had written beside it. "Just before he died. RIP."

Paulik quickly looked up Mme Falzon's phone number and dialed. "Come on," he said into the phone. "Pick up, dear old woman." He waited, counting the rings. When he got to ten he sighed and hung up. "Not even an answering machine." He turned back to the notebook and flipped through another two pages of small photographs and stubs. There were handwritten annotations by Corinne Falzon noting who came into her café and when. He turned another page and saw the review he had started reading of the *West Side Story* WWII musical. Setting his elbows on the desk and resting his chin in his folded hands, he continued to read, chuckling at a few of the more sarcastic sentences. He rubbed his eyes and yawned.

A second later, he sat up, his back rigid. He reread the sentence, just to make sure. "I don't believe it," he said, quickly grabbing a colored pen, circling the name. "Hello, you. There you are, as big as day."

Chapter Twenty-eight

❧

Friday, August 18

They were an odd trio, sitting in a four-place *carrée* on the TGV in a first-class car. A beautiful tall black woman, well dressed in imaginative and colorful clothing, was reading a book about van Gogh's life. From time to time she reached out and took the hand of a much older white man, well into his seventies, with a long aristocratic face and a head of thick white hair. He wore a pale yellow linen suit that was miraculously not creased. He read *Le Figaro*. Across from them, a white man in his late thirties or early forties who bore no resemblance to either (he looked like his deceased mother) flipped half-heartedly through a real estate magazine, stopping frequently to fuss with the many parcels on the empty chair beside his.

"Sébastien," the older man said. "Do you mind?"

"Mind what, Father?"

"Stop fussing."

"I could swear I forgot a parcel," Sébastien said.

The woman smiled. "You brought enough gifts, don't worry," she said, looking at the pristine white and pink bags from Paris's best children's shops. "It was so kind of you." Her French was very good, marked with an Anglo accent.

The older man smiled and squeezed her hand. "Rebecca, we have a gift, I hope?" he asked, now worried. He'd never bought a baby gift in his life.

"In my suitcase," she said.

The older man looked at his son and snorted. "At least we didn't have to buy an extra seat, just to be sure there was a spot for all the gifts."

Sébastien ignored his father's remark and picked up his magazine. Rebecca leaned across the table. "I'm a posh client from the United States and want a hundred and twenty-five square meters in the seventh arrondissement, no ground-floor flats please, with a balcony and two bathrooms. At least two bedrooms."

Sébastien looked at her, only now noticing her sparkling purple eye shadow. "One point seven million euros," he answered without hesitating.

She sat back and made a whistling sound.

"Academia isn't paying you enough," her partner said. "Even Yale."

"I'll say," she answered.

Silvery olive groves whizzed by the window. "We're coming up to Avignon," Sébastien said. He reached for the bags, taking them by their fine silken corded handles and rearranging them once again.

"It's twenty more minutes to Aix," his father said, flicking his newspaper to straighten it. He sighed. "You remind me more and more of Antoine."

Sébastien looked up, shocked. "That's impossible. We have nothing in common."

His father huffed. "You never used to, until this baby business. Now you're acting every bit as much the anxious uncle as he is the besotted father. I could make no sense of him the other night on the telephone. Complete gibberish."

"I think it's called sleep deprivation," Rebecca said.

The tables and chairs belonging to the Place Richelme's cafés and bars were already installed for business, the morning's market washed away and forgotten until the next day when it happened all over again. Paulik and Officer Goulin—he wanted a woman present, and it was required by the law—left the Palais de Justice knowing exactly what needed to happen next. They walked quickly, purposefully. In the next square, just a few meters north, stood Aix's seventeenth-century Hôtel de Ville. When Léa was little, the Pauliks had spent Saturdays outside its doors watching the wedding parties file out, after signing the official documents but before (for some of them) the church service. Léa would jump up and down, trying to see over the heads of the friends and family members so she could rank the brides' dresses. When the commotion was over, the Pauliks would go for a hot chocolate in a café. Sometimes they'd splurge and buy Léa a thick bridal magazine at the kiosk opposite the Hôtel de Ville, and she would mark the pages of her favorite dresses with her precious Post-it notes. Bruno and Hélène, although they themselves had had a very simple wedding—Hélène had worn a pale pink summer dress and he his only suit—enthusiastically took part in this ritual with their daughter. Hélène would feign exasperation when Bruno pointed to a dress in the magazine with too much décolleté or a revealing open back. "Papa!" Léa would say, agreeing with her mother. "C'est trop vulgaire!" Léa was now thirteen, and it felt like they hadn't been downtown on a Saturday morning in years.

As they walked down the rue Cordeliers, Paulik was thankful that there was still a street in Aix with small locally owned shops. On the way back up, if he had time, he decided he'd buy some spices and nuts at the Middle Eastern shop that Hélène loved. And maybe if he bought some phyllo dough she'd make them baklava.

Waiting at the traffic light to cross Sextius, they both pulled out their work cell phones and checked their messages. Paulik realized that he often did this now while waiting for a light to change. What had he done before the small phone had become an appendage? "Should we cross against the light, sir?" Goulin asked. He could see she was impatient, rolling back and forth from her toes to her heels. He was about to answer when the light changed. They picked up their speed. Paulik looked at his watch— it had taken only ten minutes. At number 19 they stopped and Sophie Goulin rang the bell. A head poked out of an open upstairs window and Paulik looked up.

"Mlle Gastaldi," he said, shielding his eyes from the sun. "Do you have a few minutes?"

Sandra Gastaldi sat primly across from him, her hands folded on her lap, her eyes wide. Wide with what? Paulik mused. Fright? Excitement? Or relief?

Sophie Goulin sat on the edge of a chair. Her face was bright with attention, her long thick black hair tied into the usual bun. Bruno Paulik had been tempted to stand but he sat as well, across from Mlle Gastaldi in a second armchair.

"I hope you like chamomile," Sandra said, pouring out the tea once it had steeped.

"Chamomile is fine," he said. Somehow Paulik had known that they would be served herbal tea. He preferred hot drinks with caffeine, not *Grandma's piss*, as his father called it. He knew now, after years of experience, to accept the offer of tea, or water, or coffee, whatever it was. It was an obvious attempt at stalling, but it gave the police the chance to look around the suspect's surroundings. Here, he took in the comfortable but worn and out-of-date furnishings; the thread-bare carpet; the small vase overstuffed with plastic flowers. The art on the walls wasn't much better. Framed posters, mostly. He almost laughed out loud when he saw the identical picture—the blue-and-white village—that was in the Italian restaurant that he and Verlaque liked so much. Only it wasn't in Italy, as they had discussed that day. It was Greece.

Officer Goulin thanked Sandra but left her tea on the coffee table. Paulik leaned forward, also ignoring the tea. "Ms. Gastaldi, why didn't you tell us you were involved in that *West Side Story* musical all those years ago?"

She lifted her cup, her hand shaking. He continued, "You worked on that play, along with your best friend, Anouk." He remembered the musical's review, and the critic's sentence: *The only thing that saves this play are the colorful and imaginative costumes designed by Sandra Gastaldi.*

"It wasn't a secret," Sandra said. "No one asked me."

"And you didn't bother telling us," Sophie Goulin said.

Silently thanking Mme Falzon and her black notebooks, Paulik went on, "Anouk told you about overhearing Liliane and Gauthier's conversation, didn't she?"

"What conversation?" Sandra asked. "That was a long time ago."

Paulik paused, figuring out his next move. "Anouk protected you," he said. "I asked her if she'd ever told anyone about overhearing that conversation, and she said no."

For the first time Sandra Gastaldi looked downcast. "I'm sorry. You're right, we both heard Liliane and Gauthier that night."

"Go on." He wondered how she'd lie—or act—her way out of this one.

"And I was protecting Anouk. I thought she . . ." Sandra choked and began to cry. Paulik and Goulin waited, and after Sandra blew her nose, she was able to continue. "I thought Anouk might have been responsible somehow for one of the deaths. When they showed up here, in our little theater, I was worried that Anouk had arranged it and was bribing them."

"Didn't they recognize you?"

Sandra laughed. "A costume girl from a short-lived musical put on twenty-five years ago? No." She looked at the officers, her eyes red with tears.

Paulik began to lose his patience. He asked, "Why did you suspect Anouk?"

"Her debts," Sandra replied. "The building is paid off but they have trouble meeting the bills, and have been behind in property taxes for two years. She's even spoken to a realtor about selling. I didn't see how putting on *Cigalon* could resolve all that. But if . . ."

"If someone died," Paulik said, "there would be publicity."

"So even if *Cigalon* was canceled, people might come to the next play, in droves. Out of morbid curiosity," Sandra suggested. "Anouk told me she's already been contacted by a few magazines for interviews."

Paulik, weary now, decided to speed things up. "Before we came here," he said, "we interviewed Anouk in our offices. We told her that we know you were involved in that play in Paris. She's confessed that you overheard the conversation between Gauthier and Liliane, but you forced her to stay quiet about that fact."

"You bullied her into saying that!" Sandra said, her voice shrill.

He saw that Sandra was losing her cool. A good thing. "She was exhausted, that's true," Paulik said. "But more because of what you've put her through, not us. Anouk said you'd convinced her that it looked obvious that she was guilty. You even tried to convince us of that. In the end it almost drove her mad, to the point that an innocent person and their unborn child were put into danger. Because of you."

Sandra quickly stood up, causing one of the flower-patterned cushions to fall off the sofa, narrowly missing capsizing the teapot. Paulik glanced over at Sophie Goulin. He saw her leg muscles tighten, ready to spring if needed, but she stayed calm. Paulik continued, "And if we were to check your phone messages and emails, I think we'd find quite a bit of contact between you and someone in Greece." He looked up at the photograph of the blue-and-white village, and pointed to it.

"That's nonsense, and you need to have a warrant."

Sophie Goulin pulled a sheet of paper out of her pocket and showed it to Sandra, who threw it on the floor. Sandra ran to her bedroom, flinging open the door. Goulin quickly followed, with Paulik close behind.

"You fool!" a man shouted from the bedroom. "You stupid idiot!"

Paulik knew in an instant, even having never met him, whom the voice belonged to. What amazed Paulik, as he relived that moment in the days to follow, was just how easy it had been. True, it had been a long haul, perhaps too long, but much of that was because of Sandra, who'd had them looking in all the wrong places for the guilty party: She'd set up Anouk, and even got Jean-Marc to think it was Liliane herself who had killed Gauthier. But he wished all cases ended like this one, with two guilty people in one room, handcuffed by a very adept police officer named Sophie Goulin, on the force for fifteen years, married, mother of two boys.

Chapter Twenty-nine

~⁓

Saturday, August 19

The night before, it had poured rain, as it usually did in mid-August in Provence. Hélène Paulik made lamb chops with oven-roasted potatoes and opened one of her vintage Syrahs. Léa made a salad with a walnut vinaigrette that contained far too much vinegar and mustard. Paulik had been too distracted to buy phyllo dough on the way home from Sandra Gastaldi's, so they ate jelly beans out of the bag while watching a very funny movie about Astérix and Obélix in ancient Egypt.

That next morning Bruno Paulik felt refreshed, and the weather had cooled. Sophie Goulin was at the coffee machine when he got to his office.

"I hope you had a relaxing evening," he said.

Sophie looked perplexed, as if she'd already forgotten about yesterday's events. "Oh yes, we did," she answered. "We played Monopoly." She poured her boss a cup of coffee and handed it to him. "I just got off the phone with Victoire Tasset," she said. "She'd wanted to call last night but was too caught up with her family."

Paulik nodded. "Totally understandable. But I want her here later today."

"I told her that."

Alain Flamant entered the room waving a piece of paper. "I just got off the phone with MDM's head accountant in Luxembourg."

"Excellent," said Paulik. He winked at Sophie. "Sit down, Flamant, and have a coffee."

"No thanks, I've had three already," Flamant said. "Once we were approved by Interpol, I was able to speak to the mining company's head accountant, who was already at his desk. Liliane Poncet and Stéphane Breton together bought stocks in the company when they were married twenty-four years ago. Nothing much has happened since then, and in fact, because of an accident at one of the mines, the stock value has gone down. Until this spring."

"Aha," Paulik said.

"When the mine in Canada struck gold, the lawyers sent letters to the stockholders informing them of their sudden wealth. Stéphane Breton's letter was returned, though; it was an old address in Paris. And the only address the company had for Liliane was her Paris apartment. Luckily that apartment still has a concierge, whose phone number I was able to get from the company that runs the co-owners' association."

Paulik gave him a thumbs-up. "Well done."

"The concierge forwards all Mlle Poncet's mail here, twenty-nine rue Cardinale. Anyway, the accountant didn't hear back from

Liliane, which he thought was odd, given all that money, but then he read in the papers about her death."

"So our hunch was right," Sophie said. "Gauthier opened that letter without telling Liliane. But Gauthier told Stéphane Breton, naturally. He had to; only Breton could sign the papers to get the money."

"That's not all," Flamant said, sitting down. "Are there any more pastries?" Kévin shoved the bag in the direction of Flamant, who mumbled thanks and took a croissant. He went on, "But still no one has cashed in those shares. Odd, right? And, as we know, Stéphane Breton promptly disappeared from Greece only to show up here in Aix."

"Why not cash in and flee?" Paulik asked. "We could go next door to Breton's cell and ask him, but I think you know the answer, Officer Flamant."

"It certainly wasn't out of any love for Sandra," Sophie said. "Breton doesn't seem like a caring or honest person. Or do we have him wrong? Did he come to Aix to fetch her? That's what she obviously thought, having him hiding in her apartment like that."

Flamant brushed the croissant crumbs off his jacket, smiling. "The pin code."

"What?" the three other officers asked in unison.

"To get at the stocks, the accountant sent out a secret pin code by letter," Flamant explained. "You receive a pin code and it allows you to send MDM your bank information. But that code was sent to Liliane. The accountant told me."

"I went through her papers," Goulin insisted. "I would have found it."

"Gauthier?" Paulik asked. "He was seen arguing with her."

"She would have received the pin code *after* the letter telling her about the gold stocks," Flamant said.

"But she never got the letter," Sophie said.

"Right. So she realized what had happened and hid the pin code somewhere. She would have followed up, but then was killed."

"I bet it was Liliane, who was heard arguing with Gauthier in his apartment. She wanted to know what happened to that letter. She was no dummy, and would have guessed that Gauthier stole the letter somehow."

Paulik stood up. "Can we get someone over to Liliane's apartment as quickly as possible?"

Kévin put up his hand. "I'll go! I'm looking for a handwritten four-digit number, right?"

"Exactly what the accountant told me," Flamant said.

"But where should I start?" Kévin asked.

Sophie smiled at Paulik, who suggested, "Try looking in her paperback copy of Pagnol's play *Cigalon*."

Kévin flew out of the office as Sophie Goulin called after him, "They have the keys downstairs! You need to sign for them!"

"D'accord!" Kévin called back from the stairwell.

Paulik laughed and turned to Sophie. "How much of this did Victoire know?"

Sophie replied, "She told me she didn't know about the gold mine, but she'd overheard Stéphane and Gauthier talk about getting rich and *not* telling Liliane. She also said she thought there was a woman in Aix involved, someone who visited Greece once this spring. We'll show her a photograph of Sandra Gastaldi when she gets here."

"Why would Gauthier include Stéphane in on the deal, and not Liliane?" Paulik asked.

Sophie explained, "Gauthier and Stéphane were in the same boat—both rejected by Liliane. A team. And Victoire told me that Gauthier idolized Breton. Breton was highly influential, don't forget."

"Why wasn't Liliane killed first?" Paulik asked.

"That may have been the plan between the two men," Flamant offered. "But Gauthier was double-crossed by Stéphane Breton. With both of them out of the way, Gauthier and Liliane, Breton would get all of the stock money."

Paulik grabbed another pastry and turned to Sophie. "What else did Victoire say? Start from the beginning."

"I'm having another pastry, too," Flamant said, reaching for the bag.

Sophie began, "Victoire met Stéphane in Greece, when her parents had a vacation home there. It was when her sister Aurore was ill, and Stéphane pretended to be sympathetic and under-standing. Victoire realizes now that he was just manipulative."

"What did he want?" Kévin asked.

"Guess," Sophie said. "What men usually want."

"Oh, right."

"After Aurore died and Victoire fought with her parents, she snuck off to Greece using her sister's passport. The detective her parents hired didn't figure that one out. She was vulnerable and found herself under the grip of Breton. The longer she stayed, the deeper she became involved in his life, to the point where she agreed to come back to Aix and help him with this scheme. She knew Aix, after all, and she liked the idea of coming here and dressing up."

"Greta Garbo," Paulik suggested.

"Yes, and Breton knew how to make Victoire look like Liliane," Sophie said. "Anyway, Victoire liked getting away from Breton, and walking around Aix incognito. She was beginning to come to terms with coming home. She says she had no idea about what was going on—she only thought this was about getting money from Liliane, and trying to make it look like Liliane walking the streets at night, having her look crazy. He said Liliane was keeping the money from him illegally, and of course he promised to share it with Victoire. She knew that by now he had a new girlfriend, this woman in Aix, but Victoire was relieved to be through with that part of their relationship."

Paulik sipped his coffee but said nothing. Sophie went on, "But Victoire started getting scared. She took the bus out to the country one day, because she wanted to walk by her family's country house, when she got a frightening text from Breton. She fell, having fainted from the heat, and was helped in from the side of the road by a neighbor."

"Marine Bonnet."

"Exactly."

"And that was Victoire leaving the theater the night of Liliane's accident?"

"Yes, she was supposed to go and frighten Liliane in the theater, but got there later than planned and found Liliane lying at the bottom of the stairs. She screamed and ran out. The next morning she was going to come straight here but instead caught a flight back to Greece, deciding to play cool in front of Breton in order to collect evidence."

Paulik asked, "Do we have proof that Breton rented a car in Ancona?"

"Affirmative," Sophie replied. "But what's better yet is that Victoire managed to crack his computer password and gain access to his account. She's scanning us the proof of Breton's trip to Aix and the hotel he stayed at. She even has receipts for the vintage suit she bought, and handwritten instructions that Breton left for her. But the best bit is his emails back and forth to Gauthier Lesage. It shows their entire plan."

"How did Mlle Tasset break into his computer?"

"She said it was remarkably easy, especially as Breton's password was very simple to figure out."

Paulik drained his coffee and smiled. "So what was it?" he asked.

"Patrası."

By the time the second pot of coffee was made, Victoire Tasset's emails began arriving. Sophie downloaded and saved the documents, sending them to the printer in the next room. Flamant was in the printing room muttering about computer paper and they heard him open and close the printer's paper drawer with a bang. Sophie cringed. She hated when people were rough with objects, especially expensive ones.

A few minutes later Flamant returned with a stack of paperwork in his arms. "We should hire this Victoire," he said, setting down the stack. "She's very thorough. Luckily we had enough paper as *some* people don't bother to refill the paper tray."

Sophie winked at Paulik as she got up and began arranging

the documents by date across a large table. Paulik walked over and shifted some papers, seeing Breton's hotel bookings for Aix. "Breton stayed at that modern hotel on the ring road."

"Practical," Sophie replied. "It has parking, and he could still walk all over Aix on foot."

"I ate there the other day with Judge Verlaque," Paulik said. "Breton may have been sitting at the next table."

"So we did," a voice said from the doorway.

"Speak of the devil," Paulik said, smiling.

"I'm on my way to the clinic and thought I'd stop by and say hello," Verlaque said.

Sophie reached out and shook his hand, hoping that the judge wasn't going to show them any more baby pictures. But he was too busy getting filled in on the backstory of Breton and Lesage's plan. "What will happen to Victoire?" Sophie asked when they finished the debriefing.

Verlaque winced. "Victoire was an accomplice, even if she claims she didn't know that murder was part of the deal. However, she voluntarily aided the police, and will no doubt do more to help incarcerate Breton. Sandra Gastaldi, on the other hand, is in more trouble."

Verlaque left, mumbling about the ridiculous number of presents his brother had bought for Rosa. Paulik went into his office, saw Mme Falzon's phone number, and dialed it. "Ah, oui, Mme Falzon," he said. "It's Commissioner Bruno Paulik calling from Aix-en-Provence. How are you?"

"I'm fine and waiting for my first-class ticket!"

Paulik laughed. "I've been enjoying your notebooks, and they've been a huge help."

"Humph," she said. "I knew they would, someday."

"I noticed a very nice Polaroid of you at work, taken by *G.M.* Would that be Guy Minoux? It was in the notebook numbered . . ." Paulik flipped the notebook over to read the spine. "Fall 1991."

"Ah, yes, but it shouldn't have been in that notebook. He'd been dead for years. But sometimes I found loose photographs and things and had to glue them into the notebook I was working on at the time."

"I see," he said. "Were you good friends?"

"Oh yes, great friends. He liked his martini blancs, and would come into the bar and tell me everything. Heavy smoker. Gitanes. Guy never had much money. He was married to Liliane when neither of them were well known. Why?"

"I visited Mlle Poncet just before she died," he replied. "And she whispered his name." He paused for effect. "And then she said, *I'm sorry.*"

Mme Falzon sniffed and blew her nose. "Ah, so the kid is right."

"Kid?"

"A young film student," she said. "You're lucky I still had notebooks to loan you. *Loan,* do you hear?"

"*Oui, madame.* What was the student looking for?"

She said, "Information on Liliane and Guy Minoux. This kid is smart, and so sweet that I loaned him a stack of my notebooks."

"What's he interested in?"

"He claims that Liliane may have used Guy's unpublished manuscripts to write her Montmartre series. The films that made her famous."

"*Mimi in Montmartre*," he said. "They won her many awards."

"The kid says he can prove it," she said. "He's been doing research for his thesis or some other thing. Then he tried backtracking, afraid he'd told me too much. People have always trusted me with their secrets. I swore I wouldn't tell anyone, but you're a policeman and have to solve two murders."

"That's right," Paulik replied, smiling. "Did you keep this boy's name and number?" It didn't have any bearing on her murder, but Paulik was relieved it at least explained why Liliane sent Gauthier money every month. He must have known about Guy's manuscripts and was blackmailing Liliane. Perhaps she'd even threatened to go public and confess.

"Of course!" she cried. "He has some of my notebooks!" She put the receiver down and he could hear her walking around her tiny apartment, its wooden floors creaking. Coco barked and she hushed him. "Okay, I found it." She read out a name and number with an address in Aubagne.

"Aubagne," Paulik said. "That's down here."

"Home of Marcel Pagnol," she replied. "The boy told me that's where his film school is. It's attached to the Aix University."

"Yes, it is," Paulik said. One of Hélène's nieces had attended that school, and now she was a film editor in California. "Thank you so much for this, Mme Falzon. You're an angel."

She laughed. "That's what my clients used to call me! Ciao, Commissioner."

Paulik then phoned Jean-Marc Sauvat. He thought that Sauvat should be brought up-to-date, and perhaps he could go and gently tell the other actors. Paulik himself, with Sophie Goulin, would go and speak to Anouk and her parents. Jean-Marc answered just as Paulik was about to give up and leave a message. "Commissioner," Jean-Marc said. "Hello!"

"You can call me Bruno. Do you have a few minutes?"

"Yes, and no. I'm out buying baby presents." He paused. "I'm the godfather."

Paulik grinned to think of Verlaque having to lug yet more parcels up the four flights of stairs to their apartment. He went on to explain the events of the previous day while Jean-Marc listened. "I was a fool," Jean-Marc finally said.

"Sandra fooled us all," Paulik said. "She set you up to see Victoire Tasset leaving the theater that night."

Jean-Marc stayed silent. He then said, "She did invite me to dinner, that's true. But we both saw the girl, at the same time."

"It must have been arranged beforehand."

"Ah, *merde*."

"What is it?"

"Sandra did look at her watch a few times," Jean-Marc said, sighing. "I thought she was tired. And, now that I think of it, she did want me to come to the window to look at the view."

"No worries," Paulik said. "Take care, and when you see Marine, tell her I'll come to the clinic tomorrow with Léa and Hélène, if that's all right."

He hung up and his cell phone rang in his hand; it was Léa. "Hello sweet pea," he said. "I just have a few seconds. Is it fast?"

"Yes, Papa," Léa said. "I just wanted to tell you that we got our grades today. And I got the second-best grade in math!"

"Hey! Wow!" Paulik said. "Congratulations!"

"Are you disappointed?"

"Are you joking?" he asked, thinking of his own dismal math grades at the same age.

"It's just I used to be the best," Léa went on. "But now it's Charles."

Paulik said, "I'm proud of you." And then he thought of Antoine Verlaque and Marine and Rosa and he added, "My heart is swelling. It was the day you were born, and it still is."

"Ah, Papa!" Léa cried. "That's so corny! Are you all right?"

ALSO AVAILABLE

DEATH AT THE CHÂTEAU BREMONT

MURDER IN THE RUE DUMAS

DEATH IN THE VINES

MURDER ON THE ÎLE SORDOU

THE MYSTERY OF THE LOST CÉZANNE

THE CURSE OF LA FONTAINE

THE SECRETS OF THE BASTIDE BLANCHE

A NOËL KILLING

PENGUIN BOOKS